IT'S IN THE BAG

J. C. ADLEY

Copyright © 2021 J. C. Adley
All rights reserved
First Edition

NEWMAN SPRINGS PUBLISHING
320 Broad Street
Red Bank, NJ 07701

First originally published by Newman Springs Publishing 2021

ISBN 978-1-63881-024-7 (Paperback)
ISBN 978-1-63881-025-4 (Digital)

Printed in the United States of America

*To my family, P, T, Z, M & C, I love you, always.
To Dr. Michael K. Newcomer and Dr. Colin Bird,
thank you for everything, even the bag.*

CHAPTER 1

Well, if there ever was a Monday that would make a Monday scowl and turn up its nose, this was the Monday. Anna Dawson had felt every, single, solitary minute of this day. She glanced up at the clock on the wall then down to the schedule on her desk. Thankfully, she was able to take a gigantic sigh of relief; only one more appointment stood between her and her leaving the corner office in the town that she had called home most of her forty-five years.

Anna had done well for herself. She had sworn that she would leave this haven in the mountains of western North Carolina once she was old enough, and she did just that. She left Pressley Heights under the spell of the man she thought she would spend the rest of her life with. She married him, for goodness's sake. That was usually the plan when one married, but all good plans are subject to fail miserably as much as succeed. Anna had been taught that whatever she set out to do in life, to do it to the best of her ability… She took that to heart. When she succeeded, she did it beautifully and to all the acclaim it could possibly muster. Failures were accomplished with the same amount of gusto and critique, and they always provided abundant fuel for town gossip. She had definitely had her turn at keeping the rumor mill going a time or two, or twelve.

Anna glanced at her watch and gathered the notes she needed for the consult she was about to do. Anna was an attorney, a well-admired attorney in the 28th Judicial District of North Carolina. She handled family law, estates and wills, divorces, and property settlement cases. She enjoyed helping the people of her community, and they trusted her ability as an advocate for their interests. She was tenacious, sassy, and stubborn when she needed to be. Perfect combination for law. Her father, Jake Dawson, had hoped that she would follow in his law enforcement footsteps, but being the sheriff of Pressley Heights was never in her life goals. Heck, growing up the only daughter of the sheriff of the town, he ought to be happy she didn't rebel and become a permanent resident of the local lockup. Anna eventually compromised with her father's plan, added an extra four years of college after her own very unhappy and contentious divorce, and finally took her version of his advice and entered the law field, just in the courtroom rather than the patrol car.

A knock on her office door startled her for a moment. Usually her assistant just buzzed on the phone, but hey, everything else had been off today; what was one more abnormality?

"Come on in, Shellie. What's up?" Anna noticed the perplexed look on Shellie's face. "Please tell me the last appointment canceled!"

Shellie, a beautiful blond lady in her midforties, came in and slowly closed the door behind her, as if she was on a secret mission to steal the crown jewels while navigating through the Matrix. Shellie had been Anna's assistant and her best friend for over ten years now. Her father had been a deputy with Anna's father as they worked their way through the ranks. It was fate that Shellie and Anna would forge a friendship and a wonderful working relationship. Anna would be lost without Shellie; sometimes Anna thought that it was Shellie who did all the work and Anna got all the praise.

"Shhh! You can't be loud. I don't want them to know I am in here talking about them. I had to come warn you. This next trio is a doozy. I am so sorry that I scheduled them…they sounded so normal on the phone," Shellie whispered as she came around to Anna's side of the desk. "They are not your average folks. Well, two of the three are not your average folks. They must let the nice-looking one do all the talking. As a matter of fact, the 'normal-looking' one, quite handsome actually, asked to speak to you by himself before they all join in. That okay?"

Anna let out a low groan and rubbed her temples as if that would help alter what was to come. "Why not? It's not as if this has been a banner day so far. Hey, maybe he—or the trio as you call them—will jazz up the afternoon. Send him on in. Oh, what is his name again?" Anna rose and followed Shellie across the room to the door. "And hey, if I send you an IM asking for you to call security, could you please handle that quickly as possible this time? I would hate to have a repeat of what happened with old Mr. Mahoney."

Shellie nodded her head. She had failed in the past to call security, and it had resulted in Anna punching a little old man in the nose for coming on to her and trying to give her a smooch. "Watch for IM, send him in. And his name is Mr. Logan, Mr. Richard Logan." Shellie scooted out the door, and Anna could hear her summoning Mr. Logan to come into Anna's office.

Anna adjusted her skirt, smoothed out her blouse, and gave her long, light-brown hair a toss. Normal people or not, Anna wanted to try to look her best at all times. Anna's mother, Darcy Dawson, had tried, albeit unsuccessfully, to instill in her daughter the knowledge that the "pretty people" got further in life, made better grades, got better jobs, never had to wait in a line at the grocery store, were always let out in traffic, and basically lived on a different level than others. Something like that was her main thought process. BS was what Anna called it, but Darcy had been quite the beauty when she was younger and she used that to the fullest. Apparently, she never had to wait in a line and she wanted to bless her daughter with the same time-saving gifts that she was blessed with. Anna wasn't a good student of her mother's vain ways; she had thought it best to let her mind and ability do the talking. Besides, waiting in line at the grocery store was Anna's chance to read the town gossip. She never bought the *Town Tattler*, but she sure got the highlights waiting in those lines.

Anna walked to the doorway and was met by a handsome man, midfifties if she had to guess, with gray sprinkled through his dark hair. She paused, stopped dead in her tracks, and actually and made eye contact with his cool-blue eyes. Holding out her right hand to shake the hand of her newest client, she thought this might not be so bad. "Hello, Mr. Logan, I am Anna Dawson. Come on in and pull up a chair at the conference table. My assistant mentioned that you wanted to talk in private before the others joined us."

The seemingly nervous and off-kilter man took a seat across from where Anna would be seated. He fumbled with his folder of papers and searched his suit jacket for a pen. "Can I get you some coffee, water, or a soft drink? We have a small fridge in here just for our clients. You seem a little nervous. I promise there is no reason to be. I don't bite, and never mind what you may have heard about me, I can be pretty nice and helpful." Anna hoped that a little humor or some liquid refreshments would help calm the man down. No such luck, it seemed. Mr. Logan seemed rattled to his core. This was going to be interesting if nothing else.

"Um, no, um, Ms. Dawson. I'm good. Please call me Richard. Look, you know why my family and I are here to talk to you. It is about our father, his new wife, how she convinced him redo his will. We think she is trying to kill him." Anna nodded as she glanced over her notes; he had just hit the major bullet points of his phone consultation. He continued, "You see, I am the youngest of us kids. My brother, Jimmy, is fifty-nine, my sister, Opal, is fifty-five, and I just turned fifty. I thought it would be better if we all came here and talked to you in person, as a team, so you could hear the story from each of our perspectives."

He finally stopped messing with the paperwork he had with him and he looked Anna in the eyes. "You see, my team…my team has let me down. Two-thirds of my legal team here today is straight out of the holler back in the eighteen hundreds. I told them to be professional and that this was a very important meeting. My sister, bless her, she smokes like a freight train, is wearing what looks like a Hawaiian muumuu and her best flip-flops. And my brother… I knew I shouldn't have let him come. He forgot his teeth at the house."

His head was now propped up in his hands on the conference room table. Anna actually felt sorry for him, and she was about to burst out laughing. He may be in dire straits for a legal team right now, but man, he sure could tell a story.

"Look, can we just do this another time, or never. There is no way we are going to be able to get the help we need when I have Mo and Larry out in the waiting room and I am sitting here in my three-piece suit. Hell, I don't even know if he showered, or she for that matter. She is probably out there about to set off the smoke alarms and sprinklers just by her stench. This was a mistake. I am so sorry to have wasted your time." Mr. Logan began to stand and gather his things.

Anna sat back in her chair and motioned for the befuddled man to sit back down. "Mr. Logan, I assure you, I will help you and your family any way I can. It makes no difference to me if they are wooly as all get out or wearing the best that Madison Avenue has to offer. This great big world is full of all kinds of people, and I am not going to be one to judge any one of them. I am not Jesus, and I have yet to become a judge…so you are good with me. Let's get your siblings in here and see what we can do."

With that, Mr. Logan sat back down and seemed to calm a little while Anna hit the button on the intercom. "Shellie, could you send in Mr. Logan's siblings, please. Thanks!" Anna went toward the closed door and looked back at Mr. Logan. "Everything will be fine, no judgment, and I promise that. Remember, I will not judge anyone. I am not Jesus and I haven't heard that he is hiring."

As the door opened, Anna saw exactly what Mr. Logan had been talking about and knew instinctively that her "no judgment" clause was about to be tested. Ms. Opal Logan, a well-rounded woman, wafted through the door, seemingly riding on the scent of five hundred cigarettes, but her Hawaiian muumuu looked beautiful. Royal blue with large white flowers, accents of bright pink and orange, it had to be an authentic piece. Her hair was long, with a pattern of black and gray stripes, accented with a gigantic orange flower just as in the dress's print, it seemed. Her hair looked like something a much younger person would pay high dollar for in a salon. She had an air about her, sure, confident, not one care in the world. A tough ole bird.

Next was Mr. Jimmy Logan. A force all his own. The oldest of the trio, Jimmy seemed to have lived hard, partied hard, worked hard, and drank a little too much at each opportunity. He was a tall, slender man who wore his white T-shirt and overalls with pride. He was a very ingenious man; he must like to keep his hands free for whatever may come for him to do, so he used the pocket on the front of his overalls to hold the cup. Anna assumed was for him to spit in, since it was obvious his cheek was full of—what do you say—snuff.

Handy… Anna had always thought those pockets were pretty much for decoration, or for less disgusting purposes. Shaking her head, Anna put on that million-dollar smile. She needed to concentrate on the purpose of their very interesting visit. Anna swore not to judge, so to each his own; good for them.

Anna introduced herself, shook hands, and showed them to their seats beside Richard. She made sure they had their waters and took her seat directly across from the interesting crew. "I am very happy to meet with you all this afternoon." Anna shifted in her seat and gathered her notes in front of her. "Richard has given me a little information to start with, but I want to ask some questions to get started and go from there. It is paramount that we delve into the reasons that you think that your father's new wife is trying to kill him. His safety is of the utmost importance, and we need to take care of that first. Why, exactly, do you think, or what have you witnessed, that led you to believe that your father is in any grave danger?"

"Because she is a money-hungry old bitty, that's why," Opal started with a shout. "She wants him dead so she can have the house, the land, and all his money. She is just a gold-digging bitty." Anna knew from that moment that she would not have any problem with withholding opinions when it came from Opal. She shot straight from the hip and didn't seem to care whom she hit in the process. "She had her eye on him before our mother was cold in the ground. She scouted him out, set her sights on him, and wooed him with her womanly ways."

"Good Lord, Opal, can you act like you have some sense? Please act like a lady!" Richard snapped at his sister, turning red as a tomato in the process. "And please do not talk about Daddy being wooed by womanly ways. That is disgusting. He is old, and I do not want to think of him being wooed by anything." Richard stared at his sister for a moment and then turned his attention to Anna. "Look, it's true that Melanie probably had her eye on Daddy from way back, when Momma first found out about her cancer and how bad it was. The doctors all told Momma and Daddy that there was really nothing that could be done since it had already gone too far. That is neither here nor there. Melanie is a widow about five or six times over, always the surviving spouse in the ordeals, and her husband always seemed to die not too long after the wedding. There has to be something up, something a little wonky or fishy…if you know what I mean. Or that lady has the worst luck at picking men in the world."

The wheels in Anna's head started turning, and she quickly came up with an idea that just may help out this trio on all accounts. "That is a couple of very interesting facts about…what is her name exactly?"

Richard spoke up first. "Her name is Melanie Buxton Logan. I am not sure what her maiden name is. Seems like it must have been lost in the many marriages. Chambers was the last name of the gentleman she was married to before my dad. His name was Vernon, Vernon Chambers. Poor guy didn't last long at all. About six months, if I remember correctly. Melanie hasn't been too forthcoming with information since I started asking a lot of questions about what she and Dad's plans were and why the big rush to change the will and all. She can turn mean and hateful pretty quick."

"I think I will do some digging with some help from the Sheriff's Department to look into Melanie's past, any record of run-ins with the law. I will also do some investigation into these marriages, however many there may be. I can go to the Register of Deeds and pull the marriage records. Were all her marriages here or close to Pressley Heights?" Anna was sure she could find out some interesting facts on this Melanie character with some help from her friends in the county.

Richard and Opal looked at each other, and then Opal voiced her ever blunt opinion on Anna's inquiry. "Four of her victims—I mean husbands—all lived in and around Pressley Heights. Heck, three of them were friends of our family in one way or another. That is probably how she got her feelers all in a tizzy about our daddy dealing with our mother's sickness. I never knew I lived in a town with such idiots. Stupid, stupid men. That is why I don't bother with a man. They ain't no good, just a bunch of trouble. They will run off with the next pretty little thing they see and take a fancy to. These old men see Melanie, shiny and perky, they don't pay no attention to anyone trying to talk some sense into their crazy minds. All they see is her all made up, listen to her go on and on about how she is in love and wants to live with them happily ever after. Well, you see what happens when someone blows smoke up someone's rear…they end up dead. And my daddy better not be dead any time soon unless the good Lord calls him home himself. Amen and hallelujah." Opal took a long, deep breath, looked at Anna, and stood. "Now, is there anything else you need me for, honey? Not to be overly rude or anything, but I sure could use a smoke."

Wide-eyed, intrigued, and entertained more than she thought she could be with this group, Anna had nothing else to get from Opal and was scared of what else she would say. Shaking her head, Anna said, "No, no, Ms. Ledford. You go right ahead and head on outside for that break. We have a nice courtyard just off the first floor and to the left of the double glass doors. Enjoy, and thank you for your candor and honesty. It truly is nice to talk with someone so forthcoming. I only wish more people were such a joy to speak with. I will work to try to find out all I can and see if we can get to the bottom of this and try to figure out what and who we are dealing with. It has been a pleasure."

"Can I go too?" Jimmy popped up like a spring. "I ain't much of a talker and I don't know any more than has already been said. You make me nervous because I know your pa is the sheriff. I can't say all my dealings have been on the uppity-up, but I ain't never been caught. Seems like the longer I sit in here the more likely it is that I will be moved on down to the lockup. Nice meeting ya, Ms. Anna. We do appreciate your help in not getting our pa killed. I will be out here with Opal in that courtyard you mentioned, and Rick"—Richard looked as if he was terrified what might come out of his brother's mouth next—"you just come get us when you are done conversin'." Jimmy didn't wait for an answer; he said his form of a goodbye, spat into his paper cup in his overalls pocket, and scooted right out the door, hot on Opal's heels.

They both looked at the door for a moment, and then Anna turned to finish up with Richard Logan for this appointment. "Mr. Logan, it has been a pleasure meeting with you and your siblings. I mean that. Quite frankly, this has been the best part of my day. I hate your family is going through this, but it was a joy to meet with you all." Anna glanced over the notes she had taken while they had been talking. "I will reach out to some people and get them working on tracking down just who Melanie is. I cannot say for sure. These kinds of stories are all unique, but usually they all have one thread of similarity. Someone is running from something or someone. I will do my best to find out and maybe we can get some answers that will convince your father to take off his rose-colored glasses, start thinking straight again, and make sure changing his will is exactly what he wanted to do and not just by influence of a pretty lady trying to take all he has while keeping him distracted and Lord knows what else."

Anna stood, and Richard did the same. She started toward the door to walk him out. "So if that plan is acceptable to you, Shellie has the papers you need to sign to retain my services and the fees that will be incurred. She will get all your information should I need to reach out via email and not just by phone. Feel free to call into the office anytime with any questions you may think of or information you think would be helpful while I am checking into Melanie."

Anna stopped at the threshold of the door to her office. "Have a good day, Mr. Logan, and try not to worry. Stop and see Shellie on your way out. I will be in touch soon." With that, Anna shut the door to her office, happy and satisfied that she had done the best she could with that meeting. Tomorrow she will start an investigation; too late in the day to start now. Ah, the end of the Monday that would not quit. Official end of the day workwise, that is. Now on to her second shift job, her most favorite one: being a mom to her two boys. The best part of her marriage that ended in a devastating disaster, her boys were the best parts of her and their father. For that, she would always be thankful to the man she thought was going to be her forever and ever. Some say, "Never say never," but Anna would like to add another line to that quote: "Never say forever!"

CHAPTER 2

Anna loved her home. She loved everything about it. It wasn't the biggest house known to man, but it had been her refuge for almost ten years. The two-story brick house had been the home she and the boys had moved into a few months after she and Mark had separated. The house had three bedrooms, a finished basement, a white picket fence, and a beautiful yard with mature trees. She was closer to her parents, a few streets removed for her sanity, back in the neighborhood that she had grown up in and knew so well. She was close to her office and their church, and the boys were close to school. She had a lot of friends still in the area and she loved the fact that her boys could grow up in an environment similar to her childhood experience, same schools and areas to explore. The three of them loved the outdoors and spending time with their family and friends. Pressley Heights was the perfect setting for that.

Anna's boys were her heart. She loved them more than she ever thought it possible to love someone. When she had Johnathan, she remembered looking over at him while the nurses weighed him, and simply said, "He is perfect." He was, and he had grown into a wonderful, intelligent, kind, and strong young man of sixteen. Jack had come along a couple of years later and he was just as perfect as his brother had been, with the only difference being a pound more on the scale. Jack, at fourteen, was his father made over. All the best parts of his father and her, rolled into one smart, funny, and athletic young man. Anna was truly blessed, and she knew it. She may have been through a lot in her life, and she would walk each day back through it a million times for her boys.

Neither she nor Mark wanted a long, drawn-out divorce, so they handled most things rationally and to each one's benefit. They both cared the most about the boys, who had been the glue that had held them together for the last few of the thirteen years they were married. With things between the couple getting worse and Mark's participation in a few things that Anna could not stand anymore, she felt it best to leave. Little did she know that that would be the best decision she could make.

Anna had signed over the family home to Mark; he gave custody of the boys to Anna without a fight, with visitation rights when he could work it out. Mark was a high-profile surgeon and was well known and in high demand. Mark paid Anna a healthy alimony each month and what the child support worksheet said he should pay for both boys. In turn, Mark got his freedom to do that which he wanted without having to come up with wild stories to explain his not coming home, missing special occasions, and calling in the middle of the night to have Anna pick him up because he was too drunk to drive home.

For years, Anna had blamed the bad behavior on the pressure of the job, but it all got too much. Anna had helped out and worked as the manager of a doctor's office while Mark had been going through medical school and his internship. She had left college after her Christmas break of her senior year of college to follow Mark. She would have followed him anywhere. She gave up a great deal; her parents were none too happy. They accepted Mark into the family, but there was always something that her daddy just didn't like, or trust. It must have been his instincts as a sheriff, but if Anna had listened to him right before the church doors, when her daddy offered to help her escape and walk out on her own wedding, she wouldn't have had her boys. That was worth everything.

Anna never did do things in life the easy way. Love, school, any decision that required thought of any type, she made with her heart. She finally grew up and learned that the heart can sometimes be the worst thing to base any decision on. She was stubborn, sassy, and hardened by experiences she had lived through. Her faith ensured that she knew that the Lord would be with her through anything, and she was certain she kept him fairly busy. She made a promise to herself when the divorce was final that she would focus on herself, on raising her boys, on school, and on building a career she could support herself in and love. She vowed never to let a man interfere with her plan for a happy life. So far so good.

Anna hit the button to close the garage doors and walked through the door that led from the garage to the kitchen via a small mudroom. Her purse, briefcase, and her keys quickly found their spot on the table inside the door; her phone she propped up on the island in the middle of the kitchen. It being Monday, the boys would be home around 6:30, after marching band practice. She needed to figure out what they were going to have for supper. Spaghetti: that was a favorite of the boys and so easy now she could make it with her eyes closed. Quickly she gathered two pots, the noodles, tomatoes, ground beef, French bread, and tomato sauce. Her phone rang, and she swiped across the screen with her finger, quickly putting it on speakerphone.

"Hello," she said in the general direction of the phone on the island.

"Howdy, sweetie, you home?" Her father's voice, booming and strong, seemed to fill the room.

"Yes, Daddy, I am home. Just starting supper." Anna kept right on working on her gourmet supper. "How was your day? Did you bust any drug rings or finally defeat the deep dark world of crime?"

Jake Dawson's laugh was legendary, boisterous; it always brought a smile to Anna's face. "Why, yes, honey, I kept everyone safe in the metropolis of Pressley Heights and now I am hungry. Your momma is at one of her high-class ladies' meetings at the club. You know I hate those. I ain't never invited."

"Well, you are of the male persuasion," Anna said, laughing. Her father never had understood why her momma liked those ladies, but he always used it as an opportunity to spend time with his grandsons. "You wanna come over and have an Italian delight with us? Spaghetti and some fresh French bread. The boys should be home in about forty-five minutes. They would wonder where you were, since it is Monday and all. I need to run something by you anyway. Had a very entertaining consult today. I may need some assistance from your fine department for this case."

"Sounds good, honey. Be there in a few."

Anna kept right on making dinner, humming as she went. With the ground beef browned and in the pot with the sauce, the tomatoes, and the other ingredients, she set the stove top on simmer. All she would have to do was boil the water for the noodles and brown the garlic bread when the boys got home. As if knowing that Anna had a moment to herself, Murphy, the family's obese cat, sauntered into the kitchen as if he was the one who paid the mortgage. *Meow! Meeeeeooooowwww!* "Hello, Murphy, nice to see you this evening. Hate that I woke you from your slumber when I arrived home. It isn't your suppertime yet." Anna bent over and scooped up the ball of white fluff. "You, my friend, need to skip a few meals. You have certainly made yourself into quite the ball of joy."

Murphy wiggled and made it clear he didn't like the judgment and most certainly didn't appreciate being picked up. He hopped down and looked up at his aggressor as if to say, *You, my master, need not to talk about me needing to skip a few meals… You are quite plump yourself.* Anna swished his tail, and off he went to wait until his appointed mealtime.

The truth of the matter was, Anna knew that she could stand to lose around twenty pounds. She looked great, beautiful even, if you listened to her family and friends, healthy. And with her health history, that was a compliment. She was curvy in just about all the right places and had long, brown hair with beautiful caramel highlights. She dressed in near enough to the latest fashion. She got compliments almost everywhere she went, and she was settled in her mind that, right now, she was going to enjoy feeling good for once. Her boys didn't seem to be embarrassed by her; they still went and did things with her, so in her mind, she was good.

Five years before, Anna had to make a life-and-death decision. Her own life hung in the balance. She had let things get too bad, all because of her vanity and pride. The Lord had seen to it to have a surgeon move to Pressley Heights, just the surgeon she was going to need. Anna was twenty-one, still considered newly married, working hard to keep both her and Mark's heads above water, that she started to feel really bad, really fatigued, and then the bleeding started. She didn't say a word at first, but then she had to.

She mentioned in passing to one of the doctors she worked for that she had been noticing some blood when she went to the bathroom. Usually not a conversation you had with your boss, but he just so happened to be a gastroenterologist. Apparently, it was just what she needed. *Well played, Lord.* After a few tests and a lot of blood work, she was diagnosed with Crohn's disease. She had heard of this before because her momma had it, but it had never been that big of a deal to her because Darcy didn't have the disease to the extent that Anna did.

Over the next few years, all while Anna was a single mother trying to hold it all together with the single thread of sanity she had left, trying to get a law practice started and increase her client base, she tried every medicine that the doctors knew to try. She was either allergic, or her body would have a reaction that her doctor could not identify or explain, or the medication failed entirely. Her doctors here in Pressley Heights sent her to UNC Chapel Hill and Duke, even offered to send her to the Mayo Clinic to try to get answers. With options running out and already three near-death hospital stays, Anna made the decision to meet with the new surgeon, the new rectal surgeon in town.

She was horrified that she was in her thirties already having to get a rectal surgeon. She thought those doctors were special order, reserved just for the elderly and those unfortunate enough to have cancer or have a terrible accident befall them in life. She would never forget her dragging Shellie to the initial appointment with Dr. Patrick Hyrd, from Texas. In her digging and general snooping, she had found out that he was a younger doctor, had studied at the best University in Texas, and had done a residency at Chapel Hill. Seemed legit enough to meet with him at least.

"Nice office, I suppose. Nice enough. Looks like the carpet is pretty new." Anna was making small talk with Shellie, trying to find a reason to run screaming from the office waiting room. "Clean too. I don't really see any dust around. It doesn't smell like the dentist

IT'S IN THE BAG

office... Dr. Garrett's office smells like a sterile autopsy room. I hate the dentist."

Shellie needed Anna to stop talking; she was beginning to notice the others in the waiting room looking at her friend with side-eyes and whispering to their companions. "Can you please be quiet? You are scaring the others. They are looking at you like I am the transport guardian from the ninth floor of the hospital. You know about the ninth floor of the hospital, right? Now be quiet."

Anna looked at Shellie. "Is that any way to talk to your boss?"

Shellie laughed. "Right now, you are not my boss. You are my best friend who needed a companion to the rectal surgeon to find out how he is going to fix your unruly arse."

"I should really look into giving you a raise. This seems, ummm, a little beyond the scope of your employment. Above your pay grade, as you say. Make a note of that and remind me when we get back to the office." Anna had been so blessed to have Shellie.

The door opened to the hallway, and a cute, perky, slender, beautiful blonde dressed in light-blue scrubs stood with her iPad and looked down to call the next name. "Ms. Dawson." Glancing around the room, she said the name again. "Ms. A. Dawson?"

Shellie elbowed Anna in the ribs, and Anna let out a small squeak. "Right here, sorry. I was so intrigued by this article in—what magazine is this—oh, yes, *Bikers Weekly*, I didn't hear you at first." Anna stood and put the magazine under her arm and grabbed her phone and purse. She and Shellie followed the all-too-happy-seeming nurse through the door.

"Right this way, Ms. Dawson. My name is Penny and I will be doing your vitals and getting your information for the doctor. Let's stop here first and grab a weight. You can give your purse and things to your friend and hop on up." Penny motioned toward the scale.

Anna handed off her purse, her phone, and her newly acquired *Bikers Weekly* magazine. "Okay, Shellie, close your eyes. I don't want you to know my weight and yap it all over town." She did as she was told and hopped right onto the scale. Anna watched as the digital numbers flashed and went up and down. Thank the Lord the weight was shown in kilograms. Taking a mental note of the number, she would remember to convert later. "I usually deduct five pounds for my brain, three pounds for my clothes, and six pounds for my boobs. Also, I am wearing really heavy shoes today. They make a difference." Anna looked directly at Penny the nurse and seemed to will her to write all that down or change the weight altogether. No luck.

Shellie, shaking her head, grabbed Anna's arm as she stepped off the scale. "You are impossible. I am never coming with you again. Here, take your stuff!" Shellie handed off the purse, phone, and magazine. "I can't take you anywhere."

"Ladies, we will be in room two today. You can come on in, and I will get your vitals and go over your medical history and medicines. Then Dr. Hyrd will be in with you in just a few minutes. You came on a good day. He isn't running behind today."

Anna busted out laughing. "Ha ha! That is awesome. We came on a day when the *rectal* surgeon isn't 'running behind'! Get it? That is a really good one!" Shellie and Penny looked at Anna and gave her a pitiful smile. Anna stopped laughing abruptly and sighed heavily. "I am a wee bit nervous about this."

Penny smiled and waved off the comment and poor joke. "I understand. This is not the first place people want to go when they wake up in the morning. Who wants to first have a problem bad enough to see a surgeon, much less a rectal surgeon, and second, who wants to come show a total stranger their bottom?"

Anna thought Penny was a sweet soul. She was a sweet, young soul with not one problem with her perfectly shaped and perfectly sized rear end. Penny could go now. Anna smiled. "Thanks for your understanding with a very understandable fear of being here. I appreciate it. Just let him know I am scared to death."

Penny smiled as she got up to head out. She grabbed the vitals cart with the BP cuff and all things vital. "He understands. All his patients are, but not one has regretted meeting him." With that, Penny was gone. The door shut softly behind her. Now silence.

"I tell you one thing," Anna said, turning to Shellie. "I tell you what. If Doogie Howser walks in here, we are walking out. No young high school kid is going to work on my plumbing. Deal?"

"You are impossible. Would he have a job here if he wasn't a proven surgeon? They just don't hand out medical school degrees to high school students. You were once married to a doctor, for goodness's sake. Doogie was a TV show. Fiction, remember? He wouldn't even know who Doogie Howser is, and don't you ask him either. Poor thing. I bet he gets all the weird questions this Podunk town can offer a new doctor. Bless." Shellie slapped her hands down on her lap and laughed. "I don't understand how you can be so confident in the office and in the courtroom and fall all to pieces in here. You are still you. Gracious, girl, act like you. Yours ain't gonna be the first behind he has seen and it ain't gonna be the last."

Two swift knocks stopped Shellie's rampage. The door opened, and in walked Dr. Hyrd. A young, early- to midthirties clean-cut man walked in followed by his assistant, seemingly around the same age, beautiful and very kind-looking. "Hello, ladies. I am Dr. Patrick Hyrd. This is my assistant, Jenna Cooper. It is a pleasure to meet you both." He glanced between the ladies as if trying to figure out who was who by their actions. "I take it you," he said, walking directly toward Anna, "are Ms. Dawson. I can always tell who the patient is and who the support person is. The patient is the one squirming in their seat." Dr. Hyrd held out his hand, and Anna shook it, and then shifted one more time in her seat.

Anna leaned over to whisper in Shellie's ear. "Go! Go! Go! I told you I wasn't going to be seen by Dr. Doogie, and, well, Dr. Doogie has arrived. Go *now*!"

Shellie gave Anna yet another quick elbow in the ribs. Anna needed to stop or she would look like she had been in a terrible accident after this visit. Shellie then said, loud enough for Dr. Hyrd to hear, "Stop it, Anna, just stop. He is not Doogie Howser." Shellie continued, turning her attention to Dr. Hyrd and Jenna, "You will have to forgive my friend and boss. She is a little terrified about being here, and she is a little intimidated by your apparent young age. She will get over it. I assure you, you have been vetted by the best detective in the South. This lady is not only an attorney, she is the daughter of the town sheriff. I assure you if there is anything you don't know about yourself, or your past or education, just check with them. Now, feel free to carry on."

Anna thought again to herself that she just had to give Shellie a raise.

Dr. Hyrd chuckled and smiled at both the ladies. "I assure you I have heard it all before. Since I have moved here to this wonderful town of yours, I have heard just about everything. I do appreciate a patient who wants to be so informed. I will definitely check with you in case I can't remember something about my past. Now, why don't we jump on in on these issues that have brought you to see me."

Dr. Hyrd spent a great deal of time going over Anna's medical history, as long and crazy as it was. He talked about the discussions he had been involved in with her primary care, and even more in depth with her gastroenterologist.

"I take it that Kevin—I mean Dr. Oldgoins—told you why he was referring you to me. I know that this surgery is not what you had wanted and have been putting off for quite some time." Dr. Hyrd sat back against the wall. "I know no one wants to lose their colon and have an ostomy. No one wants to have a bag attached to their abdomen that collects their waste. Look, I get it. I have looked at your MRIs, your CTs, and I really don't see another way to give you back your full quality of life and, to be honest, years of that life. You can live a full, healthy, and productive life with an ostomy. Your life would change in very few ways as to what you can and cannot do. If you do a little more research into just how many people live with an ostomy, I think you would be shocked."

Dr. Hyrd sat quiet for a moment as he watched the color disappear out of Anna's face.

"I see that this will take some time to digest, and it has to be a decision that you can live with. I can tell you right now, I will not be your favorite person, but I am okay with that. I want to do what is best for you, and this surgery is it. You can hate me, you can yell, cry, scream, but in the long run, it will be one of the best decisions you can make. You have two sons, right?"

Anna nodded her head, silent.

"I understand that they are ten and twelve years old."

IT'S IN THE BAG

Another nod from Anna.

"I want you to be the best mom you can be. I want you to be here to see your grandkids. I want you to be present for many, many more years to come. I fully think that this surgery can help you achieve that."

"Wait, what?" Anna muttered a phrase that she had heard too many times from her children. Nothing else said, just that teenager comment that meant, *Hey, I am kind of listening, hearing the words, but it might be important, so I had better check.* Then just silence, as if no other words would form in her brain.

Anna, still silent, turned and looked at Shellie. Shellie took the reins. "So you are saying that surgery for sure, bag, and good to go. No more medicines, no 'we will wait and see,' no other intervention out there. Surgery is what is left, and with surgery, then good. Right? Condensed form, of course…much more involved in between the surgery and good to go." Shellie was so good at summing stuff up.

"Let me do an exam, but yes, I feel that, in discussion with her doctors, seeing her files from the hospital and scans, that yes, this would be the way I would treat her if she were my mom or my sister. No doubt at all. The sooner the better. Once the surgery is done, recovery can begin, and while the Crohn's cannot be cured, it can begin to go into remission, and maybe some new medicines can be added to help keep it in remission. I don't have a magic ball—no one does, of course—but I have done this surgery and I have seen patients benefit from it." Dr. Hyrd spoke to both ladies even though he knew Anna had long since tuned him out since the mention of bag. He didn't seem deterred at all. "Look, let me get Tammy, my scheduler, in here to talk to you about what all this entails, time-wise, and then we can go from there. How does that sound?" Dr. Hyrd looked at Anna for a response; nothing. "Is she okay?" He looked to Shellie, the only one of the two who was still responding to him at this point.

"Yes, she is fine. She kind of shuts down for a bit when she is faced with something crappy. She is fine. She already knew this was what you were going to say. Now, she just has to *deal* with what you have said. Bring on Tammy. I got this." Shellie was ready to get the heck out of there. The doctor was nice and all, but she had had enough. "Oh, one more thing, can we take this magazine? Seems she has kind of destroyed it with all the twisting and folding. We can replace it."

Dr. Hyrd laughed. "Keep it, no worries. I didn't think she looked like the *Biker Weekly* kind of lady. Interesting choice, though." With that, he was off to another waiting patient.

*****

Anna heard a quick knock, then the opening of the front door, and a yell from that direction. "Just your daddy, don't shoot!" Jake Dawson could make an entrance like no other.

Anna yelled back, "Glad you told me, Daddy. I was just grabbing my gun." Anna giggled. "Get in here, old man."

"Old man, my ass, Little One. I have you know that you are still my little girl and I am still your daddy, old or not. Older, I can settle for older. Distinguished, even. Wise." Her daddy came in and set down a salad and some dressing.

Anna noticed the addition to the island. "Thanks for the salad. You made that awful quick since we just got off the phone."

"Well, you said it yourself, this is where I usually end up on Monday nights. So this week, I came prepared. Thought I would add a little green to this dinner extraordinaire." Jake winked at his daughter as he pulled out a bar stool to sit at the island. Picking out a couple of croutons off the salad and popping them in his mouth, he sat back and looked at Anna. "So, you mentioned something about a new case you may need some help with. Tell me what you got."

Anna could hear the garage door open. "Boys are home, Daddy. They are just about to burst through the door, talking a mile a minute and smelling of teen angst and sweat."

Anna shot her dad a look with a wink and said, "I think that we will have to wait to discuss the case until after dinner when I can concentrate again. I can say this for the moment, I do believe there is a true black widow lurking in this town, and we both know I cannot stand spiders."

IT'S IN THE BAG

"Good. I was done talking to you for now anyway. Where are those grand boys of mine?" Jake stood and waited on the boys to get into the kitchen.

Johnathan came through the mudroom door into the kitchen first, throwing his car keys down on the table and his book bag onto the floor. Johnathan was sixteen going on thirty. He was an old soul. He was tall, like his father, and very handsome. Johnathan favored his mother, her dark eyes and her coloring. He was long and lean, smart; once girls started catching his eye, watch out. He was kind, levelheaded, and responsible. He loved his mom and his family and would go to blows over any one of them.

Jack followed his brother about a half step behind. His book bag joined Johnathan's on the floor below the coat hooks, and he stepped in and gave his mom a hug. He was fourteen and could look his mom in the eye, if he ducked down a little. Jack was tall for his age, long and lean too, and seemed to grow a little more each night. He was the more athletic of the two boys. He was smart, funny, and also kind. He shared his mother's dark eyes, but he favored his father. He was the spittin' image of his father at the same age.

"Hey, Gramps! Best part of Monday is that we know you will be here for supper." Johnathan gave his grandpa a wink as he went to give his mom a hug. "Mom, you should feel privileged that Gramps likes us better than hangin' out with all those old ladies at the club. I bet some of Gramps's friends would like schmoozing up with the fancy ladies while they sip their tea and eat their grilled chicken and kale."

Jake laughed as he grabbed Jack in a bear hug. "I will take Monday evenings with you guys a thousand times over an evening with your grams and all her old bitty friends. All they do is get together to gossip and eat fancy food. I swear, just been to church yesterday, morning and night, preached the Good Word, which is against gossipin' as I recall it, and then eighteen hours later, she is off flappin' her jaws to the snooty of the town. I will never get that, but it makes your grams happy to be with her friends. Heck, she doesn't mind, nor does she understand my fishing trips with the guys. So what do you do?"

"Will y'all set the table for supper? I am just about finished up and I know you guys are hungry." Anna looked at her handsome boys.

Both boys nodded. Jack grabbed the silverware, and Johnathan took four plates out of the cabinet. Soon the table was set, the food was placed in the center of the table, and all four were seated in their normal seats. All joined hands, and Jake said grace. This was one of Anna's most favorite times of her week, every week. All three of her favorite men, sitting, talking, and laughing with her about life, school, friends, work, and just normal, everyday things. This was what family meant to Anna.

*****

With the table cleared, the boys happily upstairs doing their homework, Anna and her father worked together to clean up the dishes and the kitchen.

"So, tell me about this consult you had today. What kind of help do you need this time?" Jake was looking forward to this story. Anna usually kept to herself about her cases, but when she was forced to ever ask for his help, you bet there was always a good reason. A very good and entertaining reason.

Anna dried her hands and threw the dish towel down on the counter. She turned and leaned her back up against the cool marble. "Bless it, Daddy, this one is going to take all kinds of help from all kinds of people. Most from you, though." Anna giggled as she recalled the trio that had graced her presence that afternoon. "I think we may have a woman who is killing off her husbands, one by one, making it look like accidents, and then moving on to her next victim, I mean husband."

"Do tell. I haven't heard a good one like this in a long time." Jake was actually intrigued. Most of the time, Anna just needed help getting a client a restraining order. That or an officer to pay a visit to a dad who was getting a little behind on child support and needed a friendly reminder of his obligation to his child, not the woman. This sounded almost fun. "We don't get many possible cases of a woman killer in these parts."

"Only because of your dedicated service to Pressley Heights all these years, Daddy. Criminals are usually too scared of the wrath of Sheriff Jake Dawson." Anna rolled her eyes but felt pride in her heart for all her father's hard work over the years. "I bet they talk about you in all the surrounding counties and states even. Bad people try to plan heists and robberies, killings and shenanigans, and none are all that excited to come into the metropolis of Pressley, not with that Big Jake around."

Jake shook his head. He loved his daughter and he loved her picking on him. He loved she could take it and could dish it with the best of them. "Okay, give me the highlights, names and such, and I will get to work on it in the morning. Well, to be honest, I and some of the other guys will get to work on this in the morning."

Anna and Jake looked over her notes from the office. He took down some of the information in his notebook, enough to get him and his deputies started, and told Anna he would be in touch with her as soon as he had something for her to work with. He then stood and got his things together to head home. Anna walked with him to the door. Jake stood at the bottom of the stairs and yelled to the boys that he would see them later. Both boys ran down the stairs like galloping gazelles and exchanged hugs and said their goodbyes. Jake then left, and Anna smiled as she locked the door and settled herself down for the evening.

CHAPTER 3

Five years ago, Anna was waking up to a new world, new body, and new way of life. A seven-hour surgery the afternoon before had left her body without a colon, rectum, anus, appendix, and fallopian tubes. She had three incision spots and a drain coming out of her abdomen. She still had the catheter. Pain medicine and the little button she could press every ten minutes were her only friends at the moment. Ten minutes was an eternity when it felt like a dump truck had been driven through your abdomen. Along with her handy-dandy drain, Anna could feel the newest addition, the permanent one, to her right side, just below her ribs. She felt the bag through the sheet and blanket covering her. She couldn't yet bring herself to look. She was far too drugged up, too much in pain, and not quite mentally ready to accept that reality at the moment.

"Knock, knock." Dr. Hyrd's head peeked around the door of her hospital room. "How is the patient doing this morning? Feel like you were put through the ringer yesterday or what?"

It took Anna a few extra seconds to actually focus on him as he seemed to keep moving about the room, then she just shut her eyes and decided it would be best to converse as if blind. "Well, remember when you said I would probably hate you? Well, we are just about there. I know you said it wouldn't be rainbows and unicorns, but I expected maybe a crazed clown or deranged elephant. This is so much worse than when I had the boys. So much worse."

"Well, I can understand that. I had a front-row seat to your experience yesterday and I know you have been through it. I told your family and friends last night how I was elbow-deep in your abdomen, and I thought your father, sheriff's uniform and all, was going to go down in a heap in the floor." Dr. Hyrd started to pull back the sheet to check the incisions. "Okay, let's check my handiwork." Dr. Hyrd took his time and checked each incision and the bag.

"The drain will have to stay for a few days. We will know by the output. I have had to send a few patients home with the drain before, but only in certain instances. Everything is looking as it should. The output into the bag still hasn't started, but it will take your small bowel a little while to wake up and start to function again. We will slowly add soft foods to your liquids, see how that goes. Once you start to show proper output and are able to take meds and food by mouth, we can talk about getting you out of here." Dr. Hyrd took out his cell phone and seemed to be searching for something. "Here it is. Remember you asked me for your colon in a jar to take home? Well, you can't really do that, so I did the next best thing. I laid it out and took a picture for you. Isn't that awesome?"

He could see that she couldn't really see, and her attention span was failing.

"On a totally positive note, all the tissue samples that were sent to the lab came back showing no signs of cancer, just active Crohn's. That is wonderful news."

Anna, still having a hard time focusing, looked in the direction of his phone and nodded and tried to smile. "That's great. Thanks."

Dr. Hyrd gave her a pat on her shoulder and a squeeze of her hand as if to tell her she would be okay, it would take time, and he understood all that he possible could, but that in time she would be okay. "So, do you have any questions? You seem to have quite the fan club gathering outside your door. I told them I got to be the first visitor today." Anna shook her head as if to say no. "If you don't have anything for me, then I will unleash the masses on you. And hey, for what it's worth, not all of my patients have such a fan club. Let them do things for you, let them help you as you heal. You don't really strike me as the type to rely on others very easily. Learn that. That is an order." With that bit of advice, Dr. Hyrd headed out the door. He glanced back and promised to check in later that evening.

Anna fought hard to recover and learn her new way of living with a bag, but despite all her best efforts, she fell into a depression. The disease had been a battle for years; the surgery had been a hard thing for her body to endure. The hardest part for Anna was the mental mountain that she had to climb to be okay with being different now. She had to come to terms with the fact that forever she would be different, this would be something she didn't think she would ever get over.

She thought she would never be able to go out again. What if it leaked? What if people knew? Would she smell? She fell into a dark place and shut herself off to her friends and coworkers; she only let in the boys and a chosen few. She thought she would never be able to live that wonderful life that she was promised she would have after the surgery. It took months, determination, and the unfailing love and support of friends and family to slowly draw her out and help her realize that her life was there just waiting for her to start living.

*****

Anna couldn't, for the life of her, understand why women felt the need to wear high heels. Of course, she had about thirty different pairs in a rainbow of colors, heights, and styles. Church heels, cute heels, fancy heels, chunky heels that Shellie said were in style eight years ago, prim heels, sexy heels (which didn't get much action), court heels, and wear-to-work heels. Anna had also fallen victim to buying a pair of Jimmy Choo heels, and those were the pick of the day. These shoes, ungodly expensive as they may be even at 55 percent off, might just be the death of her. The walk from the parking garage to her office wasn't extremely long, and on warm summer days, cool spring evenings, crisp fall afternoons, all is well and good. But this day, in these shoes, it was not well with her soul or her soles.

Anna's office was a three-story brick building that she shared with two county departments. The first floor was home to the County Planning and Permit Office, the second floor was Anna's law offices, and the third floor was home to the County Management offices. To the second and third floors there was an old, wooden, one-hundred-year-old staircase that flowed up the right side of the building with door access to the second floor that opened to the lobby upstairs. She loved her building; the history of it and the character that was saved during the renovations a few years back made it feel almost cozy. It was professional and clean, perfect for each of the entities that it housed, and it seemed to sit directly in the center of town, in proximity to the courthouse, other county offices, and restaurants and shops. The only thing that Anna would change was its lack of on-site parking. She would give her left Jimmy Choo for a parking space closer to her building.

The weather was perfect for a late spring morning. Al Roker, Anna's secret weatherman crush, had promised some storms later in the day for her "neck of the woods" of Pressley Heights, NC, but right now the weather was perfect. She took a moment before she opened the glass doors to her building, just enjoying the breeze and letting the sunshine warm her face. Well, Anna thought, better go see what mayhem and joy she had awaiting her this morning. Anna also couldn't wait to hear from her daddy. She just knew that there was something fishy with Melanie, and she never had a feeling like this unless it turned out to be a doozy. She wanted so bad to help the trio who had brought her so much joy at their consult. She needed to call and give an update when she had more information.

"Good morning, Shellie! I see that you are already hard at it this morning." Anna stopped by the break room and noticed that Shellie had her piping-hot, jumbo-sized mug of coffee, probably twenty-five dollars' worth from Starbucks, and the paper laid out like she was going to wrap presents with it. "Anything worth reading in the paper this morning? I see that you have thoroughly examined it for anything worth my time."

Shellie came running in from her office, stopping to turn on the lamps in the waiting room. "No, nothing good at all. I checked the obits. No one we know in them, so that's good. How was your evening?"

"Good, good. Just a regular Monday night. Daddy came for dinner, pouted about Momma and her high-society friends and enjoyed his time with the boys. Nothing out of the ordinary, which suits me just fine." Anna pulled a cup out of the cabinet, retrieved a Mountain Dew from the fridge, and cracked it open. Anna didn't like coffee, except the smell of it brewing, so she substituted Mountain Dew for her morning shot of caffeine. "What does the morning look like?"

"Your first meeting is at ten. A man who is upset with his parents and wants to sue them, something about his birth. And then your daddy called and said he would like to meet with you sometime this afternoon, something about the Logan case." Shellie made her way to her desk and double-checked the calendar. "You have a couple of calls to return and calendar call at the courthouse this afternoon. We will be able to get the dates for the cases that we still have to get before a judge. Nothing too bad today."

"Thanks, Shellie." Anna glanced over the paper. Shellie had been right; nothing in there to spark enough of an interest to pick up and read, so on to bigger and better things. "Hey, Shellie, want to call Peg and Gigi to see if they want to do dinner Thursday night at the Broken Twig, the one downtown? We haven't all been out together in a long time."

"I am good for Thursday even if they aren't. I will shoot them a text and see what they say. Sounds good to me."

"Okay, just let me know. Either way with them, we are going. Their loss if they can't come. I bet they will, though. The last time I talked to Gigi, she seemed ready for an evening out with the girls." Anna was already looking forward to Thursday. "I am going to return those calls before my ten o'clock gets here."

Anna went into her office. First things first: shoes *off*. Her feet were angry with her, and she didn't care how good they looked in those shoes. Anna kicked off her Jimmy Choos and slipped on her trusty flip-flops. She had quite the stash of flops under her desk. Her desk, the massive dark-cherry desk, was probably the most cherished thing in the whole office. It was once her grandfather's. Once he had passed away, she had inherited his house. The one piece of furniture that she wanted most was this desk. Some of her fondest memories of her papaw was of him sitting at his desk, working, looking very important and smart. She remembered that her papaw, no matter how much work he had to do or how hard he was working at his desk, he would always push his chair back, help her to climb up in his lap, and talk, laugh, read, and draw anything she wanted. As she grew, he would still push back from his work, she would pull up a chair, and they would talk, laugh, and discuss her life. He was never too busy to push back from that desk and spend time with her. She wanted that desk to be part of her, her work, and so that she could hold on to a part of that memory that was actually tangible.

Other than the desk, she had purchased a large conference table at an antique store down by the river. The table sat six easily but could sit eight if needed. It was made of reclaimed timbers from an old home from the area. The legs were made to match with other pieces of the same home. Each chair that sat around the table was different. Anna had chosen each chair personally; all had their own personality. They were different in size and material but all were sturdy, comfortable, and gave the look of class, professional, and different. A talking piece when taken in altogether or separately. *Thanks, HGTV.*

She made the calls; for some she left messages, and two she could mark as done. Anna tried to make all her calls herself. She tried hard to keep her clients happy, keeping their trust and making them feel as if she was working only for them. At any time she could have many cases going at once, but she tried to make each client feel as if they were her one and only. She tried hard, and she sometimes had to turn down cases. Being from the town, sometimes the cases, or the participants in a case, caused her a conflict of interest and she couldn't be their counsel. Sometimes she had a full plate, but she never overextended herself. She made a good living; she was trusted and respected. She and Shellie had built a good business and made a good team. She was proud of what they had accomplished together.

Shellie appeared at Anna's door. "Your meeting this morning is with a Mr. Cam Hendrix. He wants to speak with you about his parents and his issues. He wants to sue them about a very personal matter. He wanted to explain it to you himself, wouldn't divulge a lot of information to me, but I think it may have to do with his birth." Shellie raised her eyebrows and leaned up against the doorframe. "He kept referring to something that wasn't done and how it wasn't handled properly after his birth." A sly smile came across Shellie's face. Nothing brought her more joy than giving Anna cases that would or could cause some giggles…or discomfort. "Can't imagine what that might be. Good luck with that."

"Thanks, Shel. So I have a little time here before Mr. Hendrix arrives. Let me just look into some common issues for suing parents after your birth. Google should have a lot of information about that." Anna looked at Shellie and sat back. "Give me a couple of minutes after he arrives and watch him in the lobby. Let me know if he looks like a creeper, okay? I will come get him once I have the go-ahead from you."

"Gotcha. I will give you a heads-up on any creeper material I can tell. You are so lucky you have me."

"Lucky may be too strong a word." Anna winked at Shellie. "Lucky would be if you had gotten all the information out of him before the morning of his meeting. That would be lucky. I will leave it as I am blessed to have you deal with him first." Anna smiled, and with that Shellie retreated to her desk.

Anna worked diligently, trying to find and be prepared for whatever Mr. Hendrix was going to throw at her, until her IM popped up with the report from Shellie.

>   9:54 A.M. SHELLIE T. HARPER
>   He is well dressed, suit/tie. He is clean-cut, well-spoken, and his train seems to be 100% on the rails. Could go off at any moment, but right now, he seems calm, cool, and collected. He has some papers with him, but nothing else. My official Nut-O-Meter is giving him a normal score.

Anna quickly typed back.

>   9:55 A.M. ANNA N. DAWSON
>   You had so better be right about this. I will be out in just a few. I have to put these death trap shoes on and collect myself. I will be right out. Thanks. If this goes bad, you owe me lunch.

IT'S IN THE BAG

Anna got up, leaving her flip-flops under the desk, and headed over to retrieve her heels. She took a quick look in the mirror, smiled, and fluffed her hair like her momma always said to do. Anna took an extra moment. Her hair did look, well, good, fluffed and all, and she looked good today. She felt good, and she liked that very much. Maybe her momma was right. Nah, that couldn't be it. Maybe she was just having a good day.

Anna took a chance for one more deep breath as she turned the doorknob on her office door. She exhaled and put on the million-dollar smile that she had worked years to perfect. She took two steps out of her door, and the gentleman in the leather chair looked up from his phone and began to stand. "Hello, Mr. Hendrix. It is very nice to meet you. My name is Anna Dawson. I am very happy you were able to come and meet with me this morning." Anna shook the man's hand and turned to show him into her office. "Right this way. You can take a seat at the conference table or in one of the chairs in front of my desk. Whichever you feel you would be most comfortable in is fine with me."

Mr. Hendrix walked into Anna's office, and she closed the door behind them. He seemed to take in the room, looking at the conference table and at the chairs at her desk. He walked toward the table, chose a chair, and pulled it out. "I think this will be fine, Ms. Dawson. I appreciate you agreeing to meet with me today. My problem, or my issue, with my parents is not one that I think gets talked about too often. I appreciate your time." With that he took his seat.

Anna walked over to her desk and gathered her pen, her cup of Mountain Dew, and her legal pad. "Well, Mr. Hendrix, that is exactly what this meeting is for. For me to understand your issue with your parents and to see if there is any way I can help remedy that issue." Anna set down her things, pulled out her own chair, and looked again at Mr. Hendrix. "Can I offer you some coffee, water, anything at all?" Mr. Hendrix shook his head, thanking her for the offer, saying that he had just finished a breakfast out. "Well, if you change your mind, just let me know." Anna got settled and decided to jump right in. "So tell me, Mr. Hendrix, tell me what brings you in and how meeting with me can help you resolve that issue."

Mr. Hendrix looked a little nervous. "Well, you see, I am upset with my parents for how they failed to secure my afterbirth and how they did not properly bury it. I strongly believe in that practice and feel I have been the recipient of ill-favored treatment. I feel that this matter is something that should be made right by my parents." He looked straight at Anna, steadfast in his convictions.

Anna had so many questions that she needed the answers to in order to know the why, what in the world, and the just how he thought his parents could make this up to him. Anna was fairly certain that after the birth of a child, unless the umbilical cord was being preserved for stem cells or such, the hospital would dispose of that material. Whether by incineration or as medical waste, it wasn't like she was going to be able to have his parents produce the placenta from what seemed like it would be thirty-plus years ago. She also made a mental note to remember this for future reference. This was not something that she had googled in her premeeting research.

"Well, Mr. Hendrix, let me get some information from you and we will see where we stand." Anna was going to need to be a little delicate with this. She had a feeling about Mr. Hendrix now and she wasn't so sure that Shellie's "Nut-O-Meter" was working properly; it might just need a trip to the shop. "Let's start with this. What is your date of birth?"

"March 14, 1983. I was born in the local hospital here, in Pressley Heights. My parents are from here and we have lived here, or in the general area, my whole life. My father is a mechanic and my mother works at First Federal Bank as VP. My father is sixty-one, and my mother is fifty-eight." He seemed willing to give information that Anna hadn't even asked for yet. "I am not a weirdo. I am not some guy with ideas that are so totally off the wall. I am just a little pissed that they didn't bury my placenta."

"Okay, I see." Anna quickly made some notes. "I would never call you a weirdo at all. Never. I have heard that in some cultures that the burial of the placenta after a child is born is quite popular or a general practice. I understand that the Navajo Indians practice this. Also there are some people in New Zealand—the Maori people, I believe—that also follow this ritual." Anna wasn't seeing any reaction from her client across the table. "I have read that the reasons that some peoples do this is they believe that the placenta is in fact a living part of the child, the home it grew in that helped sustain life. They believe that the placenta, once the child is born, should be buried to show that it had served its purpose and could now return to the earth."

"Exactly! That is exactly what I am talking about. My parents did me a huge injustice when they did not do this for me. That is why I am seeking to make them pay for their failure to do so." Mr. Hendrix seemed dead set on this. "I need you to make them understand and make them make this right."

"Well, while I feel that I understand where you are coming from, and I can sense your hurt toward your parents, let's keep going and see where I may be able to help you. First, do you have any siblings?"

"Nope."

"Do you or your parents participate or are you involved in a religion that practices this as a norm or a teaching of its doctrine?" Anna was grasping at straws here.

"No, we are all Southern Baptist." Mr. Hendrix wasn't anything if he wasn't direct in his answers.

"What about how your parents handled your birth makes you the most upset? Is it just the placenta nonburial, or is it something else too?" Anna continued to try. "What exactly are you asking for your parents to do to make this right in your eyes?"

"I feel I was wronged that they didn't care enough to bury the placenta that was part of my birth. I have researched, and there are more people in the States here that practice this. They have to get special permission from the hospital, but many do this with a midwife, or after a home birth. It is done. I am not crazy. I wanted this for me."

Oh, Anna knew she was in for it now. Anna had been an attorney now for a little over seven years, hearing what she thought was just about everything, between being raised by the town sheriff and now her current occupation, which she was starting to question. She was going to have to tread lightly with Mr. Hendrix. His crazy train seemed to have started to derail, with him as conductor, right here at her conference table.

"I see. Your last statement you just made, 'I wanted this for me,' that is where I take a pause." Anna knew that she had just pushed the rest of the train off the tracks. "I understand that now, sitting here in 2020, that you say back then, in 1983, just after you were born, that you wanted your placenta buried and treated differently than it was." Anna paused. "I am just a little bit older than you, but I haven't met anyone yet, in all my life, who has a crystal-clear recollection of what they wanted right after their birth. Except for instinct to eat and be held and kept warm, I know not one infant who consciously knows where they are, what had just happened, or why they just went on that crazy trip called birth. I fail to believe that you can honestly recall or believe that you wanted that for you at that moment." Anna just laid it all out there. "I feel that this is something you believe more now rather than at the time it could have been done."

"You think I'm crazy, don't you?" Seemed Mr. Hendrix could lay it all out as well.

"I do not think you are crazy. I think you have a belief that a placenta is something that should be handled in a certain way. I think that you wish, or you would have preferred, that your parents handled the placenta differently when you were born. Is that correct? Am I close to what you are feeling, where your feelings of being wronged come from?"

"Yes, precisely. I feel that they should have taken in to account the possibility that I would have wanted it handled differently or with more care. I am very upset that it was simply treated as medical waste and destroyed."

Anna thought for a moment. "Okay, I just want to ask a few more questions about you. I see from your ring I can assume you are married."

"Yes, Lora and I have been married for eight years. We have two children—Hope, who is six, and Tyler, who is four." Mr. Hendrix beamed with the subject of his family being brought up. His wallet was out of his back pocket too fast to know what had happened. "Here is a picture of Lora. This was taken right after we were engaged.

It is one of my favorites of her. And here is Hope. She was around five here. And this here"—he pulled out one last photo to share—"this is Tyler. They are just a pleasure, my pride and joy."

"Your family is quite lovely. I have children myself. They are wonderful. You all look very happy. So tell me, where did you bury your children's placentas after their births? Did you do it on your property or on some family land?" Anna just had to know.

"Oh, we didn't do that with Hope's or Tyler's. My wife thinks the whole idea is gross and would not have anything to do with even thinking about it. She told me she would leave me, take the children, and have me evaluated if I pushed the issue or even talked about it with the doctor or nurses. The hospital took care of the disposal, and that was that." Mr. Hendrix shook his head. "Lora told me she thought that doing that was very barbaric and from the Dark Ages. She would not budge."

Anna was instantly bewildered, and it came out with astonishment and her best teen expression. "Wait, what?" Anna could feel her eyebrows come together as she furrowed her brow. "You mean to say that you are here talking to me about wanting to sue or to recoup some sort of damages from your parents for not taking your placenta home and burying it in the yard, even though it was your desire when you were all of five minutes old? That seems a bit hypercritical, if I do say so myself, and I just did." Anna really needed to work on her delivery sometimes. The filter that most people have, hers always seemed to be missing.

Anna wasn't done. Even though the look on Mr. Hendrix's face said that she should be done, she had more to say. "I do not think that I can help you, sir. Well, on second thought, I think I can. I do hope that you don't take offense—well, I don't really care if you do. Just hear me out. You need to go directly to your parents, offer an apology for being so childish, and try to move on with a relationship with them. They did not do you any harm, not at all. You owe your children a relationship with their grandparents, who seem to have raised you in a good home, except for the whole thing about hurting your feelings with the placenta. Go to Lowe's, to the nursery in town. Buy a tree. Go plant that. Let it go." With that, Anna got up, marched across her office, opened the door, and saw Mr. Hendrix out. She shut the door behind her and kicked off her shoes.

As Anna started to google new careers, Shellie came to the door and told her that her daddy was on the line, waiting to speak with her. "He said it was really important and that he had to speak with you directly. He said that he would wait. So he has been on hold for about ten minutes. I thought he would give up and hang up, but I keep checking on him and he is still there."

Anna picked up the phone and pressed the flashing button to pick up the call. "Hello, Daddy. Whatcha got for me?"

"Hello, Little," Jake said in his booming voice. "Little" had been his nickname for Anna since she had been a baby. It stuck to this day, even though she wasn't that "little" anymore. "You need to get down here to my office today. Seems that lady you had me check into has quite the past—and present, really. As usual, you have really stepped into it this time. We will need to sit down and discuss some aspects of this. We will have to work together with a couple of different divisions to stop this crackpot from doing any more damage. She is quite the conniving woman."

Anna's countenance perked up immediately. "Really, like what? What did you find out?"

"I really think that we need to talk about this here, at my office. Tony, a detective I have placed on this case, can be here around three. Do you think you could make it around then? Bring Shellie with you. We will need all the eyes and minds on this one."

"I am sure we both can be there at around three. But please give me a hint, please?" Anna needed her daddy to throw her a bone.

"All I will say is that someone is here from Homicide. See you soon. And bring me one of them iced froufrou coffee things you youngsters drink now. Those are so good, and your momma says I shouldn't drink them on account of my blood sugar. Last time I checked, she ain't a doc." With that, the line fell silent.

Anna made a note to pick up an iced café latte from Starbucks and walked barefoot out to Shellie's desk. "Please tell me nothing has been added for in-office meetings for this afternoon. If so, please call

IT'S IN THE BAG

and reschedule. We are due at Daddy's office at three, and don't let me forget to pick up an iced latte for him."

"We don't have any in-person meetings this afternoon at all, any phone calls we can handle elsewhere, and one iced latte, check!" Shellie looked happier than she had all day. She loved going to Jake's office. Shellie would never admit it, but she had a thing for Eddie, Lieutenant Eddie Mullins. Shellie would be useless if he was present, but still, it would be entertaining. Both were single, both were intrigued by each other…both were spineless when it came to letting the other know.

"Okay, sounds good. Let's go grab a late lunch. I need to stop by the courthouse and file a couple of things, then we will grab the latte and head to Daddy's. That sound okay?" Anna walked toward her office door. "Oh, and grab your umbrella. Roker promised some rain this afternoon."

*****

Anna would have to give it to Al Roker; he was almost never wrong. Today was no exception. As if on cue, the torrential thunderstorm set in at 2:58 p.m., just as Anna was parking her Honda Odyssey next to her daddy's car. "I don't understand why Daddy has to park so far across the parking lot. He is old, he is the sheriff, and he has worked his way up to a better spot. Right? I mean, geez. Looks like they would give him a spot by the door." Anna needed to find a valid reason for her being upset at having to walk in the rain, with a contraband latte, and somehow do it in her most expensive shoes ever. "I should have kept my flip-flops on. Let's just sit here for a few and see if this lets up any."

"I don't think we should keep your daddy waiting. I don't like it when he is upset and yells. He makes me nervous." Shellie was getting her purse and coffee balanced in one hand as she reached to the floorboard for her umbrella. "Write one of your scathing letters to your best friend Mr. Weather Pants Al Roker and ask him to drum up some decent springtime weather for us down here. This is getting to be an everyday thing."

"Although I love Al, he is neither Jesus nor does he do any special-weather orders. I shall pen him a love letter, to Savannah, Hoda, Jenna, Carson…" Anna was getting sidetracked in her love of *Today*.

Shellie opened the door and opened her umbrella. She looked back at Anna. "I certainly hope I am the only one you obsess over *The Today Show* to. Anybody else and they would think you are talking about actual people you know. Come on. I am not waiting on you. Meet you inside." Shellie was out of the car, slamming the door shut, and halfway across the parking lot before Anna even had time to be offended by her comment.

Anna really didn't want to go out in the rain, really…but the curiosity was greater than her want to stay dry. She was nothing if she wasn't dedicated to the law and to helping out the trio of country bumpkins who were trying to keep their father alive and their inheritance intact. Anna tried that same trick that Shellie did, balancing the cup carrier of lattes (she had given in and gotten one for herself; no sense in her daddy's blood sugar skyrocketing alone), her purse, her workbag, and umbrella. Easy-peasy.

Anna made it across the parking lot, dodging most puddles, and only getting her feet and her legs wet. Not an issue at all. She managed to punch the handicapped access button to make her no-free-hand-available entrance easier. Inside the building, she put the cup holder down on the table in the entrance, shut her umbrella, and leaned it up against the wall so it could drip onto the rug. Hopefully, no one would steal it, certainly not from the sheriff's department; one would think it would be safe here. Tell that to about six other umbrellas that had mysteriously disappeared during her lifetime of doing the same thing. Anna had a particular fondness for this umbrella; it was covered in puppies and kittens in all different colors. The boys had gotten it for her birthday that past year. Anna picked it back up and started toward her daddy's office. She would be darned if the hoodlums of Pressley Heights, or any of the employees of this fine establishment for that matter, stole her umbrella today. Not today, suckers!

Shellie came out of Jake's office and met Anna in the hallway, grabbing the cup holder from Anna as she turned and fell into step

IT'S IN THE BAG

with her. "Wait till you see what's in your daddy's office. Just wait till you see. It won't matter that it's raining buckets outside, not when you see what your daddy has got in there."

"Well, my Lordy in heaven, Shellie, does he have the sunshine itself in his office or just one of them lights they use to interrogate people? I hope he has had one of those wall dryers installed. My feet are freezing, and my pants are drenched." Anna laughed. Shellie was one who was easily excited. "Maybe a dozen puppies, and he wants to let me pick one out for my very own, then he can see the joy on Momma's face as he brings the rest home with him."

Anna should not have been quick to be so snarky; she had been the recipient of some swift karma in the past, swift judgment from the Lord and some very quick failure of her own devices. This was going to be one of those times. Anna should have just turned around and marched right back out to her car, sans umbrella and her discount Jimmy Choos. She should have just retreated before what was about to befall her. *Fall* being the relevant word there.

Shellie went on ahead of Anna, entered the door, to the right, and headed to a chair in front of Jake's desk. Jake's office was a sort of museum of sorts, a large room with mementos, awards, and photos of Jake with dignitaries, state officials, past presidents, the family, and even his dog, General. General was an old, clumsy, long-eared, short-tempered basset hound. The dog simply would not die. It came to the office every day with Jake, had a bed, an opinion, and a constantly full dog food bowl. General had the oddest relationship with Anna. General loved Anna from the moment Jake had brought him home as a pup, seemingly a hundred years ago. General took an immediate liking to Anna, a liking that neither Anna nor anyone else could figure out.

Anna entered the doorway of her father's office. She had been there a million and one times before; she could walk in there blindfolded. Nothing was ever moved; nothing ever changed. Her father liked it that way; he was a creature of habit. Anna made her entrance, starting to take her bag off her shoulder, digging into it to pull out her phone and a pen. That was the moment she glanced up, took a sweeping look around the office at the ones gathered around, and smiled at each face with the million-dollar smile, the one that her momma had ingrained in her head that she must enter the room with.

Most of the people present she knew; a couple she did not. She noticed a uniformed officer whom she did not recall ever meeting, but she looked totally badass in her uniform. Anna then eyed a tall, dark-headed man and she took a little extra time checking out the man in the attractively cut blue suit. Burgundy tie, button-down collar, pressed shirt that fitted his body well. She was intrigued, caught off guard by the look and the face of a man. It was something that had not happened in a very long time, her being stopped in her tracks by a man just by his looks. Anna definitely noticed the man with the blue suit and the piercing green eyes.

What Anna failed to notice was that General had gotten his ancient sack of bones up and started toward the door. At the exact same time as she was crossing the hardwood floor, General decided to sit down almost directly in her path. Anna stepped and immediately felt something odd under her foot, something thin and hard, even through the sole of her shoe. It was at that exact moment that General let out such a high-pitched yelp that probably woke a few of the dead in the cemetery across town. The corpses probably thought that Jesus had sounded the trumpet and it was time to go. This instantly set off an unfortunate series of events, with Anna as the main attraction.

Anna jumped when General made such a fuss and landed on her left foot, only to have her left ankle give way and turn under her. With the force of her jump, the forward momentum of her movement, and the direction of her fall, it seemed to propel her so much that when she hit the hardwood floor she slid for quite a ways. The only thing that helped to stop her from going all the way to her daddy's desk was the fact that she took out the trash can. Papers, empty coffee cups, candy bar wrappers, and used tissues flew everywhere, including all over her. When she came to a stop, she collapsed the rest of the way to the floor, not caring that she hit her head and was lying now at the feet of the good-looking man in the blue suit. She shut her eyes and felt her body begin to hurt.

Before Anna knew it, Shellie was at one side and Mr. Blue Suit was on the other. Jake was over by General, who was licking his tail. "Good gracious, Little. I think you broke his tail. Look at him, he is in pain. What in the world were you thinking?" Jake was bent down by his dog, checking his tail and petting his head.

"Daddy, what are you doing? General about killed me. His tail is fine. I didn't break it off, I see no blood. If I see you take out your cell phone and call the vet, I will knock you in the head. I am your only child, lying on the floor of your office, and you are checking the tail of a dog who has three paws in the grave. Bless." Anna was sitting up but not happy. "Are you even concerned if I have a concussion, a broken bone, or if I am injured in any way?"

Jake sat down by the dog, still feeling his tail. General had already forgotten about his tail and was just loving the fact that he was getting extra attention. "Little, I have seen you fall so many times, believe me, this one was not in the top ten of your all-time best. I have said it before and I am sure I will say it again. You, my dear, sure know how to make an entrance." Jake was now laughing and playing with the dog. General's tail was wagging and seemed unscathed.

Anna looked at Shellie. "Thanks. Nice to know the people who truly love me." Anna then looked Mr. Blue Suit. "Hello, my name is Anna. I am Jake's daughter, and General's older sister. I am not the chosen one." Anna took off her shoes and looked at her ankle. She rubbed it and deemed it turned but not broken. She began to try to get up.

"Here, let me help you stand up." Mr. Blue Suit held out his hands and helped Anna to her feet. "There you go." Anna brushed off her hands on her pants as Mr. Blue Suit reached out his hand to introduce himself. "Hello, I am Detective Tony Phillips. I am relatively new, but I have heard about you." Tony laughed.

Anna smiled. "Well, I hope that the little episode just now doesn't make me out to be any worse than you already think. I can only imagine what you have heard, but get to know me for yourself…and don't listen to anything this man tells you about me." Anna walked over to her daddy and helped him back up with help from the other officer she needed to meet. After getting her daddy on his feet and patting General on the head, she turned to the lady officer. "Hello, I am Anna Dawson, his daughter." She motioned over to her father, who was sitting back down at his desk and slurping his latte.

The officer was prettier up close than Anna had first thought. Beautiful red hair, fair skin, and young. "Hello, I am Officer Sue Jackson. I was called in to this meeting. I have had some experience with this lady in question and your dad—I mean, Sheriff Dawson—thought I would be of help. It is very nice to meet you."

Anna needed to check herself in the bathroom. She quickly made certain of where General was: circling his bed, apparently tired from all the excitement. "Look, everyone, I need just a moment, and then we can get started. I will be right back. Going to run to the potty." Anna slipped out the door. She turned to the right but needed to be going to the left. She had made it almost all the way to the doors leading outside before she realized her mistake. Making a U-turn, she headed down the hall toward the bathrooms. As she got closer to her daddy's office, she saw Detective Phillips standing just outside the door.

As she went to pass by him, he grabbed the upper part of her arm and stopped her. They were facing each other, just about as close to face-to-face as one can get without knowing someone a little better than they did. Their eyes locked, and she felt a jolt go up her arm into her brain. She could not move.

"Are you sure you are okay?" His voice went right over her head. She saw his lips moving, heard a voice, but was not catching what he was saying. "Anna. Anna, are you okay?" He let her arm go and stood directly in front of her now.

"Wait, what did you say?" Anna closed her eyes and shook her head. "Yeah, I think I am. I just need a moment to myself in the bathroom. I will be right back."

"Okay, I just wanted to make sure. You took quite a tumble, and when you said you were going to the bathroom, you went toward the main entrance. Just needed to make sure you weren't lying out in the hallway here. I am going to send your assistant in with you." Detective Phillips called out for Shellie. The two ladies made their way to the bathroom, and he went back into the office.

IT'S IN THE BAG

Anna had never felt like that before. Never felt such an electric feeling when she was touched by another person, male or female. His touch, his strong hand on her arm, scrambled her brain and sent a current through her that she just could not explain. Maybe she had fallen harder than she had first thought. Maybe she had hurt some nerves in her back or neck. That was the most amazing feeling in the world, obviously because she was having to splash water on her face and neck to calm herself. It was probably a deadly nerve disease or a brain injury. That could be easier an explanation than her feeling something for a man she had just met, just at his touch. She had obviously jarred her brain.

Anna talked to herself until she had gotten herself back to a calmer version of herself. She told herself she was filled with a mix of embarrassment, adrenaline, pain, and a feeling of betrayal from a dog she had loved all of his ninety-nine years. That was it. She was fine. Just banged up, a little bit embarrassed, and now she needed to let that go and get it together. She had work to do.

Shellie stood off in the corner of the bathroom, as if watching a horror movie, anxiously waiting for something horrid to happen and for her to run screaming from the bathroom. "Are you okay? You are really freaking me out. Do you need to go to Urgent Care? Hospital? Did you hurt your bag thing? How is your head? I saw it hit the floor, I think. So much was happening, I didn't catch it all."

"I am fine. I am just embarrassed." Anna was smoothing out her shirt and her pants. She tucked in her shirt and checked her makeup and hair in the mirror. "Do you have any lip gloss on you?" Anna pinched her cheeks to force some color back in her face. "I just need a little something to hide the fact that I just fell out on the floor, something to perk up the looks here."

Shellie reached into the pockets of her dress pants. She always had lip gloss. She was addicted to it. If they didn't lock her away in a drug treatment facility, Anna would call and report the amount of lip gloss that Shellie consumed. But Shellie was too much of an asset. As was just proven again.

"Here you go. I believe this is called Cherry Jubilee. May be just a little darker than you like, but it will do in a rush." Shellie handed it over and watched Anna apply some to her lips. Anna wouldn't agree, but it made her face light up. "Perfect. Now I am sure Detective Phillips will notice you for sure, especially since you will be totally upright. Hopefully."

Anna huffed as she handed the lip gloss back to Shellie, took one last look at herself, opened the door, and held it as both ladies walked back out into the hallway. "I will have you know that I want to look good for everyone in that room, especially since my…umm… entrance went so well. I want to look my best, always. My momma ingrained that in me. Here you go, the best I can do today. I have no interest in Mr. Blue Suit, no matter how good his behind looks in it, or how well that shirt fits his broad chest. No interest at all." Anna stood outside the door to her father's office. "Now behave."

CHAPTER 4

"Well, I want to thank everyone for meeting here this afternoon, and thank you, Anna, for providing some entertainment for us. I have always been able to rely on you for that." Jake grinned as he gave his daughter some ribbing.

"You are quite welcome, Daddy. I aim to please," Anna snapped at her father.

Jake, not paying her any attention, kept the meeting on track. "It seems that we have the makings of a doozy of a case on our hands. With just the little bit of information that Anna gave me, and with the help of Detective Phillips and Officer Jackson, we have been able to dig up some dirt on a one, ah, Melanie Green. Seems to be as if you stepped right into a big one, Anna. Why don't you catch everyone up on how this all came about, and we will go from there?"

Anna told the group about the consult she had had with the Logan family. She talked about how the children had raised the concern that their father might be in danger. She talked and finally felt in her element. All clumsiness and joking by her father aside, she was an excellent attorney with a sharp eye for cases that might have an air of criminality; in other words, she knew when to bring in the boys in blue.

While she talked, the others took notes, and one in particular took note of just how professional Anna could be. Anna finished up her summary, thinking about how she promised this family to focus on the safety and health of their father. Then she looked to the others to share what they knew, hoping to find out a little bit about their suspect's history.

Jake took the helm. "Thanks, Anna, great job. All right, Detective Phillips, why don't you fill us in on what you have on her and then we will hear from Officer Jackson."

Detective Phillips began to go over the facts that he had with him. "It seems that Ms. Green has been doing this to families for quite some time. I have five cases, where she was married at the time of her husband's passing. Two of the cases were brought to our attention by the children of the deceased. One or two, okay, you have bad luck and you outlived the man, but when you start adding up four and five instances, all with a great deal of money to be had from inheritance and homes and property to be sold, you can be talking about quite the motive." He took a moment to let that sink in for everyone. "I have talked to the two families who brought this woman to our attention, took their statements, tried to track down anything to pin a crime on the lady, but she is apparently good, really good at her schemes."

"So you guys have had your eyes on her for possible homicides of her husbands for, what, years, and nothing?" Anna couldn't hold her tongue anymore. From the moment he had mentioned that he had spoken with the families, she knew she would be all over that as soon as she could get a word in. "If you have only talked to two families, that seems like it would be enough to at least open a case. What is up with the other families? Have you tried to talk to them at all?"

"Oh, yes, we have. We found out about the fifth one just recently, from a group of friends of the family who never had a good feeling about Melanie. The friends said that their friend only knew Melanie for three days before getting married to her. His name was Vernon Chambers. He was sixty years old when they married. His wife of thirty years had passed away six months earlier from a long battle with cancer. He was an antiques dealer, well-established, and was sixty-one when he died in a drowning accident while boating alone with Melanie. His date of death is August 10 of the year before last." Detective Phillips flipped over his notepad. "They were married for fifteen months at the time of his death. Mr. Chambers had no children from his previous marriage, was an only child, and had no heirs to speak of. Best we can estimate, Melanie cashed in on a two-hundred-thousand-dollar life insurance policy, collected the profit from the sale of the antique business, well over a million, and until recently was living in the home that they shared. It went on the market approximately two months ago."

"And why wasn't there an investigation? Into the boating accident?" Anna questioned Detective Phillips to find out more information mostly, but she was enjoying watching and listening to him.

Detective Phillips was starting to feel like he was on the stand giving testimony in a trial. It seemed that he and Anna were the only ones speaking, although he was having to do most of the talking and answering. Everyone else seemed quite entertained and not about to butt in. "There was an investigation, by our department as a matter of fact, and it all fell in line with how she said that it had happened. They had been out for a day on the boat, enjoyed lunch, a little wine, maybe too much in his case. They went swimming without life jackets, and she was the only one to return to the boat. She made a call to the authorities, and his body was found the next day. We had no reason at the time that it happened to think it anything else than a horrible accident."

"Humph, likely story." Anna couldn't help it, but she also couldn't defend her comment. "Sorry, sometimes my mouth speaks before my brain catches up. Always been a problem of mine." Anna shot a look at her father. "Not one word, Daddy." Anna looked back at Detective Phillips. "I am sorry." She turned on the charm and the big eyes and the smile, hoping to get his forgiveness. Anna was thinking she may need a lot more of his help. "Can I talk with these friends? Can I have the information you have and maybe I can talk to the families of the others, if I can find them, and see what I can come up with?"

"I can give you all that I have—the contacts, the names. Good luck with finding the ones that I couldn't. I kept running into dead ends. If you can find out more information, go for it. It would go a long way into trying to figure this woman out. Honestly, I think you have something here."

Detective Phillips copied the information that he had in his file. Officer Jackson had some background information about Melanie

Buxton Logan. Her maiden name was Buxton, a popular name just a little south of this area; maybe some of her family still lived in the area and could answer some questions. This was a good start.

"I wanted to give you my cell number and the number to my office. Please keep me posted on anything you come up with. This is a case I will keep open since I know that you are working on it and it will stay that way until you say it is done. I will keep checking out things too. I can run a few reports on the maiden name and try to flush out some family." Detective Phillips handed her his card with his office phone on the front and his cell number written on the back. "I look forward to working with you on this. This lady sounds like a real piece of work. Hopefully, no one else will be hurt by her."

He started to walk off and then turned back to Anna. "And you can call me Tony. The whole 'Detective Phillips' thing gets a little old. I prefer my friends to call me Tony." He flashed a smile that made her knees weak. "Talk later, Anna." With that, he said his good-byes to Jake, shaking hands and laughing at some crazy comment Jake had said in a whisper, and he was gone.

A few minutes later, Officer Jackson got a call on her cell and excused herself to her office upstairs. Anna looked forward to getting to know her better. She seemed witty, smart, and fun. She could be someone good to get to know.

"So, Little, tell me what you're thinking? Do you think you can do anything more to check this lady out?" Jake sat back down in his big leather chair and spun so that he could lean his elbows up on his desk. "I personally think you could be sitting on a big, big case of a black widow."

Anna sat back down in a chair across from her daddy, Shellie at her left in a matching chair. "I don't know, Daddy, but I think we have our work cut out for us. If Tony and Officer Jackson gave all the information they could find, and this is what they do for a living, I hope that we can dig a little deeper, use our brains, and figure this lady out. I want to stop anything bad from happening to Mr. Logan if at all possible. There is so much we don't know and so much to find out. We need to try to go back to before the beginning and see if she does just have terrible luck or she is helping these men meet their demise to help her bottom line."

"I don't know about this lady, but I can tell someone has the hots for Officer Tony. That is what I got from today, that Anna can't walk into a room without falling, and she got up off the floor and fell for your detective." Shellie was one to offer her opinion whenever she saw fit. "I wasn't paying too close attention to the notes on this Melanie lady, Lady Midnight, or whoever she is, but I haven't seen Anna act like that in quite a while." Shellie smiled at Jake.

Jake shook his head and smiled. "Shellie, my dear, you and I think a lot alike. You, my dear, you would make a great detective. If you ever get tired of working for my slave driver of a daughter, you call me anytime, and I will put you to work. Very perceptive, Shellie. I too saw my girl eyeing Tony, and I will tell you what, she could do a whole lot worse. Tony is a good man, been through hell and back, but a good man."

"Well, as much as I love sitting here listening to you both give a play-by-play of my meeting skills and how my love life apparently needs to be jump-started, we have work to do, my friend." Anna motioned to Shellie to get her things and get ready to go. "And if you don't stop with your banter about Detective Phillips, you may be down here working for my daddy very soon. Understood?" Anna walked behind her daddy's desk and gave him a kiss on his cheek. Shellie gave a quick wave, and they both headed toward the office door.

"How does that song go? Anna and Tony, sitting in a tree, K-I-S-S-I-N-G." Jake had a great singing voice, and his laughter was legendary, but Anna grabbed the doorknob on her way out and slammed the door so hard the glass shuddered inside the panes. Jake's secretary, Matilda, jumped a mile off her seat and stared as the two ladies walked by, one laughing and one in a huff. Anna could still hear Jake laughing almost all the way to the outside door.

CHAPTER 5

Wednesdays for Anna could be stressful. Not work stressful, mind you, but lunch-with-her-momma stressful. Anna was an accomplished, smart, intelligent, kind, honest, law-abiding woman…who was still terrified by her momma. Anna loved her momma, very much, and perhaps they were so much alike they clashed sometimes. A lot of the times.

Anna shared her momma's stubborn streak, her fierce love of family, and her tenacious work ethic. Anna just had different ways of putting the personality traits that she shared with her mother to work in her life. That was where the differences started. Everyone knew that Anna was Darcy Dawson's daughter, and everyone seemed to envy Anna for that. Anna had heard it a million times of how just wonderful and loving her momma was and how people just loved to be around her. Anna didn't always see it in her personal relationship, but she had to give it to her momma; Darcy Dawson made a life for herself by being good to others. That part of her was genuine. Anna knew her momma loved her and was very proud of her. Anna also knew that her momma also didn't approve of all the things Anna did in life, love, and parenting.

Darcy Dawson was a force to be reckoned with. She was a beautiful woman, inside and out. She was elegant and polished but could also work circles around most people in the yard, doing the work that most women left to the men. There was not a person who ever spent time, even just a moment, with Darcy who didn't walk away with a smile on their face. She was a kind woman who felt the need to help anyone who needed it. This was a wonderful trait, but it was a trait that had gotten her into trouble with Jake a few times. Once he found out about her picking up hitchhikers, taking them out-of-

IT'S IN THE BAG

the-way places, and giving them money, sometimes with Anna in the car as a child. Darcy loved people. She loved to laugh. She loved life.

As Anna had grown into her own woman, she realized there was quite the method to her momma's madness, as she called it. Anna had softened toward her momma, especially since she had had her boys. Anna had given her momma two grandsons, two pieces of kryptonite, as Anna called them. Darcy could not say no to those boys. Anna sometimes could not recognize the woman her momma was around her kids. Things that were downright forbidden for Anna to do as a child, like eat in the car after going through a drive-thru, or just handing out money without having to do a minute of work for it, or buying them whatever they mentioned, or jumping on the furniture in the house—nothing was denied them whatsoever. If Darcy heard of Anna saying no to something, Anna felt like she was on trial thanks to the questioning she would have to endure from her momma. All the whys, "what's so wrong with it," the "why nots," and the "really, what would it hurt?" questions.

Anna often heard about the apparent buffets they would have driving down the road with their "Nonny" at the wheel, french fries going everywhere, and her just laughing at the shenanigans of the little guys. Who was this woman? She had obviously had a stroke of some sort or had been replaced by aliens. An exact replica of the woman who bore her was sent by aliens, which had to be the explanation. This was the one and only reason Anna believed in life on other planets.

How many times had Anna walked into her childhood home and was welcomed by the glorious smell of freshly baked cookies? Anna had thought back once to all the freshly baked cookies she had eaten in her home baked by her momma. Didn't take long to think of all the times that had happened...a big, fat zero. Zero times had there been cookies, cakes, brownies, any known goodie to a child. None. Pop out a couple of grandkids, and Darcy became Betty Crocker; surprise! Her father had noticed as well; his waistline had been a victim of this culinary expert he was suddenly married to. Anna and her daddy had taken a liking to this new skill that Darcy had put into practice.

The one area of her momma's life that Anna was very proud of, and a bit jealous as well, was her marriage. Her momma had been the pick of her father from the moment he first saw her. The story goes that Darcy was helping her mother work in the flowerbeds that ran in front of their house. Jake and some buddies were driving down her street, and at just the right moment, Darcy bent over to pick up a tray of flowers, her jean shorts cut short and tattered around the edges, worn and dirty. At that moment, when Jake saw her, he slowed the car and stared in her direction until she turned and their eyes met. He went on down the street, dumped his friends off at the library, and made his way back to introduce himself to the woman he would marry.

Their marriage had been a good, solid one. It hadn't always been sunshine and birds chirping like in fairy tales, but this one came about as close as you could dream of. Anna could always count on her parents; they were good, fair, a little stricter than most of her friends' parents but fun, decent, hardworking people. She never worried that her parents would get a divorce like some of her best friend's parents. She knew all too well the schedule her friends would have after their parents split up: a weekend here, a weekend there. Some had to spend summers away. It was rough. She was always thankful for her parents' love.

Her momma worked hard, took care of her daddy, the family, and the house. When they had gotten married, Jake and Darcy had dreamed of a house full of children, but the good Lord only blessed them with one, and one was just perfect for them. One child was just fine. When Jake began with the sheriff's department, he worked all the odd-hour shifts, worked most of the holidays, and worked the longest hours. During those years, Darcy was happy to have Anna to keep her company and to keep her mind off the fact that her husband was out doing a dangerous job. Those were the years that she and Anna had been the closest. Darcy couldn't rest easy until she heard his patrol car pull into the driveway. She knew just the sound that only his car made, how he turned into the driveway, and how he would walk up the sidewalk and open the front door. She knew him.

IT'S IN THE BAG

After ten years, and as a retiring sheriff, Jake threw his hat into the ring to fill the empty seat. He had no real experience in the politics of the sheriff's department, but he was a quick learner. Jake had become well-known in the area, partly for his hard work, his knowledge, and his commitment to the community, but just as much for his personality, his way with people, and his laugh. Jake shot from the hip and told it like he saw it; no one ever wondered where they stood with him. Darcy threw herself into his campaign, and together, he won in a landslide. Darcy was Jake's biggest cheerleader; she always had his back and was the best at hosting parties for all the deputies and their families many times during the year. They were the best team.

She helped Jake build the department into one that all the new recruits wanted to come work for, the one for which employees in other departments around the state kept their eyes open for an opening. Darcy and Jake made a good team, seeing each other through the hard times and celebrating with each other the good times. Theirs was a true love story.

Enter a source of struggle in Anna: her failed marriage. Anna felt like she had failed her momma, her daddy, her children, and herself. The morning she decided she couldn't take it anymore, the lies, the hurt and betrayal, the drugs and the drinking, where did she go to first? She stood on the doorstep of her childhood home, knocked on the door, fell into her momma's arms, and cried like she hadn't done since she was a young child. Darcy stood and held her daughter, held her close, and then they sat on the back porch in the wooden rocking chairs, watching the boys play in the yard, and talked for hours.

Together, Anna and Darcy worked to get her and the kids moved closer to the neighborhood she grew up in. Darcy helped take care of the boys while Anna finished her law degree and built up her business. Darcy was the one who sat by her daughter's side when she was fighting for her life in the hospital, back before Anna finally gave in and had her colon removed. Darcy was Anna's advocate while she was unconscious. It was Darcy who worked so hard with Anna's doctors to try a new biologic medicine. Darcy had to make the hardest decision of her life as a mother. The doctors told Darcy that this medicine they could give Anna would either kill her or cure her from her current situation. Darcy gave the go-ahead, and she sat and held Anna's hand, come what may.

Darcy had called it correctly. Within six hours, Anna had come out of her unconscious state and began to talk, and while she was still extremely weak, she was trying to move. Over the next six days, Anna continued to improve, began to eat again, and relearned how to walk on very unstable legs. Anna had let this latest attack of Crohn's go way too far, almost costing her everything. Anna had tried to hide just how bad she was, the bleeding, the constant crippling diarrhea, the nausea, the lack of an appetite. She had become quite good at hiding the fact she could barely go. That whole act came to an abrupt end when Anna collapsed in her parent's driveway, dehydrated and weak with the disease. Darcy had been so mad that Anna hadn't told her how bad she was doing, how much pain she was in. Darcy made Anna promise while in the hospital to never keep anything about her health from her ever again. That time in the hospital represented the closeness that Anna had felt with her momma growing up.

Anna realized that her momma was who she was; nothing was going to change that. And with that realization, Anna knew that her momma would continue to drive her insane, most of the time. Anna also knew that there was no one on the planet who would fight harder for her. In that, she took a great sense of pride knowing her momma always had her back. Anna might end up in the loony bin, but by golly, it would be the nicest looney bin; her momma would make sure of that.

*****

Anna arrived at the Country Club and gave her keys to her favorite valet, Keith. Keith was a wonderful man who had worked with Anna's father as a deputy for almost twenty-eight years. He retired a few years ago and now worked a few days a week so his wife didn't kill him in his sleep, at least that was his story.

"Good afternoon, Ms. Anna. You look beautiful today. Your momma will be so glad to see you. She is just inside the restaurant, a table by the windows. If she gets on you too much, you just send her out here to me." Keith winked. "Have a good lunch, dear."

Anna smiled. She loved Keith. His humor and genuine wonderful personality…he was one reason she looked so forward to her lunches with her momma. "I just love you, Keith! How are you doing? How is that wife of yours? I see you must be doing okay at home. You're still alive." Anna smiled as she gave him a kiss on the cheek. "Don't tell your wife I kissed you. I don't want on her bad list. You can handle that all on your own."

"Have a good lunch, Ms. Anna." Keith smiled as he got into Anna's Honda and shut the door.

Anna walked into the restaurant and spotted her momma over at the table by the window, just as Keith had told her. Her momma looked pretty today: a light-blue pantsuit, cream-colored heels, and silver jewelry. She shouldn't have expected any less. The one thing about Darcy was she was always put together. As she walked over toward the table, Darcy looked up and saw her and smiled. She pushed back her chair and stood as Anna walked up.

"Anna, don't you look lovely." Darcy held out her arms for Anna to come get a hug. "I have looked forward to lunch with you all week, honey. How are you?" Both women hugged and sat down at the table.

Anna had chosen her outfit carefully today, as she did every Wednesdays. She had pulled from a section in her closet she titled "Approved attire by Momma." A little joke she had with herself. Today she had picked a beautiful light-green button-down shirt, a black skirt below the knee length, cute black heels, and a matching light-green purse. She also wore silver jewelry and had her hair up in a cute messy bun. Not her momma's favorite hairstyle, but today it would have to do. At least it would keep the comments about Anna's hair being too long for a woman her age. Good Lord!

"Thank you, Momma!" Anna said with a smile. "I believe this is one of the shirts you got me for my birthday. I love the color. Perfect for spring." Anna placed her napkin on her lap. "How are you doing? You look fabulous, as usual."

"Thanks, sweetie." Darcy placed her napkin back on her lap. She handed Anna her menu, which they never had to use. Every week, it was the same thing for both. "How is everything going? Daddy told me you have been extra busy at work, trying to find a killer woman or something… That sounds really dangerous, honey."

"It isn't dangerous for me, as long as I don't marry the woman in question. She sounds like a peach." Anna laughed. "I am doing well. Good week. The boys are busy, school and stuff. Grades are good. Work is good. Other than that case, nothing out of the ordinary. Been a good week. How about you?"

Darcy smiled really big. "I am so excited! I have started planning your daddy's birthday party for this year. It is going to be wonderful… I am going to need your help, though, to have it come off properly."

Anna had seen this twinkle before in her momma's eyes. The twinkle of planning a wonderful party, the talk of the town, and stressing herself silly. She would work and work herself to the bone, not eat, overdo it, and pay for it with a week in bed after the big event. Been there, done that. Darcy suffered from Crohn's, just like Anna. Apparently it was hereditary. Another thing to be thankful for; her gift from her momma. Darcy's case was not nearly as bad as Anna's. Darcy got by okay with just one prescription daily, a few flares now and then when she was stressed or ate food she shouldn't. Overall, she had done well with it.

"Momma, it's only April. Daddy's birthday isn't until July. What kind of party are you planning here?" Anna couldn't wait for the answer.

Darcy's smile couldn't have been any bigger if her head split right in half. All her pearly whites (all her very own teeth, she would tell anyone who ever commented on her smile) glistened. "Yes, you are right, honey. Your daddy's birthday is officially July sixth, but I have had to reserve the club here for the Saturday before. July Fourth. It will be the best party of the year!"

Anna was already getting a headache. "Momma, while that is wonderful and all, most people are already celebrating the United States on the fourth. What makes you think they will want to come to Daddy's birthday party instead? Most people want hot dogs, BBQ, or burgers and fireworks. Not a birthday cake at a stuffy club." Anna thought that might be a little harsh, so she added, "No offense intended."

"Oh, honey, I have already talked to the club about that. We are allowed to have fireworks here, over the lake on the property. We thought that we would do kind of a big carnival during the afternoon and then for supper do hamburgers, hot dogs, and all the normal picnic fixings with fireworks and dancing into the night. What do you think?" Darcy was the engineer of this crazy train and she was loving every minute of it.

Before Anna could talk herself out of it, she could hear herself say, "That sounds great, Momma. You name it, and the boys and I will be here to help. Sounds like a lot of fun." Anna could see the immediate joy she had just injected into her momma's life. She just hoped that her daddy loved carnivals and fireworks. Anna hoped that all the excitement wouldn't be too much for his old, weary heart. She was also glad her momma was born into money. The entire town would not want to miss this.

"Okay, now that we have that settled… The boys are going to have supper with Daddy and me tomorrow night, right?" Darcy had out her day planner.

"Yes. Shellie and I are going to dinner with Peg and Gigi. We are going to the Broken Twig downtown after work. We shouldn't be too late. The boys can stay till 9:30 or so, as long as they have their homework done…and as long as they are home by ten, which should be fine. They will be there right after they are done at school. Is that still okay?" Anna was so excited about going out to dinner with her friends. It had been a long time since they had all been able to do that. Now that the boys were getting older, one driving, it was easier to do this every now and then. It also gave a change for Momma to spend time with the boys and spoil them.

Darcy took a sip of her half-and-half sweet tea. "Yes, I am looking so forward to it. I will call in the pizzas, cheese sticks, pasta, and have one of those big brownie things they love all delivered around

6:30. That will be great. Then we will have all evening to Netflix and chill."

Anna spat her full sweet tea across the table…"Wait, what did you just say? Momma, good Lord, keep your voice down. Where on earth did you hear that from?" Anna was mortified that some of her momma's stiff friends could have heard her say that she was going to Netflix and chill with her grandsons.

"Oh, Anna, don't be so prudish. Goodness, all the young adults are saying that for when they just hang out." Darcy talked as if she was an expert on the subject of young adult slang. "I know you are all professional and such at your office, but, honey, you have two teenage children. You really should spend some time learning how they talk. They have a whole new language, you know."

"First of all, Momma, I am fully aware that I have two teenage children. Second of all, 'Netflix and chill' is how I conceived both of them. During the Super Bowl halftime show, two years apart. So don't tell me about having teenage children." Darcy looked confused. "You are correct, 'Netflix and chill' is a saying that is used, but it ain't for watching TV and eating pizza, unless you are boring and don't mind getting cheese and pepperoni in certain places… Momma, that saying means to have sex. Sexual relations."

All the color drained out of Darcy's face. "Oh my Lord, I am going to hell. Straight to hell. I just said I was going to have sexual relations with my grandchildren." Darcy was being a little dramatic. "Lord, please forgive me for saying that. I didn't know what I was saying. Please forgive me."

"Momma, for all things holy and right, please quit saying that about my children. You did not know what you were saying. Jesus knows that. I don't think that will send you to hell. Compared to some of the stories I have heard about you when you were younger, I doubt that would be the reason you went to hell. Calm down, but please, never say that again." Anna needed to lighten the mood and take her momma's mind off thinking she just purchased a first-class ticket to the underworld for eternity. "You can ask Daddy to Netflix and chill all you want, just make sure he has taken all his medication first. I don't want you having to explain to the paramedics that you guys were just trying to Netflix and chill."

Darcy still seemed mortified. "Better yet, let's just agree that I never use that phrase again."

The rest of lunch went well, less controversial at least. Anna got a list of things she needed to work on for the party to end all parties. They finished up, and Darcy walked Anna out to the valet stand. Keith immediately took Anna's key to retrieve her car. Darcy and Anna exchanged a hug and kiss on the cheek and promised to talk over the weekend. Keith pulled Anna's car under the covering and held the door for her. Anna gave him a goodbye hug, a kiss on the cheek, and pressed a twenty into his hand. Keith shut her door and tapped the Honda on the roof. "See you next week, Keith!" He waved, and she was on her way back to the office.

CHAPTER 6

Thursday held promise of the weekend. Thursday was going to be a good day. Anna had a full but not overwhelming day at the office scheduled, and then dinner with her friends. She needed that time to just relax, laugh, eat wonderful food, and enjoy her friends. She just had to get through the day; she could do that, no problem. Anna repeated that to herself over and over while she sipped her third Mountain Dew of the morning.

"You do know that those are simply horrible for you, right?" Shellie said from across the break room table. "I am actually surprised you have only lost six organs and parts. I expect your liver to be next." Shellie smiled her smug smile. "*WebMD* says that is like drinking Drano."

"First of all, *WebMD* will inform you that you are dying from a horrid disease in just three clicks. Second, I failed to know that you have a medical degree. And third, while you are allowed your own opinion, I didn't ask for it." Anna smiled, tilted her head to the side, raised her eyebrows at Shellie, and took another sip. "You tell me this every other day. I get it. They are not the best in the world for me, but look, I don't do crack, meth, or smoke pot. I don't drink, and I am not a hooker or a stripper, so this is my vice. When you look at it that way, I am good."

"Yeah, yeah, but I know you are not supposed to drink carbonated beverages with your bag thing. I know that. I remember specifically Dr. Hyrd telling you that after your surgery." Shellie did bring up a point.

"Yes, he did, but I haven't had an issue with it yet, and if I do, I will address it then. Anyway, I thought he just said not to drink with a straw?" Anna did have to give Shellie points for her memory. It had saved her more than once.

"Okay, okay. Just promise me this. If you become a stripper or start doing meth, you give up the Dew? That a deal?" Shellie really drove a hard bargain.

"Deal." Anna thought that was fair. She had passed her prime to become a stripper, she didn't have the right wardrobe for a hooker, and she didn't make enough money for a meth habit. She had college for her kids to think about.

"Okay, time to start the day. The quicker we do, the quicker we get to go have fun." Shellie got up and headed toward her desk. "I've put some files on your desk. Your first meeting is at ten, the one with Mr. Logan, Richard, the one without the spit cup, and Detective Blue Suit—I mean Phillips. I envy you sometimes."

"Thanks, Shellie. I will have those files ready to go to the courthouse in just a little bit. Just wanted to look over them before we file. I'm looking forward to making some progress and some plans about the Logan case. I need to focus on that for sure. I look forward to meeting with both of them." Anna had to keep her mind on her work; she could not let her mind wander back to that moment he had grabbed her arm at her daddy's office. It had to have been nothing; just part of her reaction to her fall. That had to be it.

*****

After Anna's divorce, she told herself she needed to find out who she really was. She had so long lived to please Mark. She had left college to follow him to medical school. She had worked hard, keeping them afloat, moved far away from her parents and home, but at that time, she was doing exactly what she thought she needed and wanted to do. Her marriage to Mark hadn't been all bad; the first few years were great. They fell into a routine, they made friends, embraced the new town, and made a life for themselves. It wasn't all wonderful, but they made the best of everything.

Anna had mentioned once after Mark had graduated from medical school and started in his practice, she would like to go back to college to finish her degree. She remembered he had gotten terribly mad when he found out that she had done some research on the local college in their town. She put those thoughts aside and continued to be the working, supportive wife.

After being married for almost seven years, Anna and Mark found out she was expecting their first child. They were over the moon. They searched, toured, and worked with a realtor. They found the perfect home with enough space for their new baby and more if that was in the cards. In the fall of that year, they welcomed a perfect little boy. Anna remembered Mark being so proud of her after the natural birth. He kissed her forehead over and over as she looked over at her son. She quickly checked that he had all ten fingers and toes. She would never forget her first words after she had seen him: "He's perfect," said through happy tears.

They were a family, a family of three. Almost exactly two years to the day, they made their family grow by one. Jack was born and he, too, was perfect. They felt complete, blessed, and happy. Anna was thankful to be able to stay at home with the boys. The little family moved back toward their hometown, only about an hour west. They wanted their families to be able to see the boys as much as possible. Mark worked hard; he could end up having some crazy hours. Medical emergencies didn't go on a schedule. They made the best of the time they had altogether, and Anna soaked up all the time she could with her little guys. She was a good mother. She was a good wife.

After Jack was born, Mark began to change. Anna couldn't put her finger on it, but when she brought it up to talk about, Mark would shut her down. Until one day when Anna was doing the laundry, she found a folded paper in a back pocket of a pair of Mark's scrubs. When she read it, her world collapsed all around her. She couldn't believe what she was reading. It was a plan, in Mark's handwriting, how he was going to leave her and the boys. How he was going back to his first job, move out of their house, out of their town, back to a life he had there. He even had written how he would secure a post office box and an apartment and how Anna would have to sell the house, but he would help with the expenses for the kids, and her.

She didn't know where this was coming from, but she knew from that moment on, her life had changed forever.

Anna folded the paper back the way she found it and tucked it into the back pocket of her jeans. She continued the tasks that she had to do that day, playtime with the boys, naps, and things to keep the home running as she always did. She made dinner and had it ready on the table when Mark walked through the door that evening. On the wall beside their table was a chalkboard sign; daily Anna would write a new inspirational message or verse from the Bible. Today she asked one simple question. The boys couldn't read yet, so there was no worry about them paying attention to it. It simply said, *When were you going to tell me you were leaving us?*

Marks looked at her told her all she needed to know. It was true. At first, Mark tried to make her believe that he had dreamed it all and had just written it all down, in perfect detail. She didn't buy it.

The next day, Mark was scheduled to leave for a medical conference out of town. As she stood by the garage door, holding Jack and with John hugging her leg, she asked Mark if he was coming home. He did, and they made an attempt for a couple of years more. Anna tried. Mark may have tried some, but when the drinking and drugs had gotten too bad, and when the mental abuse got more than she could bear, she knew it was too late to fix this. Honestly, she had checked out when she read that plan she found in his scrubs. Anna knew it wasn't all Mark's fault. In any couple, man and wife, the marriage is a product of what is put in. Just like a recipe you make in the kitchen, you put the correct amount of quality ingredients in and you are going to get a wonderful dish. Same thing in a marriage: you put trust, honesty, and love in, and you may have a few burnt edges, a few crumbles, but all in all, a good marriage. She had not tried hard enough, and back then, she didn't feel as if it was worth it.

The separation and divorce had been hard on both of them, but their main concern were the boys. Over time, they worked together to understand what was best for the boys, and that was to be primarily with Anna, with visitation with Mark on some weekends and when his schedule allowed it during the week for dinner one evening. Mark and Anna came to an agreement that, yes, at one time, they did love each other, were fully in love, but now they saw that the love they felt for each other was out of respect for what the other one had given them, for who they were now, and they wanted the best for each other. While it was hard to let go of that thought of happily ever after, they both had a permanent piece of the best of each one of them, their boys. Both Mark and Anna would walk through hell again and again for those two boys, any day of the week. They were their lives.

When everything was up in the air about her future, Anna took that time to try to focus on her boys and herself. She pulled her family and friends together and made a plan. She went back to college, finished her law degree, and went to work. She also went to work on her own happiness, happiness from within her and not by making someone else happy. She had never learned so much. A very wise friend told her, "You cannot base your happiness on the happiness of someone else, no matter how happy they are or how happy you make them. You are only sacrificing your own happiness." That was a hard truth to learn, but once it sank in, there was no stopping her.

Going back to college, with two very young sons, was an adventure. She worked hard and spent every spare minute when not with the boys studying. She had found her love: the law. She was also taken under the wing of her advisor at the university. He was a retired realtor who had always dreamed of teaching. When he closed his practice in Florida, he and his wife moved to Pressley Heights and be became the legal chair and head professor at the law school at the local university. To this day, Anna and Professor Gerson were still friends. She was honored to be the keynote speaker at the dedication of the law library at the university upon his retirement. He and his wife often had her and the boys to their home for dinner. He was an avid lover of trains. Their entire basement was a model train extravaganza. They never had children but made the boys feel as if they were their adopted grandchildren. No better people ever. Anna often wondered where she would be if, on the really hard days, she had given up and just settled for mediocre. She was forever thankful

IT'S IN THE BAG

for the encouragement and sometimes blunt advice of her family and friends. She was in a very good place.

*****

The time was getting close to her appointment with Mr. Logan and Detective Phillips. Anna sure hoped that they could dive in and get some things planned and settled today. Anna really needed to talk to the father herself. Until they arrived, she had a few moments to relax. Her favorite place to relax was in the leather chair across from Shellie's desk. Anna was so in love with these chairs; it seemed like they just wrapped around her when she sat down. They were her favorite purchase for the office; well, the lobby at least.

"I signed off on all the files. If you could run them over to the courthouse when you go to the bank, which would be great. Just drop them off with Carmen in the clerk's office." Anna slid down so her head could rest on the back of the chair. "I am so looking forward to dinner. My tummy is rumbling. I have been thinking about their turkey frittata with cranberry cream cheese spread, a side of their dressing. Man, I could eat my way out of a bathtub filled with that dressing."

Shellie scrunched her nose. "You have to be the most disgusting person I have ever met."

"And yet you love me and hang out with me." Anna laughed.

Both ladies were lost in laughter when Detective Phillips topped the old wooden staircase and stood there watching them. He smiled and then cleared his throat. "This seems like the best law firm in the world. Never heard one so cheerful." He walked in and stood in the lobby just to the left of the ladies.

"Good morning, Detective Phillips." Anna stood and put out her hand to shake his. "We are just having a little fun. We were waiting on you and Mr. Logan to arrive. Do you want to have a seat? These chairs are just heaven. Best purchase I have made for the office." Anna sat back down.

"Sure, sounds good. I am a couple of minutes early anyway." Tony sat down and put his file folder in his lap. "Hey, while we are not with the clients, can you call me Tony? I like that better with friends and associates. In front of the clients, of course, that is appropriate, but when just between friends, it makes me think my father is behind me." Tony laughed.

Anna nodded and smiled. "I will, Tony, only if you call me Anna. Same deal."

"All right, Anna, sounds great." Tony smiled and met her gaze.

Anna felt that feeling again; as soon as he said her name, she felt it. She had never heard her name said by a more powerful voice; it was like it reached out and made her look at him. And see only him.

Just at that moment, the phone rang. Shellie excused herself and turned away from them to answer the call. Anna and Tony sat quietly not to disturb Shellie. Anna glanced his way and caught him looking at her. He didn't change his look, just curled his lips into a devilish smile and seemed to dare her to keep looking. Anna turned away first. She looked at the back of Shellie's head and willed her to get off the phone.

Shellie pressed the hold button on the phone and turned back around to face Tony and Anna. "Well, that was Mr. Logan. He is going to be a little late. He has had a flat tire on the interstate, out by Exit 34, the one with the truck stop. He has a guy stopped helping him, but he asked if you could just wait for him."

Anna gave a quick look toward Tony. He nodded in agreement, and Anna turned back to Shellie. "Tell him thank you for calling and we will be happy to wait on him. Tell him to be careful." Anna looked back at Tony. "Sorry about this. I have a conference table in my office that you are welcome to sit at and work, do phone calls, whatever. Or you can just sit." Anna stood. "I have a couple of calls I can get out of the way, if you don't mind, and then we will be ready when he gets here. We also have coffee, tea, and some Mountain Dew in the refrigerator. Right in here." She pointed, walking closer to his chair.

"Sounds great. I can check my email and maybe make a couple of calls as well. Show me the way." Tony stood and followed her into her office.

Anna went to her chair and stood by as she watched Tony make his way to the table, put down his things, and take a seat. She couldn't explain it, but she felt like she had known him longer than just a couple of days.

Shellie came to the door. "I am going to go ahead and run to the bank and by the courthouse. Anything else you need?" Shellie already had her purse and the files in her hand.

"Umm, I can't think of anything." Anna looked at Tony. "Tony, would you like Shellie to grab anything for you?"

"I'm good. Thanks for the offer, though." Tony smiled.

"While you are at the clerk's office, please check my box. I am waiting on some sheriff's deeds and a couple of foreclosure notices to come back. There should also be two divorce decrees." Anna watched Shellie store all that in her mental filing cabinet. "Thanks, Shellie, you're the best."

Shellie smiled. "I know. See you guys in a bit."

CHAPTER 7

Anna wasn't used to sharing her office with anyone but Shellie on occasion, so this was a little weird. She needed to make some phone calls but didn't want to disturb Tony. But this was her office, right?

"Do you mind if I return a couple of calls? Will it disturb you too much?" Anna asked as she scooted back her desk chair, took off her heels, and tossed them to the corner of the office. She bent over and picked out a pair of flip-flops that kind of matched her black-and-light-blue outfit. Good enough. "They shouldn't take long."

Tony started laughing. "I don't mind at all. But do you do that often, I mean the throwing shoes thing?"

Anna laughed. "Yes, and I don't usually throw them at people. I cannot stand wearing heels all day. They hurt my feet. They look good, but not when I am just sitting at my desk. So I have about eight pairs of flip-flops under my desk. Old Navy has about every color, so I always have some that match what I'm wearing." Anna couldn't get over how comfortable she felt with Tony.

"Go ahead and make your calls, no worries. And hey, just yell, 'Duck' if you start throwing anything else." Tony smiled.

Anna took out the files that she needed to return her calls. Her first call would be to Mrs. Rhodarmmer, or the soon-to-be-ex-Mrs.-Rhodarmmer. Seemed there had been a compromise in the dispute over some personal property that was holding up the equitable distribution from being signed. Good news; with this out of the way, the rest of the proceedings should be pretty cut-and-dried and would keep them out of the courtroom.

Anna dialed the number and waited for her to answer. "Hello, Mrs. Rhodarmmer? This is Anna Dawson. I have some information that I thought you might be very happy to hear."

IT'S IN THE BAG

Tony acted like he was checking his email, but he couldn't help but listen to Anna do her thing. He had done some checking around. Anna had made quite the name for herself as a hardworking and honest attorney. She fought hard for her clients, was respected by her peers, and did a lot of pro-bono work for the legal aid society in town. He wanted to watch her in action.

"Yes, well, let's see." Anna glanced at the file and pulled out the paper she needed. "Mr. Rhodarmmer has consented for you to have the two matching crystal lamps out of the den if you will agree to relinquish his skull collection, all of them." Anna caught Tony looking at her again. "Yes, all the skulls for the matching lamps. Also, he has agreed to let you keep the lampshades if you will give him half of the bath towels." Anna rolled her eyes at Tony.

Anna continued with her call. "I can draw up the paperwork today, and have it ready to be signed tomorrow or Monday? Whatever is best for you." Anna paused, listening to the lady on the other end of the line. "Yes, all the skulls… So are you good with that? I think it is a very fair deal. You get the lamps, and he gets his skulls. Sounds like a win-win to me."

Tony and Anna exchanged glances. Anna smiled. Tony decided he liked when she smiled very much.

"All right, Ms. Rhodarmmer, I think that is what I needed to clear up with you for now. We already talked about the visitation with the dogs. You keep them one week, him the other. Holidays to be discussed and decided on fairly. That still good?" Anna waited and listened. "Great. I will have the papers drawn up this afternoon. You can stop by tomorrow or Monday to look over them, and if you are still good with it all, sign and I will forward them to Mr. Rhodarmmer's attorney. Once they are signed by both parties, I will arrange a time for you to bring the skulls here—*all* the skulls—and his attorney can come with him to collect them and to bring you your lamps. Does that sound agreeable?"

Anna got a confirmation and ended the call. She immediately looked at Tony, who was still watching her, but now his eyes were filled with questions. "Yes, my job is just that glamourous. Skulls and crystal lamps. No wonder that marriage didn't last." Anna laughed and sat back in her leather chair. "If you enjoyed that one, buckle up, Buttercup!"

At that, Tony sat back and didn't even try to act like he wasn't listening.

"Hello, may I speak to Mr. Mullins?" Anna paused. "Hello, this is Anna Dawson. How are you doing today?"

Anna continued the small talk for a moment before jumping into the reason she called. She knew how to finesse people and she knew how to make them feel important, how to make them feel as if she wasn't just calling out of necessity, that she really did care. Anna asked about the garden they had planted, their kids, grandkids, and then she transitioned seamlessly into the reason she had called.

"So, let's talk a moment about the issue you are having with your neighbor. When I came out to your home last week, I did see the medium-size stick that was on your side of the fence. I did. I have to say that it is more than likely from your neighbor's tree since there are no trees on your property in that general area. While I did see the stick, I also saw a few other things as well. I saw numerous children playing in the yards around your home. Even in the yard of your neighbor. I saw the children playing cops and robbers, hide-and-seek, and whatever else they could think of." Anna paused as she listened to Mr. Mullins tell her a story about the neighborhood kiddos. Smiling, she continued. "Yes, Mr. Mullins, the kids are very cute, and I do remember seeing your pictures of your grandchildren when Mrs. Mullins offered me a glass of lemonade. Thank you again for that, but what I am thinking is, rather than have you spend a ton of money to me, I think there is another way to settle this." Anna spun around in her chair, twisting a piece of her hair that didn't fit back in the hair clip.

Anna went on. "So when I was at your house, I noticed those kids, right?" Anna shook her head. "And I noticed those kids were using sticks as fake guns and swords. How is it that we know for certain that your neighbor put those sticks on your property, and that they weren't just left there, innocently, by the children when their attention span switched from guns and swords to something else?" Anna listened intently. "I have an idea. You take some of the money you would have spent hiring me, go to Lowe's, and buy your wife that firepit that she mentioned to me, and ta-da, you already have a few sticks for your first fire. That would be awful cozy for you both to enjoy." Anna smiled; he must have agreed. "Yes, I will certainly come over one evening. You have my number. Just let me know when would be a good time. Have a great day!" With that, Anna ended the call.

Anna jotted down a few notes and put the paper back in the folder. She put the two files in the basket on the edge of her desk. She glanced Tony's way. "Okay, your turn. Dazzle me with your phone skills." She laughed.

"Sadly I don't have anyone to call right now or I would." He stood and made his way over to sit in a chair that faced her desk. He took a moment and glanced at the photos on her desk and then at the ones behind her. "You have some handsome boys. Looks like teenagers?" He picked up the one closest to him. It was a photo of the three of them taken at the beach the last summer.

Anna beamed. "Yes, yes, I do. They are amazing. They can run me ragged, but they are my heart and soul. I will be honest, I never knew I could love anything so much, or so fiercely, until I had them. That whole momma bear thing, it's real." She relaxed and sat back in her chair. "Do you have any children?"

Tony shook his head. "No, I don't. I always thought I would. Always wanted kids, but I have not ever been married. I came very close once, engaged, but it just didn't work out." Tony looked down. "After the engagement fell through, I was very hurt and upset, so I just poured myself into my job even more. I found happiness in helping others. I am an uncle, though, and I will have you know, they think I am the best uncle in the world." He grinned.

"Oh, I am so sorry. That has to be rough." Anna was intrigued. What could have possibly broken up his engagement? "At least you found out it wasn't going to work before you got married. I have handled enough divorces to know. It is easier that way."

Tony nodded. "I appreciate it, but that was a long time ago. She has married since and is very happy. That was my only hope for her. That makes me happy that she is happy." He looked directly at Anna.

"So, what is your story? Married, I suppose?" he said, hoping like hell the answer was no.

Anna smiled and looked at a photo of her boys. "I was, for many years. Mark and I married way too young, way before we fully knew who we were. Don't get me wrong, the first half of our marriage was great. He was in medical school. I left college early and was working. We lived in an apartment about the size of this office…we hardly had a spare cent to our names. We never wanted for anything. We had each other. The years went on, and then we did have money. He had power." Anna took a sip of her drink. "Money and power can cloud even the most wonderful minds. We loved being parents. I think that may be what held us together finally in the end, but then even that wasn't enough. We, mostly I, called it quits. I couldn't live like that anymore. I didn't want my kids to grow up in that environment."

"Wow, I had no idea. I'm sorry." Tony looked around the office. "Looks like it turned out good, though. Your sons look healthy and happy, you have a thriving law business, you yourself seem healthy and happy. All ends well, I suppose… Doesn't make the hell you walked through any easier to stomach, but it is good now, right?"

"You're right, but Mark and I can agree, we may not have made it together but together we made two pretty awesome boys. I would walk through that hell over and over just to have them. They have made it all worth it. We are good, Mark and I, still friends. He is happy now. He is remarried to a great lady. Lindie is a sweetie. She is good to my kids. Seems to be good for Mark too. It is not the easiest thing to be married to a doctor who has no set hours, no set schedule really. At times he's rarely home. She handles it well. That makes me happy for them. He seems to have gotten rid of the demons he was fighting. That was what I couldn't handle. I never wanted him to live a life of sorrow over what we lost, just like I know he didn't me. He has a practice here in town, internal medicine, and he holds privileges at the hospital also. He is a hard worker and a great dad. That is all I can ask." Anna smiled. "Want anything to drink?" She stood up and headed over to the small fridge near the window.

"Sure, a water would be great." Tony watched her move around the room. He liked what he saw, flip-flops and all. "It was really good the way you handled those calls. Especially the last one. Impressive. Most attorneys I know would have charged them and taken them to the cleaners. I suppose that is what gives attorneys a bad name."

Anna handed him a bottle of cold water and sat down in the matching chair beside him. "You know what, you are nothing like the other detectives Daddy usually has hanging around. I have worked with a few before, and you know what, they are very arrogant. They seem to think they are better than everyone else. You are not like that at all, from what I can tell so far. Thank you for that." She took a sip of water. "I think we will work well together."

Anna heard the sound of steps on the wooden stairs. She felt a little sad that their time was over, just them talking, but there was work to do. "That must be Mr. Logan. Let me run check. When Shellie is out and about, I kind of do double duty around here. Hang tight, be right back." Anna hopped up and ran over to the corner where she had tossed her shoes earlier. She grabbed them, did a quick change, and threw the flops under her desk. As she walked out the door, Tony could hear her greet Mr. Logan.

"Hello, Mr. Logan, sorry about the tire situation, but I am glad you were able to still make the meeting with us." Anna cheerfully met him in the lobby, not giving him time to sit down, extending her hand to him, a firm shake and welcome. "Come on into my office. I have someone I want you to meet. He has some information that we would like to talk with you about that has to do with Melanie. We also have some thoughts on how to proceed."

"Sounds great, Ms. Dawson. Thanks for understanding about my being late. I hate to be late to anything, and this being so important, I really hate it. I do apologize." Mr. Logan seemed a little more than just upset at being late and having a flat tire. There was something else going on.

Anna brought Mr. Logan into her office and made the introductions, and with both men sitting with her at the conference table, they were ready to get down to business. Anna still had a nagging feeling about Mr. Logan; she had to find out what he was thinking.

"Mr. Logan, is there something else that is going on? Something with your father? What are you thinking? I can sense that there is something that you are not telling us." Anna didn't mean to pry; anyone could have a bad morning or day, or year for that matter, but he was acting weird. "We are here to help you and we need to know anything that you might think is important."

Tony sat and listened to Anna, mesmerized. She was good. He was a good—no, pretty darn good detective; he knew about people's mannerisms; he knew body language. But apparently she did too. He wondered if she was catching on to his body language. He had to focus. Focus on Mr. Logan. Mr. Logan and his probable killer stepmother. "Mr. Logan, Anna—I mean, Ms. Dawson is correct." Tony glanced over at Anna just in time to see her blush. Tony continued, "If there is anything going on that you may find odd, off, or out of character in any way, we need to know about it. You never know, even the smallest little piece of information can help out so much."

Mr. Logan looked between Anna and Tony. He put both of his fists on the table and scooted his chair up to the table. "When the guy was helping change my tire, he found what caused my tire to go flat on me. He pulled out the broken-off end of a box cutter. "It had been deep in the tire so far, it had cut a good three inches before it looked like it just broke. I don't even own a box cutter. I don't know how that got in there." Now Mr. Logan had his head in his hands. "I am starting to think that crazy bat is out to get me."

Tony got to writing as soon as Mr. Logan started in about the box cutter. A million question were running through his mind. "Does Melanie have any idea that you have any question about her, her intentions, her past…anything at all? Is there any way that she could know that you and your siblings came to meet with Ms. Dawson the other day?"

"My brother, Jimmy, he talks way too much. He made the mistake of talking our father about him thinking that she was out to kill him. Daddy got pretty defensive over it and stood up for Melanie. I am not sure if Daddy knows that we came to talk to Ms. Dawson. Jimmy confronted Daddy after our meeting, and so there is no telling what he spouted off to him." Mr. Logan was starting to look pale. "I hate to ask, but can I have something to drink? I am starting to not feel too good. Like I am going to be sick."

"Sure thing, Mr. Logan." Anna stood and started toward the fridge. She grabbed a water, a Coke, and a couple of granola bars off the counter. "Here you go. If you want anything else, just let me know. I will make sure we get it." Anna sat back down. "And just so we don't continue being so formal here, my name is Anna, this is Tony, and can we call you Richard? Would you mind?"

"Anna, thank you. I appreciate that." Richard opened the Coke and took a long sip. "Thanks for the drinks. I needed that. You don't have anything stronger, do you? Hidden up in that bookcase or something?" Richard snickered, half-joking, half-serious.

"Sorry, I don't. I don't drink at all, but maybe that will be an addition to the office for those who do and for the situations that call for it." She glanced at Tony. "I think that this tire situation needs to be addressed. I find it funny that this would happen right after they came and talked with me and Jimmy talked with their father."

Tony agreed. "I will need the tire. Leave everything just like you found it. I can get if from you after we are done here, or you can follow me to the department. I can pass it to the lab and see if they can get any prints off the blade. I doubt it, but it is worth a try. I will keep it in evidence for future use with the case."

"What kind of person are we dealing with here? Do you think she could hurt my dad? This is getting all too real to me. I feel like time is not my friend right now. If she does know that we suspect she is crooked, what is keeping her from upping her game and speeding things along? What if she tried something harsher, worried that she might get caught? I am really getting worried about Dad." Richard was about to come out of his seat. "Now I am certain that she is out to get him. What have you found out?"

Tony and Anna went over the information that they had as of right then. Tony said that there was plenty of circumstantial evidence against her but nothing at the moment that was solid enough to arrest her. He needed to talk with some of the other families, the children and friends of husbands she had had in the past. Tony said that was where he would focus his time the next couple of days to try and get enough evidence to catch her.

Anna had her own idea about how she would proceed. She hadn't mentioned it to Tony, and he was just as shocked as Richard when she shared it. "Okay, here is what I need you to do, Richard. I need you to convince your father to come to my office for a meeting. It can be with just me, you, and your siblings if you want, and Tony can be here too. Do you think you could arrange that for me, like tomorrow?"

Richard shook his head, and not in agreement. "Anna, not to mean you any disrespect at all when I say this—please know that before I say it—but my dad is not going to go for the idea of coming into town to meet with an attorney about how his wife may or may not be a serial killer and having him in her sights as her next victim." Still shaking his head, he said, "There just ain't no way in the world I could make that fly."

Not fazed one bit, Anna said, "Well, I thought that would be your answer, so I have a better plan. I will come to him. No appointment needed. I will come to his home and ask to speak to him. How about that?"

Tony didn't even give Richard a chance to object. "Umm, no, Anna. That is a horrible idea. No." Tony was rubbing his temples, in awe of her audacity to think she could just waltz over to Mr. Logan's. "You can't do that. This isn't some old couple worried about who put a stick in their yard. You can't figure this out by sitting around a firepit singing campfire songs and making s'mores. This could be life and death. What are you going to say if the wife is there? Huh? Are you going to ask her straight out if she offed her other husbands, is running out of money, and is needing a refill?"

Ignoring Tony, Anna looked directly at Richard. "Does Melanie have a job, a set place she goes during the week? Is there a time for sure that she isn't home?"

"Ah, she goes to the beauty parlor down the mountain every Friday morning. Standing appointment every week. Never misses it. She is gone for half the day for sure. She usually shops a little after the appointment and is home by two." Richard was starting to get some color back in his cheeks.

Anna slapped the table. "Perfect. Tomorrow is Friday. I will be at your father's house at 9:30 sharp. Will you be there to meet me?" Her perfect hazel eyes fluttered Tony's way and then looked at Richard, waiting for an answer.

Richard looked at Tony, Tony looked at Anna, and Anna was staring a hole into Richard's forehead. It was more than a little tense. Silence ensued until Shellie peeked into the office. "Everyone doing okay? Can I get anyone anything?"

"No, but thanks, Shellie." Anna was the first to speak. "Hey, Shellie, wait. Go ahead and plan on us going out to meet with Mr. Logan tomorrow morning. We will need to leave here at 8:45 sharp. We will plan on me driving. I have a feeling we will have an extra person going with us."

"Sure thing, Anna, on it." Shellie was out the door.

"So, Richard, plan on us being there in the morning. I want to talk to your father myself. I want to give him the facts I have, see what he knows from her, and then we will decide where to go from there. He really needs to know exactly who he is married to and just what she is capable of."

Tony, Richard, and Anna spoke for a few more minutes. Richard finally consented to being there for the meeting the next day. Anna walked Richard out and to the top of the stairs. Shaking hands once more, Richard was down the stairs and out the door. Anna chalked up this meeting as a success. A short-lived success…at least until she walked back into her office.

CHAPTER 8

"Are you insane, or just plain crazy?" Tony was livid.

Anna laughed as she sat back down in the chair behind her desk. "Well, I have been called much worse. I am a little disappointed that is the best you can do. But neither—neither crazy nor insane. I am just a woman who knows how to get what I need done, well, done. I need to talk to Mr. Logan. Mr. Logan won't come to meet me, so that leaves me with little choice. I will go to meet Mr. Logan. I really don't see the problem here."

Tony glanced out at Shellie as he shut Anna's office door. Shellie said a little prayer for Tony. He had no idea what he was about to tangle with.

"Your father warned me about you. He said that you were the best attorney in town but that you were obstinate, stubborn, and quite hardheaded. I will have to say that I could not agree with him more." Tony was pacing back and forth across the office floor. "You have no business going over to that man's house, alone, without backup… That is something I should be doing. You have no idea what could be waiting for you. Do you not see that?"

"I don't see that at all." Anna started clicking on the keys of her computer. "I am fully competent, intelligent, and capable. And by the way, I will have backup. Shellie is going with me. I never go alone. Well, there was that one time, but *now* I never go alone. If you haven't noticed, Shellie is very protective of me. She is a force to be reckoned with, and she and I both have our concealed carry permits. Guns too. So watch out." Anna navigated Google Earth to find and look over the home of Mr. Logan. "Besides, this is not my first rodeo, partner, just the first one you have been invited to. So there."

"This isn't Mayberry, sweetheart. Andy and Barney have long left the air, and this is the real world. I refuse to let you do this. I will do this. I will go meet Mr. Logan. Now, just give me his address and I will head over there." Tony took out his keys.

Anna sat back, laughed, then sat back up straight in her chair, resting her elbows on her desk. "You will do nothing of the sort. You do not control me. I am not committing any crime whatsoever, and last time I checked, you ain't my daddy. So I think you just need to calm yourself down and continue on about your business of tracking down the children of the previous victims and I will go about mine. Got it?"

Tony noticed the sparkle in Anna's eyes as she stood her ground. He couldn't remember a time when a woman had infuriated him and intrigued him at the same time. Right now he couldn't focus on that, though; he had work to do. "I got something. I got the impression that you are exactly what your father warned me of. A hardheaded woman." *A very beautiful, smart, and sexy hardheaded woman.*

Anna said nothing, just glared. Tony, thinking it would be better if he just left and let them both cool off, told Anna he would be in touch. She didn't walk him out, but as he opened the door to her office, Shellie had almost made it back to her desk, obviously having eavesdropped. Tony gave a quick nod toward her and down the stairs he went.

Shellie waited to hear the door shut at the bottom of the stairs before she made her way into Anna's office. "Well?" Shellie sat down in a chair facing Anna's desk. "He seemed to be a bit upset on his way out. I take it he didn't particularly see things your way?"

Anna huffed. "Let him be upset. I have every right to go see who I need to see for my case. He is not and will not influence how I proceed. Now, I am done wasting time on that. We need to talk about tomorrow and then go meet the girls."

Anna's group of friends, her core group, were the ones who got her through her toughest days, celebrated her highs, and made her life fun. With them she could be herself. They were free to be who they were and that was what made their group so tight-knit. They knew each other's secrets, their hopes and dreams, and what made each of them tick. They each brought something different to the table, and together, even the hardest day was made easier knowing they had each other.

Anna and Shellie had known Peggy for years. Peggy was a very well-known hairstylist in town. She charged the most outrageous prices, but she was so good no one batted an eye at their total bill when all was said and done. One look in the mirror, and that was all it took. She could work magic; her cuts and color had made it into some well-known magazines, and she had made it into the "40 Under 40," a prestigious list of businesswomen making a name for themselves in their industry. Peggy was the only person that Anna or Shellie would go to for anything to be done with their hair. The joy and pride of saying that Peggy J. was your hairstylist, at a friend discount price, was priceless.

Gisela had been in real estate when Anna met her years ago. She had been the closing agent for a couple whom Anna had worked with on a very expensive second home in the WNC Mountains. At the closing, she and Gisela—Gigi—had clicked. They sat and talked long after the couple left with the keys to their plush new home in their hands. After she tired of real estate, Gigi bought a struggling furniture refurbishing business in the River Arts district and found her true calling. Her pieces went for hundreds if not thousands of dollars. Gigi would pick up older pieces of furniture at estate sales, thrift stores—heck, off the side of the road—and take them back to her shop, work her magic, and turn that piece of junk into a piece of art.

Shellie and Anna arrived first at the Broken Twig Restaurant and Bar. It was only a short walk from the office, and they didn't have to fight traffic or find a parking place. A total win-win. They chose a table for four over by the window; it was still a little too cool to eat outside on the veranda this early in April. Shellie ordered her regular, a gigantic margarita. Anna ordered her sweet tea. Anna had done plenty of drinking her first round in college. She had long given that up; not too much good came from alcohol. She was crazy enough without it. She passed no judgment about people who drank regularly, or just occasionally, but it just wasn't for her anymore.

IT'S IN THE BAG

"Good grief, Shellie, that drink is as big as your head. There is enough tequila in there to make sure you are still drunk in the morning. You are cut off after this one, and I am driving you home. No ifs, ands, or buts." Anna laughed, but totally serious.

"For what I am paying for this, it should still have me at least buzzed in the morning. And besides, with what you have us doing in the morning, a buzz won't hurt one bit. Might help." Shellie went in for a big gulp.

"Lord, girl, just remember to come up for air." Anna did think that the presentation of the beverage was almost an art piece itself. A gigantic bowl on a glass pedestal. The drink itself was the prettiest shades of blue with ice floating at the top. As you went down the glass, the blue deepened in color. There was a couple of colorful gummy fish floating around the bowl, and of course the rim was encrusted with salt that had been dyed blue. Cute, and the gummy fish were a step up from the worm floating in the tequila bottle.

Shellie paused her alcohol binge when she spotted Gigi coming through the door with Peggy hot on her heels. "Here come the other two." Shellie waved them over their way.

"Great." Anna turned to greet them as they approached the table. "Well, hello, chicks. Glad you could join us! As you can see, Shellie started without you. Hurry and sit down if you still want a chance to talk to her before she passes out." Anna pulled out the chair beside her for Peggy to slide into. Gigi grabbed the chair beside Shellie and plopped down as if she had just finished a marathon. Her life was usually crazy, so maybe she had.

"How are you ladies?" Peggy asked. She looked over at Anna's hair. "You, my friend, need to come see me desperately. You are showing your Cruella DeVille stripes again." Peggy reached over and flipped some of Anna's hair around. "Good Lord, girl, are you trying to look seventy? You will never snatch up a hot man like that…who isn't eighty, that is, and digs Disney cartoons." Peggy laughed. She loved to joke with Anna about her gray.

"I know, I know, I need to make an appointment soon. But you are, like, booked till the Lord comes back, so I might as well just let it go." Anna winked.

"Everyone in this town knows we are friends, and they all know that I do your hair. You are a walking, talking billboard for me. I cannot have you walking around looking all haggard. I can come by your house Sunday afternoon. That sound good?" Peggy might joke a lot, but she took the best care of her friends. "Hey, Shellie." Peggy waited for Shellie to look up from the bottom of her margarita bowl. "Yo, Shellie, over here… If you will meet me at Anna's on Sunday afternoon, about three, I will give you some fresh highlights. You in?"

Shellie nodded. "Sounds great, thanks. *And* you might need to really spruce Anna up. We are working with a hot detective and you can see the sparks fly—well, on his side of the desk at least. Anna must have really impressed him when she fell right at his feet the other day, literally. It was a classic Anna moment." All the ladies laughed.

The waiter came over and took the other two ladies' drink order. Gigi ordered something called a "Painkiller;" she had obviously had a harder day than first realized. Peggy ordered a glass of red wine. Classic Peggy. Gigi looked at the ladies and was fighting back tears. "I think Peter is going to propose. What am I going to do?" She gave the impression she thought this was a problem.

Gigi and Peter had been dating for years. Gigi had twins from a previous marriage, now teenagers, and he adored them, and Gigi. He was a successful financial planner and was well-known in the area. He had handled finances and made a great deal of money with smart investments for many residents of Pressley Heights.

"And you need a Painkiller to help you make the decision easier?" Peggy asked what they all were thinking. "You have been with him for years. I don't see the problem."

"I know, but I have had one failed marriage, and if I get married again, what if I screw that up? What if I am just not the marrying kind?" Gigi said as the waiter sat down her ginormous drink in front of her. "I just don't know. I might screw it up if we get married. I won't put the kids through that again." Gigi took a big sip and winced as the first taste went down.

Anna jumped in to handle this one. "First of all, your kids are the same age as mine. They are teenagers. They barely know I am still alive, so I doubt yours pay much attention to what you are doing. Your kids love Peter. He has been part of their lives since they were, what, seven. He is the closest thing to a father that they have ever known. Secondly, your boys were infants when you and Marco split up. I know, I was there. If they remember that, then I have a man they need to meet. He is upset that his parents didn't bury his afterbirth when he was born, said it scarred him. Please. Your boys do not remember any of that."

Gigi listened as she continued to sip the drink.

"Besides, he hasn't proposed, and if he does, talk to the boys then. I don't really see the issue." Anna was about to deliver her famous line; they all knew it. They all joined in: "Don't borrow trouble you don't already have."

Peggy looked at Shellie. "So tell me about Mr. Hottie Pants who wants to get into Anna's pants."

Shellie smiled, kind of crooked, but she tried. "Let me tell you. He is tall, dark, and handsome. A body to die for, a behind to swoon over, and he fills out a blue suit quite well. He fought back with Anna today. I was listening at the door, and he actually thought he could change her mind about how to work a case. It was cute. He left in a huff, and he got to Anna, I could tell." Being tipsy, Shellie could deliver the truth spot-on. "I think he has the hots for her, but you know how she is. Since she got that poop bag, she has written off romance." Shellie took the final sip of liquid courage and looked at Anna. "You find the right man, honey, and he won't care whether or not you poop in a bag, have a Barbie butt or no butthole, whatever." Shellie sat back, proud of her outburst. She must have been holding that in for some time.

"Well, thank you, Shellie, for yelling about my butthole and poop bag so that everyone in the restaurant, eating, could hear you. And for your information, I do not keep from dating because of my health issues and things. It just isn't a priority for me. I have been there, done that, have the T-shirt and sweatshirt, and I am better off the way it is now. I am happy. I am healthier than I have been in years. My kids are happy, healthy, and doing well. My faith in the Lord has only grown through all the hard times in my life. My business is going great and growing. My friends are wonderful…most of the time, when they aren't bugging me about men. I am good. I am happy and blessed. I have absolutely everything I need, and more. I have a lot more than most people do in this world."

"Sex. You don't have sex." Gigi was the bluntest and most up-front person in their group of friends. She just laid it out there and you do with the information what you will. You never wondered where you stood with Gigi, or where she stood on a subject. "You, my friend, need to have sex."

Anna knew that was coming. She just knew it. Sex. Anna missed it, of course, but she had blocked out any thought of having sex again when she had her surgery that left her with an ostomy. She could barely stand to look at herself in the mirror for long, she couldn't imagine being someone a man would find attractive with a bag hanging off her stomach, which at times held poop. The truth of the matter was it had been years before her surgery that she last had sex. There had not been anyone since her marriage to Mark had ended. She had been so hurt, then so sick, and now so resolved that sex was over for her, she rarely gave it a thought.

Until the other day when she had felt Tony's hand grab her arm. She felt that electricity, and then again she felt the same current when he had said her name.

Anna wasn't looking for a relationship. She was not looking for any reason to bring up again those feelings of being less beautiful, less normal. She did not need that stress; she had long since dealt with the fact that she was forever changed, body-wise and, in many ways, mentally too. She was very thankful for the lifesaving advances in medicine that have allowed her to still be alive, but she wished they didn't take away so much of her ability to love her body as it was now. Vanity was what they called it, with some pride thrown in for good measure. No one had ever commented about her body, her bag, only thankfulness for her being so active again, seemingly able to do much more than before. Anna had talked to her doctor and her friends about it, but no one really knew the battle that went on inside the head of someone who was different, unless it was them.

"You don't know that I don't have a revolving door of men coming and going through my house. I could be having sex more than you, missy. You don't know." Anna huffed at her friend. "I could be having wild, passionate, dirty sex. Sex that makes your insides heat up and bubble over in amazing orgasms. Yep, you just don't know."

"Well, I am married to the same man for over ten years. You probably are having more sex than me, and better too." Peggy snorted. Obviously the wine was doing its job. Peggy had been married to her husband, her high school sweetheart, for almost fourteen years. They had split up after graduation but reconnected after college. They were perfect for each other. He was so supportive of her business dreams, and she was the one who pushed him to follow his dreams of opening his own landscaping business. "We are both so busy these days we just fall into bed and practically die each night. But when we are on, we are *hot*!"

"All we are saying is that we would love to see you happy—fully happy. You have not had the easiest of a personal life…whether your marriage, your sickness, whatever. We just want to see you live it up, especially since you now feel like living. We are proud of you and we want the best for you, in every aspect." Peggy was forever the voice of reason, of kindness, and the one who could deliver a message in the way it was intended. "We love you, all of us do, even though some of us have a weird way of saying it." Peggy kicked Gigi under the table, and Gigi jumped and squealed.

Anna relented. "I get it, guys. If that ever happens, a relationship even, it will have to be on my terms. I will have to work into telling someone about my situation, to feel them out about how they would feel about that. It isn't something you just drop into someone's lap right when you sit down to your first-date dinner. 'This is such a beautiful restaurant, thanks for asking me to have dinner with you. Oh, by the way, I don't have a colon, rectum, or anus, and I poop in a bag. I think I will have the lobster.' You have to work your way into a conversation like that. Like, get them so hooked into you that no matter what, they will overlook anything and be blinded to the fact that there is something hanging off your tummy." Anna took the last sip of tea. "One day maybe, but not right now. I just don't need the stress of worrying about what someone may or may not think of me."

The other three ladies took that as their cue to cut off the relationship coaching and just keep the rest of the dinner light. The laughter continued until they were the last people in the place. Anytime they got together, they usually shut down the place. The waiters and waitresses usually let them continue laughing and talking while they did their cleaning and prepping for the next day. On more than one occasion, they had walked out with the employees. That was the way this group was. They didn't get to do this often, but when they did, they got their money's worth for sure. They stood for a few more minutes outside the restaurant, hating to have the evening end. They always left with a smile on their faces and stories to tell. That was what true friendship was, making life better, gently encouraging those who needed it to try something new, helping carry each other's burdens and, in some cases, helping them realize they weren't burdens at all.

CHAPTER 9

Tony hadn't been as mad as when he was walking out of Anna's office in a very long time. He didn't even know why. She was so stubborn. So pigheaded. So beautiful. Geez, what was he doing? Why on earth was he letting this one person, this one perfect woman, to get under his skin? Good Lord, he had so much better sense than this. He just didn't understand this power she seemed to have over him, to make his blood pressure and his temper increase exponentially. This wasn't a good sign.

Tony had put himself out there once, the one time he thought would end up being forever. It almost was, until she decided it wasn't. He had given his heart; he had fully trusted it to a woman. He had let himself fall totally in love and all the emotions that came with it. He was fully committed to Willow. He thought they would live happily ever after; only they never got a chance to see if that would be the case.

Tony had met Willow at church one Sunday morning when she had come with a friend. The two immediately hit it off and were quickly inseparable. Tony was recently back home from four years in the Navy, stationed on the West Coast. He came home with a fresh outlook on what he wanted to do with his life and career. His time out west had given him time to think, focus, and form a plan. He enrolled in the local university and began his path toward his degree in criminal justice and forensic studies. He had thought this was what he wanted to do, but it took his time in the Navy for it to become clear, along with what specialty he wanted to pursue.

Tony finished up his degree and got his first job with the local sheriff's department. He was sharp, well-educated, and liked by his peers and his superiors. He rose quickly in the department and finally felt as if he had found his calling. With his job settled, he needed to make the next step in his personal life. After a few years of dating, he proposed to Willow, and she happily accepted. They began to plan and to forge out their new lives together. Willow had gotten her degree in early education and was excited to be a teacher. She had secured a job at the local elementary school to start the fall after they were to be married. Everything seemed to be falling into place.

The pair began to search for their first home and immediately fell in love with a small bungalow that would be the perfect first home. They made an offer. It was accepted, and that was that; they were homeowners before they were actually married.

Tony's job was really taking off. He was handed the biggest case of his career. He dove headfirst into solving the first double murder in the area in over thirty years. He spent morning, noon, and night at the office pouring over the evidence, interviewing witnesses, family, and suspects. He was hardly every home, and when he was, he was so exhausted. He no longer had the extra time or the energy to go out to dinner or a concert. A movie was out of the question; he would just fall asleep, or if he did happen to stay awake, his mind would be consumed with the case. Willow had become snippy and withdrawn. She rarely smiled or laughed anymore and would get so defensive when Tony would try to talk to her. She would lash out about how he loved his job more than her, how he didn't love her and that he didn't have any time for her.

Tony understood to some extent what Willow was saying, but he tried to make her see that this would just be for a little while, just while the case was being investigated. He promised to try to do better, to manage his time better and try to be home more. He asked in return that she try to understand that sometimes his job would have to take up a majority of his time, but that did not mean he loved her any less. He was working so hard and trying to make a name for himself to better the life that he could give her. This satisfied her for a little while. They both tried very hard.

Tony had worked the case so well that it was moving along. Suspects had been arrested and they were set to go to trial fairly quickly. The date was set, and he was going to get the conviction based on the detailed investigation that he had led. This case could really set him apart in his field. This could open some doors that usually were only held open for more seasoned detectives. The date set by the court was to be the exact week that they were to leave on their honeymoon. They were supposed to get married on a Saturday evening and leave the next day. He would have to be here for the trial; there was no way around it. He knew Willow would be disappointed; he would just tell her that they could reschedule for maybe a few weeks out or even in the spring. Tony had no idea that Willow would react the way she did. She simply took off the ring that he designed himself, picked out the stone from what seemed like five hundred others, and placed it into his hand. She told him that he had a relationship with his job that she just could not compete with. She was done trying.

Tony bought Willow out of the house and she signed the deed over to him. She wanted a fresh start, and on her teacher's salary only, she could not afford the mortgage. When that was taken care of, she left. She left his life, and the life that he thought they would have vanished. He worked through the sadness, he worked through the anger, the hurt, the confusion, the regret. He finally got to a place in his heart and mind to where he promised himself that he would never put himself through that pain again. His work became his main relationship. Each case became his main priority. There were women along the way, a date here, a date there, nothing more than a sense of companionship, if only the biblical form. He made it clear that he had no intention of a relationship with the women he went out with, that it would be just for fun. This was all right for satisfying the carnal need for that closeness, the sex, but the need for an actual loving, caring relationship, he had convinced himself he could live without.

*****

That worked way into the evening after his meeting with Anna. He was bound and determined to go with her to the Logan house in the morning. He couldn't justify in his mind letting her go without someone who could spot things that were odd or that she perhaps would miss, being only an attorney. With him being a trained detective, she needed him. He kept repeating that in his mind. She needed him.

Her father had told him how accomplished she was, how she had dealt with some particularly sketchy people and solved cases on her own without a bodyguard. He could tell himself whatever he wanted; she intrigued him, infuriated him, and she was slowly becoming a constant in his mind. One thing Tony knew: over his dead body was she and Shellie going out to the Logan's alone.

CHAPTER 10

Anna waited at the bottom of the stairs for the boys to come down to tell her bye for the day. This had become the ritual since Johnathan had gotten his license and started driving him and Jack to school. Jack was down the stairs first. He seemed to grow at least an inch a night lately. He had long surpassed her five-foot-five measurement, but they got their height honest. Mark was very tall, and so were all the men on his side of the family.

"Johnathan is coming, but he is working with his hair. It is doing the wild look this morning." Jack walked to the door, picked up his book bag, and swung it around onto his shoulder. "Hey, remember I have that big biology test today. Say a prayer for me. If I do well on this one, I pretty much score an A for this grading period." He came and gave Anna a hug, bent down, and kissed her on the cheek. "I hope you have a great day, Momma. I love you. Tell him I am out in the truck." With that he was out the door, and she could hear the garage door rising.

"I am coming, just a minute…" Johnathan yelled down the stairs. "I am usually the one waiting on you, Dork Pants. An extra minute won't hurt you."

Anna giggled as she yelled back up the stairs, "Dork Pants is already out in the truck. Just your Dork Momma waiting for her goodbye kiss."

"Sorry, Momma," Johnathan said as he came down the stairs two at a time. "I assumed he was down here fussing about me running behind." He had the smallest amount of patience of any human on earth. "Johnathan stood over six feet tall and gave her a big hug. He too grabbed his book bag and over the shoulder it went. They walked together to the door to the garage. "Well, I love you, Momma. Have a good day. Remember we are going over to Truck's after school. We shouldn't be too late."

Anna watched as they backed out and left for school. God himself was the only one who knew how much she loved those boys. She continued to stand there for a moment, made sure her front door was locked, made sure Murphy the cat had enough food to make it through the day—she really needed to put him on a diet—and made sure she had turned off the stove. Fairly certain that she wasn't going to have her house burn down or be robbed today, she made her way to her van. She had hastily cleaned it up the night before, after getting home from dinner. She didn't care about Shellie, but she was almost certain that Tony would tag along today, and she wanted him to think she had it all together. Funny, she never cared about anyone else thinking that. She made a quick check to see if she had everything—files, purse, keys, phone, cup, and a feel inside her purse confirmed that she had her gun. Not that she expected to use it today; she rarely got into situations where a gun would be necessary. But you never know.

She backed out, watched as the garage door shut tight, and off she went. It was only a little after seven, so she should beat Shellie and most certainly Tony to the office. She wanted to have all her information ready to go: address into phone app thingy, check the office messages to double-check that Richard hadn't called with a last-minute change of plans, and reorganize her purse to hold her files so she would just carry her purse in with her...gun included. One day she wanted to be the hero in some outlandish happening in the town. One that would get nationwide attention and send Savannah Guthrie from *The Today Show* to interview her, asking just how she saved all those children from the madman, asking if she was scared and just how she kept it all together during the ordeal. Today, not so much, not feeling it today.

The monthly signs of her being a woman were creeping up. Her boobs hurt when she walked or put on her seat belt, her uterus was feeling like an angry T-rex, and her right leg was hurting. Well, she wasn't pregnant. That was good. Not that she had any reason to worry. If she was, then it would be yet another immaculate conception. Anna hadn't lived a good enough life for that.

The drive to her office was mostly pleasant. She usually took the interstate, but on beautiful mornings like this one, especially when she had enough time, she liked to drive up through town. Pressley Heights was beautiful in early spring—any time really; each season had its beauty, but spring held its own special magic. The trees with their new green leaves, the daffodils and tulips dotting the yards in her neighborhood, the singing birds filled the air with their songs of happiness. You couldn't stop yourself from smiling. It almost put you into a trance how tranquil the area was. No wonder people loved to visit and vacation here.

The town was filled with little stores and boutiques, anything you could possibly want to buy. Also there was the hardware store, the old-fashioned toy store, bakery, and bookstore filled one side of the street, and the other was dotted with little eateries and the cutest resale shop. Gigi's store was at the end of the block, and the Amish furniture store owned by the most amazing couple finished up the "retail block" nearest downtown. For a moment it came to her mind, *I would love to go in and explore these stores. I wonder if Tony has done that or would like to. Hmmm, that was weird. Who cares what he would like to do?*

Anna parked her van on the side street just adjacent to her office. No need to park in the deck today when they would be leaving before most offices downtown opened. She made her way up to the office and started by checking the voice messages. No call from Richard; all must still be a go. Great! This meeting was imperative to helping Mr. Logan understand what was going on with the suspicion that surrounded his wife.

Anna took out all the nonessential items from her purse and filled it with files, pens, and a notepad. She double-checked her wallet—phone and gun were present and accounted for. All she had now to do was wait. Wait and see if Tony trusted her enough to handle this herself. Deep down, she hoped that he did. Her professional integrity meant a lot to her, but on a shallower note, she kind of hoped that he would tag along. She liked looking at him, and you never know, maybe he could learn something from her.

*****

Anna and Shellie walked to the van. Shellie got in the passenger seat, and Anna got in and shut the door. Anna felt almost sad that it seemed that Tony wasn't there at the appointed time. Maybe he got over his mad act and figured she knew what she was doing. Oh, well. So be it.

"Ready for this fun excursion?" Anna looked at Shellie as she turned the key in the ignition.

"Ready as I will ever be. I sure hope this guy is not like the last guy we went to visit. Remember the hoarder? I swear, I felt so dirty when we left there. I bet I saw at least four rats and the evidence of four hundred more in just the living room. No wonder the county wanted to condemn the house. My goodness, it wasn't safe for the rats living in there much less the man. Bless him." Shellie got out her hand sanitizer to ward off any leftover residue from that house from a year ago. "I bet if people really searched that house and all the crap in there, some of these missing person cases would be solved. I would bet money on it." Shellie held up the hand sanitizer to Anna; Anna shrugged it off.

"You are such a germaphobe. Don't you think that if there was something to catch from that house, that man would have already caught it? He seemed okay to me." Anna checked her phone to make sure the app was running with the address. She wasn't too familiar with the part of town that Mr. Logan lived in, but she had a general idea. "I mean, he did have a horrid cough, but he could have just had a cold." Anna reached for her lip gloss and blush. "Some people just cough."

"Some people have a serious lung disease because they breathe in black mold twenty-four seven too. I think that was his problem. His house would have been the best place for one of those shows to find out all the different bacteria and viruses in an area."

IT'S IN THE BAG

Applying a little touch-up of blush, Anna stopped and looked at Shellie. "What kind of shows do you watch on TV? That sounds horrible." Anna went back to touching up her makeup. "Well, let's get going. Clock says 8:48, time to go." At that moment a loud thump hit the side of Anna's van, just behind her door. Both Shellie and Anna yelled; Anna's elbow hit the horn, and Shellie's head hit the window. Both women jumped and got caught by their seat belts as they turned to see what caused the sound. They both looked out the window and saw nothing. "What the…" Anna started talking but then she screamed again as the passenger-side sliding door began to open. There stood Tony, laughing and looking very proud.

"You two weren't trying to leave without me, were you? I was starting to get my feelings hurt when I saw you sitting in the car." Tony pulled the handle to shut the door and began to buckle his seat belt.

Anna was turned in her seat, staring at him, her heart still racing and fury bubbling up inside her—or was that lust? There was a fine line between the two. "Just what in the hell do you think you were doing? Trying to get shot?" Anna huffed and turned back around toward the front of the van.

"Honey, by the time you found your gun in that thing you call a purse, I would have killed you, thrown you onto the street, and been gone in this very attractive minivan." Tony winked at Anna. "Never once during all that, whatever that display was, were you ever going for your gun. You wanted to see what was going on. Proof positive that it is a very good thing I found the time this morning to grace you both with my presence." Tony sat back in the seat and buckled his seat belt.

Anna glanced back in the rearview mirror and thought to herself, *You better be buckling that seat belt, buddy, tight, and I hope you choke on it.* "I thought you were just joking about coming with us this morning. I thought you had your own research to do. I assure you, Shellie and I have this. You can feel free to stay and work on your own stuff." Anna secretly hoped he would stay put.

"I will have you know that I worked late last night doing my research, and if we live through this escapade this morning, I will

99

share it with you. I think you both will find it very interesting. Now, let's get this buggy on the road and get this over with." Tony sipped his coffee and stared at Anna. "So, are we going or not?"

Anna put the van in drive, and they were off. She had Shellie giving her the play-by-play directions, which thoroughly aggravated Tony, and Anna loved it. He seemed to be less than thrilled to (a) be sitting in the back seat, (b) not be behind the wheel himself, and (c) just seeming to be irritated in general. All of which Anna was fine with.

"What did you do last night, Shellie?" Anna was going to enjoy this drive if it killed her. "Did you ever go and check out that store I was telling you about? The one just past the library? You should see the furniture they have to refurbish. I think you could find the perfect table for your entryway there. Gigi could do anything you wanted to it, the finish or whatever."

"I forgot to tell you. I went by there night before last on my way home. I saw that table. They are holding it for me. Gigi is going to pick it up and do a distressed whitewash on it. I think that will look amazing there by the door. She is supposed to pick it up tomorrow and should have it done in a week. I am so happy I finally found something to go in that spot. Well, so happy you did." Shellie sounded as excited as if she had picked out a brand-new car. "Thanks for your help! I can't wait till you see it all done."

Tony's head was about to explode. "Okay, ladies, I am sure that HGTV appreciates all the things you have learned about redoing furniture, finding stuff in resale shops, and whatever else they do in hour-long shows…but if y'all have forgotten, we are headed to meet a man who may or may not know we are coming, may or may not appreciate us coming when we arrive, or even understand the reason why. Don't you think we need a plan, a strategy?" Tony huffed. "I am sure this man will be quite impressed with the new table that Shellie has found, but I don't think that will constitute him welcoming us into his home and giving us some information about how his wife may or may not be a serial killer. And, by the way, I vote that she is."

Anna smiled. She was enjoying seeing Tony's frantic, grumpy side. This was fun. "I have a plan, and you will see it in fruition soon enough. Trust me, Tony. Would I put you, one of my best friends, and myself in danger, knowingly? I think not." Anna glanced back just in time to see Tony roll his eyes. "Okay, help me look for 312. That's the house number. We just passed 260." Anna slowed down to be able to squint at the numbers on the mailboxes; she needed to wear her glasses more.

"All I know is that this better not be like the hoarder's house. I refuse to go in if that is the case. Catching my death because of black mold or being bitten by a rabid rat is not on my to-do list for today." Shellie doused her hands with hand sanitizer again. "We just passed 304. Shouldn't be too much farther up here."

"What in the world kind of places do you two hang out in?"

"There it is. Gosh, this is a long driveway." Anna turned onto the paved driveway, noticing the beautifully landscaped edging as they drove along. "I don't think you will have to worry about the place being too dirty or filled to the ceiling with junk. Look at this place." Anna slowly drove up toward a stately brick-and-stucco home. The circular driveway curved right in front of the main door and there was a part that followed around to the entrance to the garage. The yard was full of mature oak trees and several flowering weeping cherry trees and two white dogwoods. Beautiful; just beautiful. "From the way two of the three kids looked the other day in the office, I wasn't expecting this as the father's home. I didn't think he would have too much of a pot to piss in. Now I understand a little more about why the woman may want to off him and why the kids want to protect their father and his assets."

Anna put the van in park, turned off the van and started to grab her things. As she opened her door, she saw Richard open the front door and walk onto the covered porch.

"Good morning, Mr. Logan. What a beautiful home this is. It is so beautiful. Even though we are still in the city limits, it feels like we are off in a secluded park." Anna walked toward the steps up to the porch. "I am glad this worked out to meet with your father. I do hope he won't mind us taking up some of his time."

"Not at all, Ms. Dawson. He is actually a little intrigued by all this. Not suspicious enough for me but intrigued will have to do for now." Richard shook Anna's hand and stepped back so that Shellie and Tony could join her on the porch. "Would you rather meet out on the back patio, or in the house? What do you think would be better?"

"I do hope that you remember Shellie from the office and Detective Phillips from the sheriff's department. He has some information to share with us, specifically with your father. Hopefully to try to get him to understand where all this is coming from and why time is of the essence." Shellie smiled and nodded when she was mentioned, and Tony reached out to shake Richard's hand, the manly hello. "And as far as where to meet and talk, whatever your father prefers is fine with us. I am sure either place will do wonderfully."

"Well, come on in. Dad is in the kitchen. He insisted on having a glass of sweet tea for everyone. Don't worry, it won't be poisoned." Richard winked and walked into the house, leading the group through a beautiful entrance and into an updated kitchen with white-quartz countertops, light-gray cabinets, and a mosaic backsplash that used different shades of gray and white. The enormous island had room for six barstools and a massive workspace. The counters were clean and uncluttered. That should make Shellie feel better. As they walked in, Mr. Logan, the father, spoke.

"Well, hello, welcome. Come on in." He motioned for each one of them to grab a glass of tea, and then he continued. "Please call me Jerry. Mr. Logan sounds so old." He laughed.

"Thank you for agreeing to speak with us. We wouldn't be here if we didn't honestly think you needed to hear what we have to say. When your children came to meet with me a few days ago, I was mostly concerned about your safety first. Honestly, the more I learn about your wife—and not to sound harsh and speaking ill of her while she is not here—there are some facts I think you need to know. You may in fact be in some danger now, or in the very near future."

After taking a sip of his tea, Jerry tilted his head to the side and looked at Anna. He met her eyes. "Well, young lady, you shoot straight from the hip, don't you? I like that. Come on, let's go out to the patio in the back. It is a beautiful morning." The group made their way out onto a brick patio with plenty of outdoor seating. A

IT'S IN THE BAG

couch, love seat, and two armchairs all sat positioned around a large table. "Sit wherever you would like, where you feel most comfortable. Just put your glasses down on the table. We don't use coasters like the fancy people do. I wouldn't say it in there, but I got to thinking after the kids came and talked to me that, perhaps, if she is as devious as it is presumed that she is, that she may just be cunning enough to have the house bugged." Jerry laughed; no one else did.

They all took seats around the table. Shellie chose one of the armchairs, Richard took the other chair. Jerry sat on the right side of the couch, and Tony took the love seat. Anna sat next to Jerry, retrieved her files from her bag, and laid them out on the table. Tony put his folders on the table as well, and Anna took the opportunity to start first.

"Okay, I know we only have a certain amount of time, so let's get started. You said you liked that I shot from the hip, so buckle up." Anna smiled, and Jerry nodded. "Do you know just how many times your wife has been married prior to you?"

"Well, Melanie said she had been married before, widowed, and that was about the extent of our conversation. We didn't dwell on our pasts. I had been married before, and she didn't give me the third degree about if there was just the one or more. I didn't either. At the time, it didn't matter." Jerry answered just as bluntly as Anna asked the question. "What does that matter anyway? We were both consenting adults, not married at the time, and free to do as we please. Richard mentioned there may be more than just the one husband. Not really sure why that would matter too much."

"It isn't just the fact that she was married more than once before, it is the manner in which her previous husbands met their demise. It seems that there are some questionable circumstances to most of them." Anna tried to be a little less blunt, to lessen the blow perhaps. "Uh, Tony, why don't you share what you have with us and we can go from there." Everyone turned to stare at Tony.

Tony cleared his throat and dove in. "We have traced back and found four marriages, not including the one you know about to a Mr. Chambers. So basically, five previous husbands who all died, for various reasons, while married to Melanie. This seems like much more than a coincidence. This is why we think it is so suspicious. All the men were pretty well-off, had businesses, money, homes, and assets for her to attach herself to. In every case, the last will and testament was changed just before the deaths, leaving her everything and sometimes cutting any children out totally." Tony paused to give that a little time to sink in. "Two of the gentlemen had children who are willing to talk with me, and Anna, if she would like. I am meeting with them Monday. The last gentleman, Mr. Chambers, they only knew each other three days before marrying."

Richard, who knew his father better than anyone else there, could tell he was thinking something, something important. "Dad, you need to tell us anything that you two have talked about, anything that you may now remember and think suspicious. We need to stop her. I don't want anything to happen to you. We already lost Mom. I can't stand the thought of losing you to such a horrible lady. Not when we can do something about it."

Jerry sat silent for a moment. He looked down at his feet and let his head rest in his hands. The group stayed quiet to let him have time to collect his thoughts. "How did the others die? I mean, what was she suspected to have done?"

Tony flipped some papers, "Well, the first husband died of a heart attack. He was known to be on blood pressure medicine, but when his autopsy was done, there wasn't any trace of that medication in his blood work. None at all. The family thought that, at the time, maybe he was just being stubborn and not wanting to take his medicine, but upon speaking with his doctors, he had been on the medication for years, always faithful to take it, and knew the consequences if he didn't."

"A heart attack is nothing. Heck, that could happen to me today, or any of you for that matter." Jerry had a point. "I mean, things happen like that all the time."

Tony nodded all the time that Jerry was speaking. "True, you are so right. That one is still up in the air. The kids of—let's see, Mr. Filmer, they believe that there was something that helped that heart attack along." Tony looked at his notes. "Here you go, the next husband, Mr. Jenkins, a Skip Jenkins. He died after an awful car accident. His brake lines had been cut. After an investigation, no enemies could be identified, but no one thought to look into his wife. He was a bank executive, and the thought was that there may have been a disgruntled customer or employee. That case is still actually open."

"The next man was a *New York Times* best-selling author. He and Melanie were eating at a restaurant, and he went into anaphylaxis shock. She had told the paramedics that he had a terrible allergy to shellfish. This was a relatively new restaurant that served both surf and turf, so there was a high probability of cross contamination, especially with shellfish. She said that she had recommended the establishment to celebrate his latest book but forgot about his allergy."

"These could all be just terrible accidents. Just terrible, but I wonder why she wouldn't have told me about the others." Jerry seemed apprehensive about all this information—rightfully so; it was his wife. "Any more information?"

"Yes, just a couple more, but maybe the most compelling of them all. Mr. Reynolds owned a very popular and successful body shop. He was one of the best mechanics in the area. One Saturday, after the shop had closed and he was the only one there, the car he was working on fell on him and pretty much crushed him. He managed to get to his phone and call for help. He actually lived for about two hours, and the doctors and nurses all made statements that he kept saying Melanie's name, over and over. When they repeated the name, he would try to nod. At the time, they thought that he was just calling out for his wife, but after an investigation at the shop, it was concluded that the jack and the stand that the car was up on had help in failing." Tony paused for a moment, then dropped this bomb: "Then she sold the business for over one million dollars."

"Mr. Logan, I am so sorry to come to your home and bombard you with this awful information, but I felt that it was imperative to let you know what we know, that your children are concerned, and rightly so as far as I can tell. We want you to have all the information so that you yourself can make the best decision for you. The one that you can live with. Just know that I, Shellie, and I know Tony too—we have all worked with many people who we would have never guessed were bad, or in some cases, downright evil. I don't want anything to happen to you. Your family doesn't want anything to happen to you. You matter. You mean the world to so many people. We only have a few more minutes to stay here with you. I want us to be long gone before she is even done with her appointment. I want us to make it as though no one was here. These glasses we are going to wash and put away, not just in a dishwasher. If she is as calculating as I believe she is, enough to commit at least four to five murders and walk away the poor widow woman in each one, then we are going to cover our tracks very well."

Tony watched Anna as she talked. She was good.

"I don't need to hear anymore. I just don't. I can't believe I am even saying this, but she has acted funny for the last little bit. She has started bringing up me changing my will." He looked at Anna. "Anna, I know that you met with all my kids. Two of the three are a little rough around the edges, right? She keeps saying that if I changed the will, making her the beneficiary, and on my life insurance, that she will make sure they are taken care of." He now glanced at Tony. "What do I need to do to help you? Honestly, this all happened so fast, and I was so lonely, I let this go too far. I wouldn't listen to anyone." Jerry obviously felt foolish, but he also was seeing clearer now. "I have worked my whole life to build what little I have to pass on. I want my kids to get that, they will need it. I had always thought that maybe Richard will continue it on, or sell the company, who knows, but that should be their decision. I am not an extremely wealthy man, but I am proud of what I can leave to my children."

Jerry had founded and grown the largest bridge contracting business in three states; they did all the bridge work for the North Carolina Department of Transportation. He was rightly proud of what he had been able to do. "I can't let that be stolen from my kids. I won't."

"Look, we all can get to places in our lives where we do things we don't understand when we look back. We all have been in dark, lonely places. It is okay. The good thing is that you do realize that there is something to what we know. There is enough evidence to show that she may not be quite the woman you thought she was, and you are interested in making it better, making a difference, so that you will be okay, and that this never happens to anyone else." Anna put her hand over Jerry's. "Look, I have a plan. You said that she wanted to get to work on you changing your will. Have you done anything to make that happen? Do you currently have an attorney that you work with?"

"The will I have is the one that Stella and I made years and years ago. That attorney is long dead and buried. One reason I hadn't put much thought or work into it was that I would have to find another attorney that I trusted. I just have been putting it off." Jerry's eyes lit up when he realized what Anna was getting at. "You, you can be my new attorney. Will you?"

Anna laughed. "I was just going to offer my services to you and your 'lovely' wife. How about this. When she gets home today, tell her you have made an appointment to meet with a new attorney in town. Tell her about me, whatever. Just leave out that I am the sheriff's daughter." Anna winked. "Okay, Tony is working to talk with some of the children from the other victims on Monday." She glanced at Tony, and he nodded in agreement. "Your appointment is Tuesday afternoon, one o'clock sharp. My office." Anna dug into her purse and retrieved a business card and handed it to Jerry. "Does that sound good?"

"Perfect." Jerry tucked the business card into the pocket on his dress shirt. "I should be safe and sound at least until she knows the will is a done deal, right?" Jerry looked over at Tony. Safety was his department for sure.

"Yes, I wouldn't imagine her trying anything against your well-being, especially since your will indicates your children will get everything, and your beneficiary for your life insurance is Richard. I won't be in the meeting with you and Anna on Tuesday, but I won't be far away." Tony put Jerry at ease quickly.

"The new will won't be ready to be signed for at least two weeks, or however long it takes for us to get enough dirt on her. I am a very busy woman and I am just squeezing you in as a favor to my friend Richard. Deal?" Anna looked at Jerry for approval. He nodded. "Okay, let's get these glasses washed and back in the cabinet. We have got to get out of Dodge."

The group made quick work of washing, drying, and placing the glasses back in the cabinet. Shellie even made more tea to replace what was used out of the glass pitcher in the refrigerator. Saying their goodbyes at the front door, Anna glanced back around, and it looked just as it had when they arrived. She was glad that they did end up sitting outside; better for the lingering smells of perfume and aftershave to be as minimized as possible.

With a wave, Anna put the van in drive, and out of the driveway they went. That had gone far better than she could have imagined. It was a little before noon; Melanie wasn't due home for another couple of hours, and she should be none the wiser. Now, what Anna was getting wise to was her rumbling tummy.

"Are you two as hungry as I am? What do you say we stop and get a bite to eat before we head back to the office? We can take a minute to see where we are, where we need to get to, and the plan to do just that. How does that sound?" Anna was already headed to her favorite deli near her office.

"Sounds great, and you are driving, boss. Anywhere you want to go." Shellie was so agreeable. She needed a raise.

"Tony, seems like you are our hostage for a little while longer. That is what you get when you just invite yourself along on an adventure of mine." Anna needed to thank him for coming but didn't want him to get the big head. "I will have to say, I am awful thankful that you came. The information that you had was just what was needed to convince Jerry that he needed to be careful. Thank you. For that, lunch is on me."

Anna looked back in the rearview mirror. Tony was smiling, and he winked at her. She smiled despite herself.

CHAPTER 11

The little deli that Anna chose for lunch that day had been one of her favorites since she was just a little girl. It wasn't the nicest, the biggest, or the most popular place to have lunch in town, but to her it was the best. The deli was in the basement of the tallest office building in Pressley Heights. Anna remembered coming to work with her daddy when she was just a little girl. They would walk together to get lunch at the deli, sit, and talk; he would talk to everyone and introduce her. She was so happy that the owners had not changed a thing other than what they had to as far as equipment and sprucing it up every few years. It still had that same feel as it did all those years ago.

"Anna, where exactly are you taking me to eat? Why are we going down to a basement?" Tony was starting to look a little skeptical as he followed the two women down the stairs that led below the street. "You are crazy if you think I am eating lunch in a dungeon, even if you are buying. I don't think I could stomach what they may have down here." Tony took each step gingerly, taking in all the spiderwebs and leaves that were collecting on the steps. Anna knew this place wasn't the prettiest, or the fanciest, but its food could not be beat.

"Trust me, Tony, we come here all the time, or have it delivered. They bike lunches all over the city. I wouldn't lead you astray or toward danger, now, would I?" Anna tilted her head and smiled as she turned the handle to open the door to the deli.

The trio walked into a brightly lit, cheerful deli. The older man standing at the register with the chef's hat on yelled to Anna, "Hello, sweetie. You and your friends find a seat you like." He handed another customer his change and told him to come again. "Grab y'all some menus, and Lucy will be over there in a jiffy. Your daddy with you today?"

"Not today, Tom. He is too busy, I'm sure, keeping this flea-bitten town safe from all the riffraff like you." Anna winked at the old man and smiled. "You know how that old man is…always working. I might order him something and send it over. I will add something to go for him, thanks!" Anna smiled as she talked with the old man like he was a member of her family. She grabbed three menus and headed toward her favorite table in the place: far back corner, perfect for looking at all the comings and goings of the people in the deli.

"Okay, Tom usually has amazing specials on Fridays, so they will tell us when they come around for drinks. For now"—she handed a menu to Tony first—"get ready to have your socks blown off by the food. Your current company is awesome, but the food is to die for. I personally recommend the three-cheese grilled cheese. Yummy!" Anna closed her eyes and took a gigantic breath in. Tony almost fell out of his chair.

They all looked at their menus and only looked up when the waitress came to stand beside the table. She was older, but still strikingly beautiful, blond, thin, and had a beautiful smile. She flashed it immediately at Anna.

"Anna, what a sight for sore eyes y'all are here today! It is so good to see you. Can I get you guys something to drink while you are picking out what you want to eat?"

"Hello, long time no see, Nancy! You look amazing." Anna stood and gave the woman a quick hug and kiss on the cheek. "It is so good to see you. What in the world are you doing waiting tables? Ain't you a little too old for that?" Anna giggled, eyes sparkling.

"Well, Lucy had to go to sign up for summer classes at the university. She needed the afternoon off, so I dusted off my old sneakers. It is fun being back in here with Tom. He is hoot, and maybe this will convince him that we could stand to hire another couple of servers. Lucy is going to be in classes this summer and for the next four years…we can't just depend on her always being here. We also can't expect Mollie to cover for her sister's shifts either. That isn't fair. She has a life outside of here, and she doesn't really like the business any-

IT'S IN THE BAG

way, working for it I mean." Nancy sat down by Shellie and caught up with her for a moment. The girls introduced Tony to Nancy. They placed their drink orders, and Nancy scooted off to grab them.

Tony looked over at Anna and smiled, then at Shellie, then back at Anna. "Do you two know everyone in the town? I mean, except for a couple of people, you guys have talked to everyone in here. I feel like I am sitting at the popular table in high school. I wouldn't know that feeling from experience, but I can imagine it is a lot like this." He laughed and looked over the menu. "I think I will take your recommendation for the grilled cheese. If it is half as good as you seem to think it is, it will be out of this world."

"You can't go wrong with Tom's grilled cheese. Legend is that was how he got Nancy to marry him. She tasted his grilled cheese and that was it." Shellie winked at Anna and smiled at Tony. "They say it is magical."

Nancy came back with three sweet teas, took their orders, and went about tending to some other patrons. Tom better appreciate that his wife was the best waitress in the world.

"Shellie, what are you doing this weekend, like tomorrow, around 9:00 a.m.?" Anna needed to call in some reinforcements for her meeting with her momma to help finish the plans for her daddy's birthday carnival. "I know you want to spend some quality time with my momma." Anna was hopeful that her friend would take the bait and know she needed help.

Shellie began shaking her head before Anna finished talking. "No go, sweet cheeks. I have plans tomorrow and they do not include your mother. I love her, I would probably die for her, but she can only be taken in doses. She has been on me to go on a date with your cousin Randall." She shot a glance at Tony. "For the love of Pete, I cannot get it through to her that Randall is gay. And if she knows of his attraction to the manly species, then she need not depend on my womanly ways to bring him over to the female persuasion. He can be as gay as the day is long, but I am not the judge and jury on that and I ain't set on fixing him. I like Randall. He is funny as hell. He is perfect just the way he is." Shellie unrolled her napkin and placed it in her lap. "Maybe it won't be that bad. Take the boys with her. They

111

can run interference and keep the hounding down to a minimum. Just do what she needs you to, agree with everything she has chosen, and make your exit. Easy-peasy."

"Darcy Dawson does not do 'easy-peasy.' She much prefers difficult-schmifficult. I don't think schmifficult is in *Webster's Dictionary*...but if they add it ever, there will be my momma's photo. Enough said." Anna laughed, partly because that was funny as hell, and partly because she was off her game with Tony sitting right across from her. He threw her natural way of rational thinking off. Anna did not like that. She needed to keep her head about herself...that was the only way to protect her heart and her sanity.

"What is going on with your momma, and why is she planning a carnival? An actual carnival? For Jake's birthday?" Tony looked as lost as a little puppy.

Anna couldn't help but smile at his naivety. "Why, yes, isn't that what normal families do for birthdays? Throw an actual carnival extravaganza for the whole town to attend during the afternoon of the Fourth of July, and then have dancing and fireworks in the evening? Complete with cotton candy, some random kiddie rides, ponies, hot dog stands, and funnel cakes. Don't tell me you don't have that for your birthday?" Anna looked at Tony with her big hazel eyes and batted her eyelashes.

"Stop being so snarky, Anna." Shellie tried to explain to Tony in a more normal way, with much less sarcasm. Anna rolled her eyes. "While Darcy does like to do things, um, a little over the top, I would say, she loves doing a party every year for Jake's birthday, which is July sixth. This year the fourth falls on a Saturday, and she has gone and planned on outdoing even Darcy Big." Shellie did concede that Darcy was doing a little more this year. "The whole entire town is invited. It is usually at the Country Club, and it is something we *all*"—she looked Anna right in the eyes—"look forward to and enjoy."

Tony raised his eyebrows. "It does sound fun, very hard to pull off, but fun. I bet Jake gets a kick out of it as much as he loves all the people. No wonder everyone knows him. He is the cool guy with the fun parties." Tony smiled. "Sounds like a good time."

IT'S IN THE BAG

"I am certainly glad you think so. You will get an invitation. No gifts, please—your attendance and enjoyment is gift enough." Anna winked at Tony. He about melted right there in his seat. "I do hope that you will be able to attend. I would absolutely hate if you missed it." She turned to Shellie. "So, Shellie, are you really saying no to tomorrow? What do you have to do tomorrow morning? Can you move it to tomorrow afternoon? Then I would have a reason to leave. I would have to get you back to whatever you have to do." Anna used her best puppy-dog eyes. "Come on, help me out. If it is just me then I will be roped, tied, and made to stay all the way through dinner. With Johnathan driving now, I cannot use having to take them somewhere as an excuse anymore. I need your help."

"Sorry, Anna. No go tomorrow, anytime of the day tomorrow. I have a day booked at the Divinity Spa with my sister. We finally got an appointment to use our gift certificates Mom and Dad got us for Christmas. That place is crazy busy. I love you, but I will not give up my hot stone massage, my complimentary glasses of champagne, and my day of peace and solitude. Working for you takes a toll on this body. I need this time. Tomorrow. Not at your momma's."

Anna was about to protest, but just in the nick of time, Nancy arrived with their sandwiches. They smelled heavenly; were not one bit healthy but were totally worth it. Anna led them in saying the blessing, and then they dug in. Silence fell around the table; the food was too good to take away from with anything like conversation. Nancy came back to the table to refill their drinks, get Anna's to-go order, and leave the check. When the last glorious bite was eaten, Tony was the first one to speak.

"If you never speak it again in your life, you have told it today. That was the most amazing grilled cheese sandwich I have ever had. I could eat like three more. I swear." Tony wiped his mouth and placed his napkin in his plate.

"Tom is the best cook around. This is the best deli in town. They may not have the most wonderful location, but it has stood the test of time. This was originally owned by Tom's father, then as Tom grew, he started working here. After college, his dad got cancer and couldn't run the deli. It almost closed, but Tom knew how much it meant to his dad and to the town. He fell in love with it and is still at it today. His dad would be so proud." Anna smiled, glad that she could share this great place with someone relatively new. "You will have to order or come down here every now and then. Support the local businesses and all."

"I will. The hard part will be not wanting to come here every day. I don't think I will be able to walk back up those steps." Tony patted his belly, under another nice fitted dress shirt. "I would like to offer my help with your little predicament that you seem to have tomorrow. I would be happy to help you, um, run interference with your mother. Jake has told me more than once he would love for me to come to the house and meet Darcy, so this will kill two birds with one stone, as they say. What do you think?"

Anna perked up. "Well, that would be wonderful. Such a friendly thing to offer to do. I must warn you, though, some people who spend a lot of time with me seem to need to book a day at the spa to recoup after all the stress I cause." Anna cut a sharp look at Shellie. "Honestly, that would be great. I promise it won't take all day, and I will be able to say that you just have to get going and I will drive so I will just have to leave too. Perfect. Thank you so much! You just made my Christmas gift list."

"Wow, Tony, that is something. It took me two years and coming to work for her to make that list." Shellie laughed. "I love you, Anna, I do, but I need tomorrow." Shellie looked at Tony. "Thank you for saving me and helping out friend here, but let me warn you. Darcy will latch on to you like a bee to a bloomin' flower. She is gonna take one look at you and think her next big shindig will be y'all's engagement party." Shellie snickered.

"Oh, hell no." Anna realized that sounded harsh; she reached over and touched Tony's hand. "No offense, Tony, but after my debacle of shame, as she puts it—my first marriage—she barely lived through the embarrassment of my leaving my husband. She fully supported me of course, she knew my reasons, but she also saw the money, house, and prestige that I was walking away from. It was years before she would show her face at the club again, and she missed like a month of Sundays at church. Daddy told her she was being silly, and Jesus could take care of me and all the people who talked about me behind my back, she need not worry. I think the good Lord has done pretty well with me—well, what he has had to work with. You know with my stubbornness, being hardheaded and all."

"I don't know about that, Anna, your momma told me a year ago or so that she was tired of seeing you throw away the best years of your life to your job, that you had a lot of living to do, sex to have, and adventures to go on." Shellie smiled as if she had just won an Oscar for that performance of Anna's momma. "She only cares about you and your happiness, of course."

"Wait, what?" Anna was stunned, and that was hard when it came to things her momma did. "Well, so happy to know that my momma talks to you about my sex life... Geez, Tony, maybe she can discuss that with you too. Maybe you could discuss positions, porn, whatever...good Lord up in heaven, take me now, *please*. I cannot believe I was birthed from her vagina. Does that woman know no boundaries?"

Tony had dealt with a lot of strong personalities in his life, but he thought he may have met his match and may be meeting her mother tomorrow. This should be fun. "So do you want me to meet you somewhere, like at the gas station or something? Just let me know what you were thinking. I will be good with whatever you think is best."

"Um, I was thinking you would drive to my house, get out, and come in the house for a few. You can meet my boys. They don't think I have enough friends either. Friends of the male persuasion, I mean. They tell me all the time I spend too much time with Shellie and the other girls. They are just kidding with me, not judging my sex life, or lack thereof, I don't think?" Anna took a business card out of her purse and scribbled down her home address on the back. "So I told Momma I would be there at nine, so say you get to my house by eight. I only live a couple streets over from my parents, so it isn't like it's a long way. I might even make enough breakfast for you to have some. The boys will leave a little before nine. They have a tee time down in Etowah Valley. I would like you to meet them. I am kind of proud of them."

Tony took the card. The address sounded familiar in his head. Since moving to Pressley Heights, he had driven around quite a bit trying to get familiar with the area. All the neighborhoods and the good and bad parts of town. If he remembered correctly, this was in a nice part of town. "First of all, you shouldn't just give out your home address to men, men you barely know. Secondly, I think I can make it at eight, and I will be sure to come hungry. How about that?"

Anna enjoyed the easy banter and friendly coaxing they had between them. That was fun. "Good. I will be sure to make you my best bowl of milk. I will wait and let you pick your own cereal. I pour a mean bowl of Froot Loops, and my Cinnamon Toast Crunch isn't too bad either. Ask Shellie, she has had it."

"She's right, she has the best cereal skills I know. Best in town." Shellie laughed. "All right, you crazy kids, we need to get going. I don't know about you, Tony, but we girls have a little bit of business to attend to this afternoon back at the office." Shellie noticed the look that Anna gave her. It was the look that Shellie understood well. Anna needed to go to the bathroom.

Anytime that she ate, she would need to go to empty her ostomy bag. She needed Shellie to distract Tony while she made her way to the bathroom. Anna did this when she didn't want people to know that she had a bag and the fullness of it made a slight bulge in her clothes. Shellie had actually thought about how funny it was her eating with Tony and not caring about the bag, like she always did around some people. It was almost like she had forgotten about it and was just enjoying the time they were having. Whatever it was, Shellie jumped into action.

"All right, big fella, I want to show you something cool about this building. We will go do that while Anna takes care of the bill. So glad that lunch was on her today! Thank you, Anna, we will be right out front." Shellie literally pulled Tony up out of his chair. "You are going to love this. Come on!"

Tony's body language showed that he would rather stay and wait on Anna, but it was hard to not go with Shellie, she was so persistent and pulling on him. He gave in and stood. He looked back at

Anna. "Thanks for lunch, I guess we will be outside." With one final tug, Shellie pulled him out the door.

Anna made her way to the bathroom, took care of her bag, and made her way out to meet Shellie and Tony. Anna found Shellie telling Tony all the wonderful aspects of the town fountain. Perfect!

CHAPTER 12

Tony sat in this truck and watched as Anna and Shellie made their way into their building. Once he saw that they were safely inside the building, he closed his eyes and tilted his head back against the headrest of his truck. What had he been thinking when he just randomly offered his help to Anna, agreeing to go to her mother's with her? He was losing it. That had to be it. He knew that he was not that person who just did things on the spur of the moment—well, things like this that had to do with a woman. If it was hiking, fishing, hunting, or some other type of adventure, sure, that was great, not just inviting himself to spend even part of a day with a woman he may or may not be feverishly attracted to. That emotion, all those emotions had been shoved to the back of his mind for so long, not allowed to come to the front of his mind and control what he said and did. This was not going to be good.

It had been a long time since Tony had felt the feelings that he had since that first, albeit awkward, way that she had actually fallen at his feet. That first moment when his eyes met hers…he knew he was in trouble from that first moment when he touched her on the arm. He had felt the electricity. He had not ever felt that kind of jolt when meeting someone. He thought she must have felt something too, or maybe it was just the embarrassment of falling so hard and fast in her father's office.

Tony had loved Willow. He had given his heart, and she had given hers. In the end, she had given his back, battered, hurt, and bruised. His instinctive thoughts were to shut off that part of his life, to protect himself from the hurt and pain that he had been dealt. He didn't want to ever go through that kind of hell again. He decided that no one woman was worth that kind of turmoil. He was going to

IT'S IN THE BAG

have to be very careful around Anna. She had stirred up some feelings that he couldn't keep at bay. That feeling of longing and desire. She didn't seem to know that she was doing that, and that was what seemed so dangerous. She was just being herself. Even when she was being challenging, she was exciting, sexy, and drawing him in, making him want her.

Tony hadn't had a real relationship, one with the commitment, time, and energy put in. The passion that lasted for more than just a moment in time, the connection with someone, other than just a way to satisfy a male need with no strings attached. He was always a little surprised to know that there were women out there who didn't mind the no-strings kind of relationship... He was getting tired of that. He envied those of his family and friends who had that committed relationship. His parents were still madly in love, it seemed; his sister had a solid, loving marriage. What was wrong with him?

Tony put his key in the ignition and started the truck. He needed to go back to the office for a little while, then he would call it a week. He couldn't wait until this evening. He wanted to go to the gym, get his workout and swim in, and then head home. He would leave worrying about tomorrow morning for tomorrow morning; no sense in borrowing trouble for today. He pulled out of the parking spot and made the short drive to the department headquarters. He parked his truck, gathered his files, and headed inside.

Tony opened the door and walked inside. He loved his job and he loved his office. This felt like a place that he could leave all those thoughts about women, especially this one woman. He needed a distraction. Work. Work would be good.

There was a knock at his door. "Come in..." Tony looked up from his computer and saw Sheriff Dawson standing in the doorway. "Afternoon, Jake, how are you doing?"

Jake made his way over to take a seat in front of Tony's desk. "Going good, can't complain about anything at the moment. Not that complaining does any good. How is that case with the Logan man going? I know you went out with Anna and Shel this morning to meet with him?"

"It went good. We were able to share with him the information that we had. He did remember some actions by his wife that led him to think she may be trying to force his hand in changing the will. He does not want his kids to lose what they rightfully have coming to them and all the work he has done in his life to build up his business." Tony sat back and moved his desk chair back and forth some. "I think, all in all, the meeting was good. He and Melanie are going to come meet with Anna next week. Melanie will think it is to start the process of changing the will."

"Anna is a force, isn't she?" Jake had a weird smile on his face. "She is just irritating enough to get under your skin. She is full of spunk—sometimes dumb spunk, mind you, but she gets the job done. There are a lot of people in this area who are much better off today because of her." Tony could see the pride in his eyes as he spoke about her. "I like to think she is the best of Darcy and me. She has my personality, my brains, my work ethic, and she has her momma's looks and her momma's laugh. Dangerous combination. Perhaps more dangerous than just about any criminal we have out there, besides that Melanie lady." Jake laughed, but his message was clear.

"She is some kind of force for sure. And, yes, no offense intended whatsoever, but she can be quite irritating. Very much so actually. She just thinks she can waltz over to someone's home, tell them their wife is a serial killer, and think that they will just fall at her feet and work with her to trap the woman…the wife." Tony needed to vent; probably not a good idea to vent to her father, but still, he had to know how she was. "She didn't even spend one moment thinking about how she could be walking into some sort of danger. She thinks just because she has a gun in that thing she calls a purse that she is protected. She needs to be more careful." Lord, that felt good to say.

Jake laughed and nodded in agreement. "I have tried to talk to her numerous times about where she keeps her gun. She has this thing about it being on her all the time, but hey, at least I convinced her to take the concealed carry class and take the test. She bucked me on that for a long time. She just didn't see the need in having that for protection, especially when she takes her hardheaded, ill-thought-out trips to visit clients or people she needs to. She has never needed to use it, thank the good Lord above, but that girl can shoot. She was dead on since day one."

"I would hate for her to have to use it. I just don't want her or Shellie to get into a situation that may get out of hand and not be able to handle it. I don't want anything to happen to them." Tony had no doubt that she was a good shot…she had proved to be good at everything else so far. Tony wondered what else she was good at. He had to stop; the woman's father was sitting across from him, for goodness's sake. "She seems really good at what she does. Hey, I am meeting her and coming to your house in the morning. I offered to help with the planning of a party for someone I know. It isn't a surprise, is it? I hope not. Oops!"

Jake laughed. "No, son, you didn't tell me anything that I don't already know. About twenty years ago maybe, but not now. She has become quite famous for my birthday parties, and they have come to be something that the town looks forward to. Having a birthday practically on July Fourth was always fun growing up. I mean, who doesn't want fireworks and a huge party on their birthday? This is more about the town getting together. Good luck meeting Darcy. You think Anna is high-strung. Bless." Jake got up and started out the door. He stopped and turned. "Look, all I want to say about Anna, she has been through some tough sh———. She met it head-on and is a tough broad. Give her a chance no matter how many walls she puts up. She is probably building a few as we speak. She is a good girl, and not just because she is mine and my only child. Underneath all that tough BS is the heart of gold. You ever hurt it, and I will kill you." Jake took off his glasses and gave Tony the look of death. "Good luck with meeting my wife tomorrow. She has been known to chew up and spit out a few people Anna has brought home. Too bad I am going fishing. Have a great day!" With that, Jake was gone down the hall, whistling a tune.

Chew up and spit out people; that was ominous for sure. What kind of woman was he married to anyway?

*****

Anna didn't even make it into her office; she just plopped down in her favorite chair beside Shellie's desk. She sat silent for a few moments and then looked at Shellie. "What was I thinking accepting his offer to help me with Momma tomorrow?"

"You were probably thinking how desperate you were to not have to spend the whole day with her, being sucked in by her motherly guilt play. Or there is always the possibility you are attracted to him, as I think he is to you, and you want to spend more time with him. Either way, a win-win in my book." Shellie talked as she checked the office emails and phone messages. She knew she was right, probably in both instances.

"I will be honest with you, Shel. He is hot. He is the first man I have been physically attracted to like this in a very long time. Probably since back in college when I met Mark, and this is even stronger. He grabbed my arm that day I went splat on Daddy's floor. I swear I felt something. And then the other day when he said my name here in the office, I thought I would melt right there. He is annoying thinking that we needed someone to watch over us today, but it was nice having him there. He seems like a great guy. I don't know a lot about him, but I doubt he kills kittens and puppies in his spare time. He was engaged once, didn't end well. He never married."

"I knew something was up. I can tell by the way you act. I also think he is interested. He didn't run from here screaming—well, except that one day he left here mad at you, but other than that, you haven't scared him off. He even volunteered to help with your momma. That says something." Shellie was so perceptive.

"That says that he hasn't met her yet." Anna laughed. She hoped that the next day would go well.

Shellie got her serious face on. "You do realize that one day, whether it is Tony or not, you are going to have to tell, show, let someone in on the fact that you do have that bag. You cannot keep hiding it. It isn't to be ashamed of. You wouldn't be here gracing my presence if it wasn't for it. You wouldn't be here to raise your boys. It saved your life. Well, Jesus did actually, but he allowed you to get that operation when you needed it. He moved Dr. Hyrd here to be able to do the surgery. What business does a great doctor like Dr. Hyrd have moving to this little town in the mountains of North Carolina? One would suspect he would be at Duke or Chapel Hill. Or back home in Texas. They have some pretty great hospitals there. I tell you what business he had coming here—the Lord's business. That was part of the Lord's plan for his life, one to help you, and he found his wife here." Shellie was getting on her high horse. Anna sat back for the speech; she knew she would be here for a hot minute. "Look, Anna, I love you. You are like the sister I would trade my own sister to have. You are my dearest friend. I almost lost you. I do not know how it really feels to go through all of that, but look, if someone really cares and loves you, it won't matter where you poop from. The thing is, you have never given any man a chance to even react to it, to know that part about you. I think it makes you super cool."

Shellie worked a little, going through the mail as she continued her diatribe. "Look, there are only so many water fountains I can show Tony, or anyone else for that matter, while you run to the bathroom. You and I know that the statistics show that there are over one hundred thousand people, just in America, who have an ostomy. I highly doubt that many people just shut off their lives, sexually or whatever, after getting a bag. You are doing yourself a huge disservice by not allowing yourself that joy again."

"I get it, Shellie, but I am not ready to do that, mentally or physically. It is an overwhelming thought to just think of someone trying to still find me attractive the way I am now. Men are very visual. Visually, I used to be not that bad of a catch, but now, well… let's just say the sh— has hit the bag." Anna got the message that Shellie was trying to send, but she wasn't ready to apply that message and act on it in her real life. "I don't know, Shellie, I just don't know. I will have to think about it. I am really attracted to Tony, and who knows, he may be toward me too…at least the way he may think I am." Anna stood and started toward her office. That signaled to Shellie that soapbox time was over.

Shellie knew Anna needed some time to think, and she had approximately seventeen minutes. "Remember you have the man coming by to sign the paperwork to change his name…or whatever. You were helping out a friend. I will let you know when he gets here."

"Perfect. Thanks, Shellie." Anna went in and shut her door. She kicked off her heels, found some flip-flops, and sat down. She always knew that one day someone would come along, and she would want to get to know them better, maybe have a relationship. She did miss that part of her life, but she just couldn't bring herself to miss it enough to put herself out there enough to where she might get hurt. If someone turned her down because of her health situation, yes, they would be petty and not worth their weight in poop from her bag, but if she put herself out there, only to be hurt, she didn't think she could get over it. She knew that her putting up this wall, this protection, would keep the possibility of her being hurt basically nonexistent.

A low knock sounded on her door. Anna got up, shuffled over, and opened it. Shellie came in and closed it behind her. "Your last appointment has arrived. This one was the favor to your momma's neighbor. This should be good. Always a treat to help out Ms. Darcy. What a way to end a Friday. Whenever you are ready, I will send him in." Shellie watched Anna kick off her flip-flops, slide into her heels, and fluff her hair, as always before meeting someone.

"I will just come out with you and grab him. What did he introduce himself by, old name or new name?" Anna looked at Shellie; Shellie returned the look. Anna knew she was going to have to wing this one.

The two ladies exited the office, and Shellie made her way back to her desk. Lucky duck. Anna focused on the middle-aged gentleman waiting in the chairs. He was clean-cut, nicely dressed, and, on the outside, if looks meant anything anymore, he looked perfectly normal.

"Good afternoon." Anna walked toward the man, and he began to stand up. "It is a pleasure to meet you. My name is Anna Dawson, and you are a friend of—I believe—Mrs. Hillard. She lives in the neighborhood with my parents and attends the women's functions with them. They are the sweetest couple, the Hilliards. I have had the pleasure of knowing them for many years. She was even my Sunday school teacher when I was younger." Anna reached out her hand, took his, and returned the strong shake.

IT'S IN THE BAG

The man smiled and nodded. "Yes, it is nice to meet you, Ms. Dawson. My name is Stephan Travers. Stephan Lamont Travers, and I do appreciate you meeting with me. It seems that Mrs. Hillard thinks that a conversation with you will help me see the error of my thinking."

"Well, Mr. Travers, it speaks volumes that you would come to sit down and talk with me, and I am sure that Mrs. Hillard only had the best intentions when she told you to come see me. Let's go in and have a seat and take a look at what you have there with you." Anna showed Mr. Travers into her office and offered him a seat at the conference table, offered him a drink, snack, her usual intro. Anna rarely met someone just as a favor, without any information beforehand, but as a favor to Mrs. Hillard, she conceded this time.

Anna sat down opposite Mr. Travers, and he handed her his folder with a couple of papers in it. "This is something I have been reading about. A friend of mine got me interested in it. I thought it seemed like a good thing to do. I had this drawn up, back in Alabama, and I recorded it there with their clerk of court. When I was reading into it more, it seemed that I have to do this in every state for it to be valid."

Anna took the folder and opened it. She read the papers and took her time with each part. Okay, this was a doozy. "Okay, Mr. Travers. This looks like an order for a name change, saying that your new name would be Simon Travers Morris Bey. Is that correct?" Anna looked at him, and he nodded. She continued. "It says here that this change is granted by the Grand Sheikness in the Republic of Alabama. This is stating that you are no longer, after this name change, subject to any of our laws, of any state. Is this your intention with this document?"

Mr. Travers nodded again. "Yes, Ms. Dawson. I have done some research and I wish to be a Sovereign Moor. I want no longer to be ruled by the laws and the administration of this government. I wish to be my own entity."

Luckily, Anna had some previous knowledge of this practice. A couple of years ago a federal judge found out that a fictitious and invalid lien had been placed against him for thirty-three million dollars. Come to find out that the sovereign individual had found out about this movement while he was incarcerated. The judge only found out about the lien when he and his wife went to buy a home; he was denied a mortgage because of his ratio of debt. It took an act of Congress, literally, for this to be resolved. Now it was illegal to place fictitious liens on elected officials. This was a common practice, by incarcerated people usually, to get back at the judge, lawyer, or whomever they choose for retaliation.

"I see that you have filed this with the Register of Deeds in the state of Alabama. Your question to me is if you need to do this in all states, nationwide? To make it valid?" Anna begged him internally to please say no.

"Yes. I just need to know what I needed to do, legally, to make this official."

Anna took a deep breath, quickly asked herself why again she had given up drinking, and looked once more at the papers. "Mr. Travers. Let me see. Were you born in the United States?" He nodded. "Have you ever applied to gain citizenship in another country?" Anna paused and looked at Mr. Travers.

"No, ma'am, I have lived here all my life. I was born in Alabama, and the only other place I have lived is here, in North Carolina."

"Mr. Travers, I believe that you are free to do what you want. Being an American citizen, which you are, you have rights. We, as Americans, have rights to live our lives in the matter that we see fit, as long as those actions do not break any law. This piece of paper may show your desire to denounce the need to follow the laws or pay taxes in the United States, but that is kind of all that it does. Yes, you have had it recorded. It is in the records of Alabama, and any other state that you can file it in. You can file this here, in our county's Register of Deeds, but it will in no way relinquish your need to follow our laws and pay your taxes just as you always have." Anna looked Mr. Travers in the eye. "I understand that you may not be happy with the way our country is working right now. There are too many injustices to mention. But trying to give away your rights—that is not one of them. My best advice to you is, you can continue to believe in whatsoever you choose, that is a right, but you still have to adhere to the laws of this land, just like any other country or state you may go to."

Mr. Travers sat quiet for a moment. Anna didn't know how he would respond, and he did it eloquently. "Thank you, Ms. Dawson. Thank you for taking the time to talk to me, as a person, who tries to understand and not talk down to someone. I see why you are so highly recommended. While I don't think I will stop looking into this life change, more than just a name change, I will take into consideration what you have said here today. I appreciate your time, and mostly your understanding." With that said, he stood, as did Anna. The two walked toward the door to her office.

"Honestly, Mr. Travers, when I first read over your papers, I thought you were looking for a fight with me, seeing how my father is the sheriff and I am an attorney. I appreciate your listening and understanding my side and beliefs. I know that in some cases, sovereigns can take a strong stance against laws and law enforcement. I appreciate you. You are a gentleman." Anna touched his arm and reached out to shake his hand.

They shook hands. "I know very well who your father is. He is a good and fair man, and he should be proud of you. You should be proud too. Thank you again. Have a good weekend." He waved to Shellie, who waved and watched him pass and head down the stairs, then she looked wide-eyed at Anna.

"Nice guy. Disgruntled with the way the country and the world is now. But nowadays, who isn't really, in some form or fashion?" Anna laughed. "Okay, let's call it a day…and we can, I am the boss. Give me a second and we will walk out together." Anna went into her office to gather her things.

She was powering down her computer when she heard her phone's familiar ding of a new text. She pulled her phone out of her purse. She looked at it and about fell on the floor.

> Det Tony Philips
> Anna, looking forward to meeting your Mom tomorrow. And cereal. T

"Shellie." Anna ran out of her office toward Shellie's desk. Shellie was standing there with her purse on her shoulder and scrolling Pinterest. "Look at this text. What does it mean?"

Shellie scanned the few words. "Looks like Mr. Hot Pants is looking forward to spending time with you and meeting your momma. I could be wrong, but that is what I think." Shellie walked around her desk and stood by the stairwell. "Now it is up to you to send him a text back. That is how that technology works. Usually one sends a message, and the receiver reads it and responds in a nice, adult way." She hit the switch that turned out the lights in the lobby. "Are you coming or not? You are totally messing with my weekend. I am on spa time now!"

Anna wasn't thinking about Shellie and her spa adventure; she had a bigger fish to fry at the moment. "I am going to text him back. Give me just a second. I have to think." Anna looked at her phone as if she was holding nuclear waste. "What do I say?"

Shellie was little help at this point. "Tell him to make sure he brings some condoms with him, his most recent blood work, and credit report. That you are ready to show him how things are done. I could care less, but I'm serious about the credit report and blood work."

Anna rolled her eyes. She would never say it, but that was really good advice. "Okay, here goes." Anna started typing.

> Anna Dawson
> Sounds good. Make sure you come hungry!? A

Anna showed Shellie the phone and the sent message. "Anna, did you read this before you sent it? You told him to come to your house, in the morning, hungry." Shellie looked at Anna and raised her eyebrows. "You, my friend, may end up having the better weekend than I do at the spa."

Anna ran back into her office to regather her things. Meeting Shellie at the top of the stairs, they began to make the descent together. "So you really think I should give him a chance? It would be super awkward if I did and something went wrong."

Shellie stopped midstep and forced Anna to stop too. "Oh, but honey boo, what if everything went right?"

Damn, why did Shellie have to be so stinking smart?

CHAPTER 13

Anna was up with the chickens on Saturday, a saying she had heard her whole life. Saturdays were usually her day to be lazy. Well, lazy in her eyes. Sleeping till at least 7:00 a.m. instead of her normal 5:00 a.m. She was excited, anxious, and a little floaty on this particular Saturday. Anna didn't sleep well; she tossed and turned all night. She needed to calm herself down. She took a warm shower. After dressing up all week, Saturday was her day to be comfortable. She was not going to change that. She needed to just act normal. She needed to cook. Yes, that was it. Cooking would calm her down; always had; it would work again this morning.

Anna stepped into the kitchen. Looking out the window, she saw that it looked like a beautiful day. The sun was bright and already taking command of the sky. The birds were singing and were already congregating around the feeders she had placed near the kitchen window. She also had put up a special squirrel feeder; she hated that they always seemed to steal all the birds' food. She sure showed that squirrel a thing or two; now the squirrel had his and the birds' food to eat. Well, at least the squirrels were happy.

Anna heard footsteps behind her. Johnathan was usually the first up in the mornings, especially on the weekends. "Morning, Mom." Johnathan made his way over to the Keurig to make his morning coffee. She had her daddy to thank for introducing her sons to coffee so early. It hadn't shown any signs of stunting the boy's growth; they both towered over Anna at only sixteen and fourteen.

"Good morning, honey. How are you today?" Anna was starting to get things out to make French toast and bacon. "Are you looking forward to Etowah today? Looks like you have a beautiful day." She continued banging around in the cabinets for the right pan.

IT'S IN THE BAG

Johnathan worked on his coffee; he made a pretty good cup for his age. "Yeah, I wish Jack would get up already. I went in his room and shook the stuffing out of him. He is just so lazy." Brotherly love on display already this morning. "We have to pick up Truck, Jacob, and Fletch on our way. We need to leave here a little before nine. He or any of those other guys better not make me late, or I will leave them."

"I will run up there in just a minute to get him up myself. I keep telling myself one day, one day, I will miss dragging your brother out of the bed. At least I keep getting my arm workout in." She laughed and put all the bowls and ingredients out on the island. "A new detective I am working with is coming by this morning. He graciously offered to go with me to Gram's this morning to help me have an escape plan from the birthday planning. I wanted y'all to meet him. He is the one helping me with that case with the crazy lady. The one I think is killing all her husbands."

"Sounds good, Mom, but how did you rope him in to going to Gram's?" Johnathan actually looked bewildered.

"Well, he has never met her. He only knows Gramps. That is how… So I better get all the help out of him I can today. Will be my last opportunity for sure." Anna wiped off her hands on the kitchen towel. "Let me go rouse your brother. He needs to get in the shower." Anna started down the short hallway to the stairs.

"Thanks, Mom. Good luck!" Johnathan took his coffee out into the den.

Anna loved the fact that she was a mom; it was one of the things in her life that she was the proudest of. She may not do it all right, like other people do it, Lord knows not like her Momma would do it, but she did her best and she had good boys.

Anna pushed open the half-closed door to Jack's room. Good grief, what a mess. This looked like a party she would have attended back in college. Clothes, cups, papers, earbuds, saxophone, chords… gross. Anna carefully stepped her way over to Jack's bed. She looked at her youngest child, so peaceful, so sweet-looking, becoming so handsome… She looked over her shoulder at the mess that this little child made, and she bent down to right above his ear and whispered in her loudest Mom whisper, "My darling, Jack, sweetie, if you don't get up and get in the shower and pick up this pigsty, you will not be golfing anywhere today because your clubs will be at Goodwill. Wakey, wakey, eggs and bakie!" Anna stood up and grabbed the corner of his comforter. "Get up, lazy pants. Clean up all this crap. Love you!" She retreated just as gingerly as she had entered. The last thing she needed today was a broken ankle.

Making her way back down the stairs, Anna glanced at the time. Just half past seven; she still had plenty of time to get the food cooked. She just needed to make sure she looked at least a little presentable. She headed to her bedroom and into her bathroom. Her morning routine was set in stone now, since the surgery. Anna had the routine down to less than five minutes, a huge improvement from her twenty-minute ordeal when first out of the hospital.

Anna took off her South College T-shirt, slipped off her well-worn floral flannel pajama pants, and looked at herself in the mirror. For early forties, she wasn't bad looking. Her boobs were still perky and not dragging the floor. Her skin, thanks to her momma's genes, was still almost wrinkle-free. She had started following her dermatologist's recommendations years ago about sunscreen. She was for the most part happy with her appearance. Then there was the bag. Her scars were almost not even evident; she was happy when Dr. Hyrd at her last checkup had even mentioned how surprised he was with how good they looked. The amount of work that had to be done in her abdomen and pelvis, she was certain she would look like she had been through battle in a war, but her incisions had healed beautifully.

Her hair had just started to show the signs of gray, reminding her to text Peggy to please not forget she was coming to do her hair the next day. A hair house call…she had great friends. The length, which caused her momma to cringe, was still down below the shoulders, to the middle part of her back. She had golden-brown hair, with just a slight natural curl to it. Her nana used to say that was the best gift she could have gotten from her…her hair and its natural curl, ever so slight as it was.

Yes, Anna was still relatively happy with her looks, as a woman her age could be. Except for the bag. She was going to have to get

IT'S IN THE BAG

past that, knowing it was something that would ever be part of her as long as she was alive, if she was ever going to be intimate with a man again. She couldn't hide it, and the man would have to accept it. That was where Anna always had the most trouble believing that she still could be found attractive by a man.

Anna had to stop; she had things to do. She had to stop the silliness of thinking things could go anywhere but friendship with Tony, and speaking of Tony, she had to finish up, get dressed, and get to making the breakfast she promised. Anna chose a pair of black athletic pants, a Rolling Stones T-shirt, and decided to choose her shoes later. She brushed her hair and put it up in a messy bun—all the rage now, she read in a magazine—and washed her face, brushed her teeth. She applied some eyeliner, mascara, and just a bit of blush. Some lip gloss and she was done. Her Saturday look was complete, new bag and all. It was gonna be a good day.

Back down in the kitchen, Jack had risen, showered, and joined the land of the living. Johnathan seemed satisfied that his brother had joined them. They looked handsome as ever. John in his light-blue golf polo and khaki shorts, and Jack in his yellow-and-white-striped shirt and shorts. They looked like professional PGA players. "Good morning, Mom. I straightened up my room. Will finish up the rest when we get home. John wouldn't be quiet about me making him late."

"I see that you have made a dent in your room. Be sure to finish it tonight, and next time, invite me to the party you apparently have in your room. I am always up for a good time." She was working on the French toast and had some scrambled eggs cooking. Bacon was almost done, and the kitchen smelled lovely. "Did your brother tell you that the detective who has been helping Shellie and me with the crazy lady case is coming over this morning? He volunteered his services to help me at Gram's. He must be a saint." Anna finished up and was putting the powdered sugar on the French toast when the doorbell rang. "Told ya, he's here. Now be nice." Anna wiped her hands on the towel as she headed to the door.

Anna peeked out the glass on the side of her front door. She took in the sight of a very nice-looking man, Army-green polo shirt

133

and jeans. Her heart skipped a beat when she saw that he had on flip-flops… She punched in the code on the security system and opened the door. For a split second her heart stopped and her breath caught. He looked so good. As she opened the door, the smell of clean wafted into the house. A mixture of soap and cologne. A slight shadow on his face; skipped shaving this morning. Nice. She definitely liked what she saw, and so did all her lady parts.

"Good morning, detective. Come on in." Anna opened the door wider and allowed him to walk past her. Yep, that was his clean smell; oh dear Lord. "How are you doing?" She shut the door and turned to meet him face-to-face.

Tony stood, stunned at the woman in front of him. The woman he had only seen dressed to the nines. She was standing there in her Stones T-shirt, her yoga-pant things, and bare feet. She had never looked so beautiful. Even the powdered sugar looked good on her forehead. He smiled and laughed silently. "I'm good, how are you? Looks like you have maybe been cooking more than cereal this morning?"

She looked at him and tilted her head, questioning his comment. He reached out and wiped her forehead, showed her his finger covered in the white sugar just before he licked it. "I presume that is powdered sugar and not crack… Yep, sugar for sure. Tastes good!"

Lord in heaven, she was going to die right here. She shouldn't have worried about her momma's so much today; she was just going to die. Melt right into a puddle of lust and inappropriate thoughts.

"Um, yes, French toast, eggs, and bacon. I hope you're hungry. Come on in and meet the guys before they head out to pick up the guys for golf." Anna took the lead and they headed into the kitchen. "Guys, hello, guys." The boys came in from the den. "I want you to meet Detective Tony Phillips. He is the detective that I told you about who was helping me with the crazy lady case." Anna added, smiling, "And the one who is helping me not be held captive by Grams today."

John walked over to Tony first, held out his hand, and they shook. "Hey, Mr. Phillips, how's it going? It's nice to meet you. I'm Johnathan, Mom's favorite." He smiled. "Oh, Mom, by the way, I

IT'S IN THE BAG

turned on *Weekend Today*. I know how you love stalking them." Tony looked surprised at that comment. John quickly added, "I mean watching the show. Looks like the whole crew is there today. That should make you happy. That Dylan lady looks like she is back from maternity leave." He laughed and took a seat at the island.

"And I'm Jack. Don't listen to that kid. I am the real favorite. It is nice to meet you." Jack also held out his hand and greeted Tony. "All right, I am starved. Can we eat already?" Jack patted Tony on the back as he made his way to his seat at the island.

"It's nice to meet you both. It smells wonderful in here. I'm kind of starving too. Your mom told me to come ready to eat."

"Well, come on over and sit down. Mom won't let us eat or even put food on our plates until you sit down. You are our guest and we have to be nice. Usually we just act like it is a buffet or a food trough. Isn't that what you call it, Mom?" John held out a seat at the island and motioned for Tony to sit down. "Something about manners or something like that. Not being our normal pig selves." He laughed.

Tony took the hint and found his seat. "Gotcha." He got settled and looked at the boys. "I appreciate your manners, but let's just be friends. Okay?" The boys both nodded. "And call me Tony." He smiled.

Anna pulled three plates out of the cabinet near the sink. Tony watched her as she reached up to grab them. He didn't know what it was; he couldn't take his eyes off her. He was seeing a different side of her, and from what he could tell, he liked it. She looked so happy. Relaxed. Hot. Those yoga pants accentuated her curves in all the right ways. The T-shirt hugged her breasts just enough to make them stand out more than her other work outfits had; he really liked that. He felt like he was getting drunk on just the view. Tony knew he had to stop. He was sitting here with her children, for God's sake, whom he just met. Now he was over here looking at their mom like he wanted to dust her with powdered sugar and lick it off.

"So, your mom tells me you guys are going to play a round of golf today. Have you guys been playing for a while?" Tony decided to focus on the boys for the time being. Safer, much safer.

Jack turned to Tony. "Well, John got the idea to start going to the driving range with some of our buddies a couple of years ago. We really got into it. We went with one of our friends and their dad not long after that and been going as much as we can ever since. We both got our own clubs last Christmas, from Santa." He rolled his eyes and looked at his mom. "That was pretty cool. Etowah, where we are going today, is our favorite course so far. The one we can afford too. Mom only fronts one round a month. The rest is up to us."

Anna looked at Jack teasingly and stuck out her tongue. "You know that Santa only visits the houses that believe in him. And please do not tell Tony how I ruined your childhood years ago when I told you otherwise. That was not my best parental moment." Anna smiled at Tony. "So who's ready for some grub?"

All three guys answered in unison. Anna placed French toast, eggs, and bacon on each of the three plates. She served them and then offered coffee, juice, or tea. Jack and John were still sipping on their coffee, and she poured Tony and herself some orange juice. Napkins to each one and she pulled a stool around so that she could face the guys. It was nice seeing the three of them, all happily enjoying their breakfast and chatting about golf or whatever sport they could think of.

"Aren't you hungry?" Tony asked while he took a bite of his bacon. "This is way too good not to partake in, especially since you are the chef."

"I'm good. I usually don't eat much of a breakfast, never been much on the food. I love to cook it. I just never really got a taste for it." Anna smiled and sipped her juice. "Cooking and baking have always been a way I deal with stress, worry, anger, most of the bad emotions."

"Yeah, we really enjoy it around here when she is really stressed. Cookies, cakes, brownies, muffins…" Jack laughed as he got up to refill his plate. "We reap the best benefits when her work life is crazy."

"Watch it, buddy." Anna, even being five inches shorter than her youngest son, took him into a bear hug, and they both laughed. "One day you will miss all my stress cooking. When you are off at college, eating in the cafeteria…you just better enjoy your mom."

Jack smiled and kissed his mom on the cheek and took two more pieces of bacon and a scoop of eggs.

Tony watched the interaction and the kidding between Anna and her boys. There was an ease, a love that was almost tangible; it was so strong. They loved her, and she loved them more than anything. He liked that. He could tell she was a great mother. These boys were blessed. John favored his mother. His olive skin, hazel eyes, and even his smile was an exact copy of Anna's. He was well over six feet tall, but his features and mannerisms were all from her. Jack was also tall, with dark hazel eyes, a little lighter tone of skin, but the same hair color. Jack's nose was his mom's, and his laugh was a lot like hers. They were undeniably her boys.

"Jack, can you hurry and shove that food down your trap? We need to go. Jacob has already sent me a text. Truck is meeting us at Fletch's house. Hurry up, you bot." John put his plate on the side of the sink and went to Anna's side. He gave her the typical teenage boy side hug, but he did kiss her on the cheek as he said bye. "We will be home sometime this afternoon. Truck may head over here after, so he will probably be here tonight. That okay?"

"Sure. Just pick up a couple of pizzas on your way in. I will make a big Caesar salad when I get home from Gram's. Be careful. I love you. Let me know if your plans change or if you are going to be later than the afternoon. I worry." Anna straightened her son's shirt and adjusted his collar.

"I know, Mom. I love you too." John looked at Tony with a really serious look on his face. "Tony, beware of our Grams. She is a nut. A loving Grams nut, but a nut. Good luck with that. You are a good man for helping Mom out today. I really appreciate it. We usually have to do it."

Anna smacked her oldest son's butt as he walked past and grabbed a piece of bacon for the road. He stopped by the back door, grabbed his keys off the table, and looked back at his brother. "For the love of all things holy, man, let's go. I will be in the car." With that, he was out the door. He punched the button for the garage door to open.

"Mom, why is he such a prick sometimes?" Jack got up and put his plate on top of his brother's by the sink. "He can be so bossy." Jack came around and did the same sort of side hug that his brother had and kissed her forehead. "If he keeps it up, I am going to punch him in the nuts."

Anna looked at Tony and smiled, and then she looked at her son. "Jack, let's try not to use words like *prick* or *nuts* at breakfast, and about family…especially when we have company. I hope you have a great round. Go out and beat your brother, just don't hit him with a club. Promise?" Anna winked at Tony. "Y'all be careful. I love you so much and you know what would happen if something ever happened to you guys…right?"

"Yes, Mom, you would die a thousand deaths and never get over it. We get it." Jack looked over at Tony. "It was nice to meet you. Come more often. She cooks more when it isn't just us. Come over anytime, like tonight, tomorrow, tomorrow night." He laughed. "See ya!" Jack was out the door just as John honked the horn on the car.

"And that is what is called breakfast at the Dawson house." Anna sat back down at the island and looked at Tony's plate. "Do you want any more to eat? Anything? The boys left some crumbs over here, and I could always cook more…"

"No, thank you so much. That is more than I usually eat for breakfast. We seem to have that in common. Light breakfast." He smiled. "Your boys seem great. They look a lot and favor you quite a bit. I bet you never have a dull moment at all."

"I have more now that they are older. They do a lot with friends now. When John got his license, I knew that my life would change just as much or more than theirs. I was used to filling weekends with play dates, the zoo, aquariums, museums, and the park. Always looking for something fun, educational, and that they would like to do. Now they do that. I do like that our house is pretty much the hub for the guys. The boys have a lot of the same friends, so it works that our house is the one they tend to congregate at. I get to know their friends, I get to keep an eye on them, and I get all the hot information on girls, fights, sports teams, basically anything boy."

IT'S IN THE BAG

Anna stood and took Tony's plate, placed it with the boy's plates, and started to clean up the kitchen. "What about you? What do you usually do on the weekends in this metropolis we live in? Other than when you do a huge favor for local attorneys, of course. Have you been able to see much of the town, the actual town, not just the touristy spots?"

Tony stood to help, and Anna insisted that he sit back down, the whole guest thing and all. He did as he was asked; it was just more time to admire her as she worked. Man, when she bent over to load the dishwasher, he could look at that all day. More than once when she turned and looked his way, she caught him staring at her. She didn't seem too upset with it, so he didn't stop.

"You have a really nice home. I love this area of town." Tony did stand and start to look around. "Have you lived here long?"

"Well, when Mark and I split up, I wanted to leave the house, and he wanted it…so it made sense that I was the one to move. This house was available, and it was so close to my parents and where I grew up. You will see how close we are to them when we get to Momma and Daddy's. I like that the boys go to the same schools that I did. They are so close to their grandparents, and they get some of the same experiences I did. I had a decent childhood, even being the daughter of the sheriff, it was good. Dating was never easy, but all good." Anna laughed as she was wiping down the island. "I remember my junior prom. My date came to the house to pick me up. I looked beautiful, by the way. Anyway, I was getting ready to make my grand entrance down the stairs into the entryway where they were standing and I heard Daddy say to him, 'And remember, son, I kill people for a living!' I was home before the prom was even over. That guy was terrified he would be shot otherwise." Anna still was a little irritated by that. "It was for the best, though. That guy is serving twenty down in the state prison." She smiled.

"All's well that ends well, I suppose." Tony smiled. "So what do I need to be prepared for with your mom? The boys have me scared now." He sat down on the sofa in the den, glancing at the TV to see *The Today Show* about to wrap up. "I have to say, I love *Weekend Today*, but nothing beats Savannah Guthrie and Al Roker during the week. Craig Melvin and Hoda Kotb are pretty awesome too." He looked over at Anna, who was standing there with her mouth open.

"I think I just fell in love with you. You are my soul mate. You are a *Today Show* junkie too?" Anna looked as happy as a little girl who just got a new tutu and magic wand. "Please say you are. Don't kill my dreams of there being more like me."

Tony laughed and nodded. "You got me. *Good Morning America* has nothing on them. *Today Show* all the way, baby. I even have the mug, the one from Sundays with Willie too."

"Oh my goodness. I got the set for Christmas last year."

A very loud and husky noise came from the kitchen. Anna hopped up and walked toward the awful noise as if summoned. She came back with what looked like a white tiger in her arms. "Meet Murphy. He is our resident overweight cat. He is letting it be known that I have fed everyone in the house except him and if I don't correct that quickly, and give two treats as my apology, I had better just pack my things. He will be looking for new help. He only allows us to live here. He is the true king of the castle here." She let him flop out of her arms, and he landed with a *thump*.

"Are you sure you don't need a permit to have an actual tiger living in the city limits? They have laws against that, you know." Tony followed her into the kitchen. "That is the biggest cat I have ever seen." She got out what was obviously Murphy's bowl as he looked up at her with his big blue eyes. Another loud meow persuaded her to move more quickly as if he was going to starve if not ingesting food in the next thirty seconds. As soon as she set the bowl down, Murphy made one round of her legs and seemed to lick her bare feet as a thank-you. Lucky cat.

Now with the Murphy-the-Cat emergency handled, Anna was ready to prepare Tony for her momma. "All right, now, let me give you some pointers for you to deal with my momma." Anna started gathering her things and piling them by the door. "Follow me. I will talk as I touch up my makeup really quick." Anna made her way down the opposite hall and made her way into her bedroom. Tony walked slowly behind her, not quite sure he was supposed to enter. "Come on in, Tony. You can sit in the chair or on the bed. I am not going to attack you. I am sure you have been in a woman's bedroom before." Anna laughed and disappeared into her bathroom, leaving the door open so he could hear.

"Momma is not like my daddy. She is very opinionated, doesn't catch onto sarcasm well, and thinks her ideas are the best. She will love you. She will think you are God's gift to her and will hopefully take her lonely daughter off her hands. Just smile and nod. Get through the planning. She will make no less than three comments about my attire, especially since I am bringing someone of the opposite sex with me. She just doesn't understand that women and men can be friends, no sex. So she will obviously think we have sex at least five times a day." Anna leaned out of the bathroom, smiled, and laughed.

"Well, your mom sounds like a hoot. Can't imagine why you wouldn't want to spend all day with her," Tony said as he sat down on the bed. He looked around. It was a very nicely decorated room; not too feminine. The bed had a few too many throw pillows than needed, by any human for any purpose, but it was tastefully done. The room was nice, and he felt that it represented Anna perfectly.

Anna leaned out of the bathroom again, this time with her toothbrush in her mouth. "Anything else you want to know before this adventure you signed up for?" She disappeared once again into the bathroom and he could have sworn he heard her spit and swish. Still hot; she was still smoking hot. She appeared again, this time redoing her eyeliner; how did women do that without a mirror? "Oh, and Daddy won't be there to help you. Momma told me at our weekly Wednesday lunch that he was going fishing. That is why today had to be the day to plan the party. Not that it is any kind of surprise anymore, just the way she likes it. She lives for stuff like this."

She crossed the room and headed toward her closet. She opened the double doors, and Tony was highly impressed with the organization and the number of dress shoes. He stood up and walked over to get a closer look. He had to ask. "How in the world did you get your closet so organized, and how much is your shoe collection worth?"

Anna laughed as she bent over and picked out a pair of flip-flops. Black with red sparkles. "You would be shocked at how much of a bargain shopper I am. I think all of the shoes put together still wouldn't add up to..." *Oh no*, Tony thought to himself; *she is doing the reaching thing again.* That look is amazing to a man, a woman reaching up with a T-shirt on; the boobs...oh Lord, focus... He was getting lost in his lustful thoughts. Anna continued, "This pair of shoes, I hate to even confess how much they cost...but I had just closed a crazy case, got paid more than I ever had before, and I wanted them, and sometimes, just sometimes, a woman needs to get what she wants. Right?" She looked at Tony.

Tony didn't know what to do with that...or what was the appropriate thing to do, so he simply said, "Ready to get this fun started?" Why was he all of a sudden the biggest dork in the world?

"Let's go, mister. Don't say I didn't warn you." She grabbed her perfume bottle and sprayed a shower of a luscious scent all around her as she walked out the door. She turned to look to see Tony still standing in the exact same spot in front of her closet. "You coming or not? We must not keep Momma waiting."

He followed the woman he knew would be the death of him out the door, wondering if he would ever be able to tell her.

CHAPTER 14

Anna drove to the home that she had grown up in. It was a beautiful home. It was a two-story brick home with a gigantic wraparound porch dotted with black rocking chairs that matched the shutter accents. The ferns that hung in between each of the posts of the porch finished off that true Southern feel. Anna pulled into the spot that used to be hers when she still lived at home. For some reason, her parents had always left that spot open, just waiting for her to come home.

Ann put the van in park and turned off the ignition. She looked over at Tony. "Listen, this is your very last chance to run. You can take my car, leave it at my house, and take your truck and hightail it. I can get a ride home, or goodness knows it wouldn't hurt me to walk the two miles home." Anna raised her eyebrows, half expecting him to accept her offer to go. He seemed a little off since he had gotten to her house. She knew she was off…thinking about ripping his clothes off every other minute, she was sure she seemed a little looney.

"I'm good to go. Show me what she's got." Tony opened the door and got out first.

Anna opened her door and got out slower. Shutting her door, she looked at Tony. She went around the front of the van and motioned him to follow her up the steps onto the porch. "Here we go!"

Anna opened the door to the house, and it instantly took her back to her childhood. Always did. The smell, the look, the feels, all the same. She loved that. Tony followed her in and shut the door behind him.

Anna could hear her momma humming in the kitchen at the back of the house. She set her keys down on the entryway table, and they both walked down the hall toward the sounds. "Momma,

Momma, it's me, we are here! Good morning!" Anna kept walking, and they both heard Darcy as she let out a squeal.

Darcy came around the corner and smiled from ear to ear. "Good morning. Come on in, Anna, and your friend." Darcy let Anna walk on past her toward the den, and Darcy waited until Tony got right beside her. "Anna Marguerite, who do we have here?" Darcy put her hand out to shake Tony's, and he smiled and returned the shake.

Anna waited until they were both in the den, and she looked at her momma. "This is Detective Tony Phillips. He works for Daddy and he wanted to come with me today to help us plan Daddy's birthday extravaganza. Wasn't that nice of him, Momma?"

"Why, yes, it is very nice, dear." Darcy seemed to hone in on Anna's outfit. "Anna, darling, do you think you should have changed out of your pajamas before you came over, especially with your gentleman friend along? Appearances, darling. Appearances speak volumes, even on the weekends, sweetie." Darcy came over and gave her daughter a kiss on the cheek.

"I did change out of my pj's, Momma. It would have been highly inappropriate to come over here naked, since I sleep in the nude." She looked at Tony and smirked.

Darcy had her back to the window and the neighbors walking their dog. She laughed and threw up her hands. "What will I ever do with you, darling? Just remember this party is a fun thing during the day and a dressier event in the evening." Darcy smiled and walked back to the hallway. "Give me just a few minutes to get everything laid out and organized, then we will get to work. Why don't you show Tony around the house for a moment?" She was gone in just a second.

"Well, this is the den. It is a den like any other den, except over on the opposite wall there is what seems to be a shrine to my life. Let's take a quick look at this before you have to sit through the three-hour version with her." Anna grabbed Tony's arm and pulled him over across the room. Their eyes caught for a moment before she let go, them both standing at the wall of photos. "And that was number one. The pajama dig. Two more before we are done, I bet you lunch on it."

"You are on." They shook on it. "Now show me your life."

"Well, what you have here is a wall of photos that show my life from the moment I was born to probably one she took maybe last week." Anna smiled. "I am shocked there isn't one of the moment I was conceived, but maybe that is in their private collection that I will run across when they both move on to their heavenly reward. Stay tuned for that one." Anna giggled. "Did you know that until I was born, Momma thought I was going to be a boy? She even had a name all picked out for me. You wanna hear it?"

"I feel like I need to hear it… I can only imagine." Tony kept looking at the photos but was waiting eagerly for the name.

"Cletus Stanhope Dawson. After my Momma's grandfather." Anna looked at Tony for his reaction. He was very good at a poker face. "No wonder he went by C. S. Can you imagine me being a Cletus? I would have been a very lonely child. Just glad I was born a girl."

"Me too. I think you make a very beautiful and intelligent woman." Did he just say that out loud? He cleared his throat and said, "Also glad that you were called Anna, and not a female version of Cletus. Celotus… You know, I am surprised your mom didn't just jazz up Cletus." He smiled, and Anna smiled back.

"Well, the story goes that as soon as my daddy saw me, he immediately called me Anna. Doesn't seem to be that he really allowed any discussion on the matter. Anna it was. And my full name is Anna Marguerite Lucille Dawson. Marguerite Lucille was my grandmother on my momma's side. She was the most wonderful person on the earth. She is what makes me look so forward to heaven. She was amazing. I was her sidekick. I miss her so much. Wherever she was, I wasn't too far behind."

"That is quite a name. A beautiful name indeed." Tony really needed to quit saying *beautiful*.

Tony took his time looking over the photos. Anna was right; there were pictures of her all through school, dance recitals, vacations, swim team, ballet, piano recitals…"So you play the piano?"

he said, pointing to the picture. "I have always thought that was the most amazing skill. Very sexy too."

Anna didn't know if he was kidding or not. She decided to let that slide. "I do. Well, I did, and I used to play a lot more than I do now. I don't have a piano at my house, so sometimes I come over here and play. It is another stress-relief tactic in my arsenal. I used to play for our church when I was a lot younger, and I have played for one wedding. That was perhaps the scariest thing I have done in a while. Now I just do it for me."

"I think that is really neat. I would love to hear you play sometime." Tony said the words just as Darcy walked back into the room. She came over to them and she gazed lovingly at the photos.

"Anna, you should play something for him. That would be lovely." Darcy smiled.

"Maybe later, Momma. Don't we have work to do?"

"In due time, sweetheart, in due time. We have all day." Anna shot Tony a look, and he just shrugged his shoulders. Surely, he wasn't getting sucked into her spell. Dear Lord. "Look at this one. This is from Anna's junior prom. She looked stunning in that dress, didn't she?" Darcy thought a moment. "Isn't that the boy that your father scared the poo out of and he brought you home at ten?" She shook her head and laughed. "Your father…my goodness. He was always so protective of you."

"Yes, Momma, now that boy is in prison. Good times." Anna went to sit on the couch, leaving her momma and Tony at the wall.

"Here she is on her wedding day. That dress. Let me tell you, it was so hot that day. She had sweat rolling down her back under that veil. She looked gorgeous, just probably shouldn't have chosen long sleeves for a June wedding. Next time, darling, go strapless. I will remind you." Darcy seemed to make a mental note of that and stored it in her filing cabinet in her mind, filed under "The Way Anna Should Do It."

Anna looked at Tony and made her eyes almost pop out of her head. He laughed and then turned back to listen to Darcy. This was very entertaining.

IT'S IN THE BAG

"Here is Anna moments after giving birth to Johnathan. She only pushed for twenty-two minutes. I timed her. She tore terribly, but they repaired that. She was able to go on and have Jack naturally too. Did you know that when the anesthesiologist was done giving her the epidural that she looked him in the eye and offered to have his children for him? She was high, she had to be, and those drugs went straight to her head. Offering to have some stranger's kid." Darcy looked over at Anna sitting on the couch flipping through a magazine now. "Anna, this is one reason I am so glad you have given up drinking. No telling what you would be doing now if you hadn't."

Anna had heard enough, and so had Tony, she was sure. "Okay, let's get to work on the tasks at hand. You can come back to the replay of my life later. Tony doesn't have all day to help out, so we will need to get going." Anna left the room and walked toward the kitchen. "I am getting something to drink. Anybody else want anything? Momma, where do you keep the hard liquor?"

"Well, my goodness, Anna, you know your father and I don't drink." Darcy and a very amused Tony came into the kitchen. "Anyway, we need all our facilities to get this nailed down. I need help with a few things this year, and that is where you come in, dear." Darcy guided Tony to a seat at the table and then she went over to her daughter. "Anna, darling, you really need to think about cutting your hair to a more acceptable length for a woman your age. A cute bob maybe. My girl is always willing to take you as a client. I could get you in really quick, just a phone call."

Anna looked around her momma and made eye contact with Tony. Anna mouthed the words "Number two" to let him know that she was one comment away from calling the three comments about her look. He smiled and shrugged his shoulders. "Momma, I actually have an appointment with Peggy tomorrow. She is coming to the house to do my hair, highlights and a trim. I am not quite ready for the helmet hair that eighty-year-old women wear."

Darcy looked to Tony for some help. "I always have loved Anna with shorter hair. It was always a hot-button issue when she was younger. I liked it short, and her daddy liked it longer. Then she grew up and this is what she chooses…a mess on top of her head."

Darcy nudged Tony to look at Anna's hair, expecting an agreement to be forthcoming. "What do you think?"

"I, uh, I learned a long time ago to not say a whole lot about a woman's choice in how she wears her hair. I grew up with two older sisters. They made it crystal clear that their hair was their choice, after they get to a certain age, of course." Tony said it with a great deal of respect toward Darcy. "Although I like the look she is sporting today. Relaxed and a lot different from the usual every-hair-in-perfect-place I have seen her in before—only at work, of course."

"Of course." Darcy looked at Tony, smiled, and changed the subject. "Okay, Anna, I need you to design and get the bakery to make the cake for the party. I was thinking something with bright colors, and just big enough to feed about four hundred or so." Darcy handed Anna a list of things about the cake. "Also, I wanted to have a smallish petting zoo, you know, for the carnival part. There will be families there with their children. I need you to secure the animals and arrange with the club to do that. Of course, we will clean up after the animals and it will be like they were never there. I was thinking goats, sheep, a donkey, a couple of ducks or chickens, rabbits. Whatever the kids like to pet."

"Um, Momma, do you really think that is a good idea? Those animals poop a lot. I am not sure the Country Club is used to having a full-on nature center on the grounds. And anyway, ducks and chickens, they aren't really the first animals I think of when I want to pet anything." Anna looked at her momma, seeing her irritation build in her eyes. "Why don't you work with the local animal shelter and the rescue place, and we can do an adoption special at the carnival? That would serve a purpose, maybe get some animals their furr-ever homes. Do some good."

"Okay, Anna, you just make sure there are some cute animals there for the children to pet. I really don't care what, but that idea sounds nice. I think that would work out well." Darcy conceded that one. "I have the food. The carnival rides and the fireworks are already done over the lake. I have the DJ. It's the guy who did your cousin's wedding last summer. He was really fun." Darcy looked over her notes. "The only other thing I may need help with is getting the invitations out…so grab a pen and we will get to work."

"You do know it is April, Momma, right? Should I be worried about you?"

"Of course, honey, I know it is April, but it is never too early to let people put something on their calendar. No need in waiting. This will be great! I want as many people as we can get to come to the party. We need to give people enough notice to plan around that weekend. For vacations and such." Darcy wasn't fazed by Anna's comment.

"Well, I get that, Momma, but I think getting them out by the second week of May will be soon enough. Most people already assume there will be a party this year, at the club, on the fourth. Most people come to the lake at the club to watch the fireworks anyway, if they are in town. It is like an institution you have going every year. I don't think we will have to worry about there being a good turnout or not. Heck, most people I know consider this just the thing you do for the fourth." Anna picked up the invitation and she liked what she saw. "This is really good, Momma. I will take this with me to the bakery. Maybe they can use these colors and do something either in a carnival theme or fireworks. What do you think?"

"I just want it to be spectacular. Pamela at the bakery knows that you will be stopping by, hopefully today, to talk to her, and she knows to send me the bill. You are just in charge of the design. They will deliver and serve it that night." Darcy looked over her notes. "Do you think you can handle that with all you have going on? Oh, and do you think the boys will help with the party too? Nothing too time-consuming, just a few little things."

"You know their numbers, just text them. I am sure that they will be happy to." Anna winked at Tony. "You are being awful quiet, Tony. What do you think about all this? Oh, that's right, this will be your first experience at a Jake Dawson birthday party. You will be amazed. Trust me."

"It all sounds fun, like a lot of work and money, but fun. It sounds like something that I wouldn't want to miss for anything." He looked at Darcy. "I am happy to help out any way I can. I am great on a grill, not really good at decorating, and I love to dance." He smiled at both ladies.

"You are too sweet." Darcy smiled. "Maybe you could teach Anna here how to share in some of your sweet nature. She seems to be a little crankier than usual."

"I will do my best, ma'am. I will do my best." Tony winked at Anna. He could swear she snarled at him. "May not help out much, but I will try!" He snarled back at Anna. "Okay, I will need to get going pretty soon, and I do think that you are my driver. I am sorry to have to cut this fun short, but, Anna, I would love to hear you tickle the ivories before we leave. It would make my day."

"Oh, we don't have time for that today. Maybe another time." Anna got up and put her glass in the sink. She walked toward her momma, who was standing from her chair. "You just mentioned that you had to be going." Anna kissed her momma on the cheek.

"Nonsense, Anna. He wouldn't have mentioned it if he wasn't wanting to hear something. You can just play a short something as you head out. It has been a long time since I have gotten to hear you play." She turned her attention to Tony. "She usually comes here when she knows she will be alone and plays, for herself, I suppose. Such a waste of all that talent and lessons. Such a waste."

"Fine, if it will get us out of here, come on. But I am picking what I play. Hurry up, I ain't spending all day." Anna headed for the formal living room where her baby grand sat.

"Honey, do you really have to use the word 'ain't'? It sounds so harshly wrong. And, honey, do you own anything other than flip-flops? You really should keep up with your toenail polish choices and not let it look so drab. That is not a good color for you."

Tony smiled and made a mental note that Anna had called it correctly. There was the third dig at how she looked today. He owed her lunch. Oh well, that was one bet he wasn't upset to lose at all.

Tony and Darcy followed and took seats on the couch. The room was so fancy, much more so than the rest of the house. Just a couch and two armchairs, the piano, and a small table were in the room. The built-in bookcases held more photos and books. Anna pulled out the bench and sat down at the grand piece. She raised the cover to the keys and sat for just a moment and thought about what to play. Her silhouette was perfectly captured in the window beside the piano, the sunlight filtered only by some off-white sheer curtains. She was a thing of beauty. She gently placed her hands on the keys and began to play.

The room was suddenly filled with the most beautiful music. The notes seemed to flow directly from her hands and swirl around her and transport her to another place totally. She needed no sheet music; this was all from her mind, her memory. Her hands, her beautiful, small hands, moved about the keys with such grace but also in full command of the music. Her body moved back and forth, almost with the music, and with her eyes closed she looked more peaceful than he had ever seen her. He had never heard such magical music, ever. He sat mesmerized, totally lost in looking at her, all of her. He watched as she pressed the pedals near her feet; he watched as she tilted her head. He could tell she was fully feeling and giving something so personal and intimate of herself. She was pure perfection. The piano, without her sitting there playing it, was just another musical instrument, a gorgeous piece of furniture to some people, but to her, it was a look into her soul.

His mind went there, to the desire to make her lose herself in him as she did in the music. He wanted to see that expression on her face as he kissed her, as he touched her and held her. He wanted to make her lose herself in him, in their togetherness. He wanted to have an intimate relationship so raw and truthful with her, just like the one she had with the notes she was playing. He had never felt such a draw to a woman in all of his life. Yes, he had been attracted and wanted women in his past, but this was different. This was new. This was so much more powerful than anything he had felt before. He could sit here and watch her all day, just her playing the music in her head. She was the most beautiful, magical, and amazing woman he had ever met. He was in so much trouble.

Anna played the last note and held her fingers on the keys for probably a moment longer than she needed to, but she had lost herself in the music and she was hoping that no one had noticed, just enjoyed the playing. She looked over at her audience. Tony looked as if he had been hit by a train. He looked like he was looking straight through her. Her mother, could that be tears in her eyes? Surely not, not an emotional response from her momma? Not with company in the house. Her mother had to be sick. Something bad. Probably cancer and she just didn't want to tell Anna until after the party, and then she would have time to focus on it. It was so unlike Darcy to show any emotion, except critique. Was that even an emotion?

"Momma, are you okay? Are you sick? Do you have cancer and are not telling me?" Anna stood and walked toward Darcy. "Why in the world are you crying?"

Darcy wiped her eyes, careful not to mess up her eyeliner or smudge her mascara. "That was just so beautiful. The most beautiful music I have ever heard."

"Wait, what? You have got to be kidding. That was the same song I have played a million and one times. That is one reason I know it by heart." Anna gave her momma a side hug and didn't know what else to do. "Are you sure you are okay?"

"I am fine, honey. Just listening to you took me back to when you were still living here at home. I would hear you playing, and it would warm my heart so. Just thinking about that and all you have been through. I am okay." Darcy kissed Anna on the cheek and made her way out of the room.

"I will come play more if you promise not to cry ever again!" Anna yelled behind her. She pulled Tony off the couch and followed her momma. They needed to get out of here.

Tony followed Anna into the kitchen where she and Darcy talked a little more about the bakery and the possibility of an animal rescue/adoption event to take the place of a petting zoo. Tony stood off to the side, leaned up against the doorway, and remembered something that Jake had said to him just the day before. Jake had told him that Anna had been through hell and that he had better not hurt her. Darcy just said that she got so emotional thinking about all Anna had been through. There was something that he was missing. Something that had happened that had affected the whole family in some way. Was it just the divorce? Anna had talked about it with him and it didn't seem like that earth-shattering of an event. What could it be?

Anna gathered her things and she looked at Tony. "Well, I know that you need to get going."

"Oh, yes. I have that important, needed thing that I have to do this afternoon." He looked at his watch. "And look, if we don't leave now, I will be late. Thank you, Mrs. Dawson, for your hospitality. I am looking forward to the party. It was so very nice to meet you. I loved learning more about Anna, which was fun." Tony smiled.

"It was my pleasure. Come back anytime. I have forty years' worth of stories to tell. Raising her was quite an adventure." Darcy patted Tony on the back as they walked toward the door. "Thanks for coming with Anna Marguerite today. She always usually uses the boys as her getaway. Glad she chose you, such a handsome man, today. Y'all have fun!" Darcy winked at Tony and stuck her tongue out at Anna…then disappeared as she shut the door.

"OMG. My momma just roasted me, hard." Anna's mouth was actually hanging open.

"That she did. I like her, a lot." Tony opened the door of the van and got in. He watched as Anna just stood there looking at the front door.

CHAPTER 15

Anna sat at the stop sign at the end of the road that she had grown up on. She was going to give him one chance to bail, or she was going to take him with her to the bakery and to the local animal rescue. She liked having him with her; he proved to her that he could put up with her momma, so he passed the friend test. He also passed the test of being super sexy…and he smelled so good. Maybe she should dump him at her house beside his truck and speed away. No, that would be awkward; they still had to work together. She would just offer him the opportunity to make the call.

"So are you done with me yet, or do you want to go to the bakery and the animal rescue place with me? No worries if you want to tuck your tail and run. I know she can be a lot to take in." Anna looked at Tony, fully expecting him to tell her he had to get back to whatever he had to do.

"I am good if you are. I happen to love bakeries, and I love animals, so sounds like a win-win. I also seem to owe you lunch, since you called it right about your mom calling you out about your outfit. Which I like, by the way." Tony smiled Anna.

Anna turned toward her house. "Well, then…let's go to Heights Bakery. You will love it. Pamela is the best. We can grab a sandwich there too. They have the best, well, everything. You will need to help me with the cake. It is going to have to be spectacular…or momma will have my hide."

"Sounds good. That was a good idea about the animal rescue event at the carnival. I used to volunteer at the one back home. It would be easy to fall in love with them all." Tony looked around at the different businesses as they drove by. "I think that will be a big hit, especially with the kids, and then the kids' parents. Hey, maybe a few animals will get good homes."

Anna grabbed the first spot she saw to park. Being the middle of the day on a beautiful Saturday, the downtown would be bustling. This would be probably the closest that she would be able to get, and it was too pretty not to walk. "Do you mind walking a little ways to the bakery? With it being so busy down here, this is probably the best spot we can get."

"I don't mind at all. This will give me a chance to see some of what downtown has in the way of shops and things. I haven't taken the time yet to really come and explore…and I don't know of a better tour guide." Tony looked genuinely excited as he opened his door. "Which way do we need to head?"

"Right this way, sir. There are a lot of really neat places to see and do stuff here too. Some of my personal favorites are the library, over there on the corner, and the Hallmark shop. I worked there when I was in high school and first couple of years in college." Anna pointed out different shops and neat little hidden gems of the town. "This is Iannucci's, the most wonderful Italian food known to man. I went to school with the owner and his wife. Good people. If you ever want some excellent spaghetti or eggplant parmesan, this is where you have to come, hands down. I mean, I made a pretty close second in the spaghetti department, but they are the real deal."

"Maybe you could go with me sometime. I mean as friends, since you know them so well…and I… I think it would be fun," Tony said as they walked and didn't look at her.

"Sounds good, sir…sounds like a plan." Anna looked over and smiled. She saw the corner of Tony's mouth turn up ever so slightly too. Just walking with him and being this close to him was making her internal temperature rise by the minute. Saved by the bakery. "Ah, here we are. Heights Bakery. Here we go!"

Anna pushed the door open and heard the bells jingle up above her head. Pamela looked up and waved. She was finishing up with a cute couple who apparently needed to get to a room fast before Tony had to arrest them for indecent exposure and lewd acts in public.

They had to be getting married or trying out for a bakery-themed porno.

"Does the bakery here always have such a special floor show or just on Saturdays?" Tony raised his eyebrows as he looked at Anna. "I mean, you said this place was the best in town, but it looks like not just for the bakery part. If her cakes are this good, we, my friend, are in trouble." Tony laughed the most sensual-sounding laugh. He cleared his throat, and the couple got the hint. Perhaps they could at least make it to the car now. They finished up their business with Pamela and scooted out as the bells jingled overhead.

Anna slowly approached the counter, letting Pamela finish up her paperwork. Anna took notice of all the freshly baked cookies, cakes, pies, and the warm breads cooling on the racks just behind the counter. Anna thought to herself that she would not be able to fit her big behind through the door if she worked here, and she would bankrupt the business in a week. She would simply eat all of the product, every last crumb. Good thing she was an attorney without a colon…seemed those two things were working in her favor. Too busy to eat and too embarrassed when she had to run empty her bag after she did.

"You were right about this place. It does smell heavenly." Tony made her jump as he came up behind her. "Sorry, I didn't mean to startle you." He put his hands on her shoulders. "I know I can be scary. Sorry." He gave her shoulders a squeeze and then went on up to look closer in the cases.

"See anything you like, young man?" Pamela was the sweetest person in the world. She had opened this bakery years ago. Her husband was a state trooper, and she said that she needed something to keep her mind busy and keep from thinking of all the danger her husband was in every day. They had two grown children; their son was in the military, and their daughter was a teacher at the local high school. No grandkids yet, but those would be the luckiest grandkids in the world. To have a bakery, owned by your grandparents…*wow!*

"Yes, ma'am, I do. I do." Tony glanced over in Anna's direction. "I am here with Anna. We were sent by Mrs. Dawson to work on the birthday cake for her dad's party." Tony looked back at Pamela, and she smiled and nodded.

"Darcy called to let me know to expect Anna. You are a pleasant addition." Pamela smiled and reached over the counter to shake his hand. "Any friend of Anna's is a friend of mine." She leaned in a little and motioned him to do the same. "I will tell you this, you could do a lot worse than Anna Dawson. She is beautiful inside and out. A rare combination these days. She is one in a million, that girl. One of the strongest women I know." She put her hand on her chest and patted it. Then she got up and made her way to where Anna was standing. "Hello, my darling Anna, how are you this fine day? Let me guess. Your momma called and told me that I should be expecting you. She failed to tell me you would be bringing such a handsome helper along with you today. I am impressed for sure." She came through an opening in the cases and gave Anna the biggest hug. She then cupped Anna's face with her hands and kissed her forehead, leaving big red lipstick prints. Tony smiled.

Anna took out the invitation she had gotten from her momma and the three came up with what would be the perfect cake. Just large enough to feed everyone, and beautiful and just over the top enough to make her momma squeal with joy. Done and done. Anna and Tony ordered sandwiches and a drink for lunch. They found a cute little table outside in the courtyard to sit and eat. Always in the back of her mind, Anna was devising a plan to eat and then run to the potty. Stupid bag. Some days, she really missed her old self, but for now, she was going to enjoy her lunch with a handsome friend.

"You will love her food. She can do anything. I would be five hundred pounds if I lived with her." Anna smiled and took a sip of her sweet tea. "She has the best spot for her bakery too. Almost smack in the middle of the main drag here. A perfect place to eat outside… She is sitting on a gold mine. If she ever decided to retire, and I hope I die before she does, she will be set for life once she sells this place. I don't think her son will want to continue the bakery, but I do know that her daughter took after her mom. She is an excellent cook. I could see her doing something amazing here."

"Pamela is great. I think she will do a great job on the cake." Tony took a bite of his pimento cheese sandwich. "She is certainly fond of you too. Not that I have met anyone who isn't yet." He smiled the sweetest smile.

"Well, you haven't met everyone in town yet. I am sure there are a few people who don't share the glowing love and admiration like some of the others. I have ticked a few people off in my past. Some people are so unhappy with themselves they cannot find anything to like in anyone else. It is sad, but I figured out a long time ago that usually when someone is hateful or bitter toward you, it generally doesn't have a lot to do with you. It's them. Something that they need to work out, get right, then they can have healthy relationships."

"Very deep thoughts for a Saturday afternoon, Anna Marguerite Lucille. I don't mind, though. Your mind is kind of fascinating." He took another bite.

"Very funny, very funny!" She laughed but felt she needed to explain. "I have been there. I had a time in my life where I was not happy, with myself, for certain reasons. I wasn't my sparkly self. I pushed even my closest friends away. I only let a very few people in. I could be hateful, short-tempered, and very sad. I had to deal with that, the reasons, and move on. It didn't happen overnight. It isn't like a switch you just flip in your brain. It took time. No matter how much I pushed, no matter how much I didn't answer calls or reply to texts, the people who really love me, who understood, they never left or got offended. That is really when you know who loves you and who you can count on. That has been the biggest lesson in my life. By far."

Anna didn't understand why she just unloaded all that on him, over pimento cheese sandwiches, but there it was. Couldn't take it back now. She had to do damage control.

"Wow, that must have been a really hard time. If you ever want to talk about it, I am a good listener. Just remember that." Tony wanted to know the whole story, but he was smart enough to know that she probably had just divulged much more than she wanted to. He wasn't going to push the matter, but he felt drawn to her to find out.

IT'S IN THE BAG

Anna just fell for Tony a little bit more. Him not asking a ton of questions and pressuring her to talk about it, that was the kindest thing he could do for her. Some people pushed for her to tell more and more, without thinking that there may be a reason that she didn't want to; too personal, too hard to share. Tony must have sensed that, and he didn't ask. That was the most wonderful thing she could imagine.

To switch the subject and focus off her, Anna brought up the Logan case. "So, to do a total subject change, what do you think of Mr. Logan after our meeting yesterday? I have some ideas, but I wanted to get your perspective, what you took away from what he said."

"I think we need to catch her in the act, whatever that act is. I think Mr. Logan is somewhat okay, as long as that will doesn't change, but once that is done, I think he would be in more danger than even he realizes. What are the thoughts in that pretty little head of yours?"

Anna blushed in spite of herself; she could feel it. "Well, I thought you would never ask. Mr. Logan is the reluctant star of his own personal *Lifetime* movie. Do you ever watch those? Always a love gone wrong, one spouse trying to kill the other, good times? Great Sunday afternoon watching. Anyway, I think that he had better watch himself closely for the next little bit. Keep an extra eye on her and her comings and goings. Hey, can we look into her finances, see what she has and what he thinks she has and what she has shared with him? That will go a long way with the whole will issue. That could be a game changer for sure." Anna had just had a wonderful idea; she was shocked no one could see the proverbial light bulb that had just went off above her head. "That is the ticket. I need you to find out all you can about her finances. Can you do that for me? Under all her previous names?" Anna looked at Tony like a little girl sitting on Santa's lap who had just asked for the world.

"I, uh, yeah, of course. I could probably dig up some financials on her. I will see what I can do. I have the feeling you have a plan for the meeting you have with them on Tuesday. I will get going on that and get it to you as soon as possible Monday. Will that work?" Tony could tell something was brewing up in that mind of hers.

"Perfect! Thanks a bunch." Anna cleaned up her plate and gathered Tony's plate and stacked it on top of hers. "I will go throw these away and run to the bathroom, and if you are game, we will tackle the animal rescue and be done. That okay? Do you need to go? I could run you by the house and I can go to the rescue later if that would be better?" Anna stood with the plates strategically held in front of her bag. "I will be right back. We will do whatever is best for you. Okay?" Anna didn't even give him a chance to do much more than a nod.

Anna took the trash and threw it away and made her way to the bathroom in the bakery. She really needed to work on her exit strategy when she needed to go to the bathroom after eating. With an ostomy, eating triggered her body and her stoma, the opening surgically made in her abdomen for waste to exit into the bag, to go to work. After emptying her bag now, she would generally be okay until the next time she ate something. With that done, she walked back to the table, being careful to take in the very handsome man she had just had lunch with. She was starting to really like his company.

The two crossed the street and headed back to the van via the opposite side of the street so she could show Tony some of the other businesses around the area. There was an ease of conversation between the two, a feel of almost knowing each other more than just a little while, like their souls had met before. Their laughs came easy, they seemed to get each other, and there was a mutual respect. That feeling was too precious and hard to come by, between a man and a woman, to let a mistake about taking it to the next level ruin it. Anna's mind knew that, but did her heart? Tony knew that fact, but did he care? Was it worth the chance that it could be something great, something that they had both been looking for all their lives?

Back at the van, Tony and Anna stand across from each other, the hood of the van in between them. Anna looked and asked one more time, "You sure you are up for the animal rescue visit, or do I need to cut you loose? This is your last chance to bail." She hit the button on the key fob to unlock the doors. "I will say, if you don't go, your day will be lacking a dose of cuteness that you will never get back."

"I would hate for my day to be without all the cuteness it can possibly have. Let's go. Someone is going to have to control you. I can imagine you are one of those who would like to adopt all the dogs and cats. I bet you belong to the ASPCA." Tony laughed as he got in the car.

"I will have you know I do a monthly donation to the ASPCA. I would donate more if they could just stop playing the Sarah McLachlan sad songs. Those kill me." Anna was a sucker for a sad story…especially one about a little four-legged furry thing.

Anna pulled out of the parking spot and into traffic. It was just a short ride to the other end of town. The animal rescue sat on a beautiful six-acre property that had a barn, a main building with the offices and some classrooms, the Dog House, and the Kitty Korner. Most recently added was a thrift store that helped to raise funds for the rescue, as well as for other organizations around the country. They sold shirts, animal outfits, bowls, collars, leashes, and toys. Anything animal related, they probably had it. It was a neat idea, and it was doing well. Anna had gone to school with the woman who opened this rescue and she loved to come here to see Barbara and her daughter, Denise.

Anna pulled into a parking place right outside the main building. "Okay, let's go talk to Ms. Brenda and get this set up, then I will be done with my party to-do list. I mean we will be." Anna looked at Tony and smiled. She grabbed her wallet and phone and took her keys out of the ignition.

"Let me guess, you know these folks too," Tony said in a kidding tone. "You seem to know every single person in this town." He grabbed her by the arm and stopped her from opening the door. He stepped ahead and pulled the door open. "There, let me get a door every now and then. Makes me feel like a man."

There it was again, that electric feeling right where he had touched her. Now she knew without a doubt it was him. It was him who was giving her those feelings; she hadn't fallen down in days, so it wasn't just a reaction to her falling or embarrassment, just him. She was dumbfounded. "Well, thank you. It is nice to have a door opened for you every now and then. I really appreciate it." Anna looked at Tony and let her gaze stay steady for just a moment longer than it probably should have. She forced herself to walk into the facility instead of pushing him up against the door and kissing the fool out of him. She needed to concentrate. She needed a distraction. She needed to see cuteness, all the fluffy and wonderful cuteness.

"Anna!" A beautiful older woman came around the counter and wrapped Anna in the biggest hug. "Well, what a wonderful surprise. I have missed you, sweetie!" Barbara looked her up and down. "You look absolutely gorgeous. So much better than the last time I saw you. You look so healthy. The good Lord sure answered my prayers for you, honey." Barbara hugged her again and then looked at Tony. "Well, hello there, handsome. You here with Anna or can I take you home with me? You are so cute, my husband wouldn't mind. We would just set another place at the table." She winked at Anna, then at Tony.

"Easy there, Barb. I don't think Dan would go for a threesome. Simmer down. This is Tony Phillips. He is a detective who works with Daddy. We are here on a mission from Momma." Anna smiled and laughed when she caught how red Tony had turned. "You know about Daddy's party, right?"

"Well, of course, hon, doesn't everyone? Why, we plan our summers around the Dawson birthday bash every year!" Barbara walked back around the counter and leaned up on her arms to talk. "Let me guess, she wants to know if I have any llamas or an ostrich? Tell her I am fresh out, but I have a couple potbellied pigs she can have!"

"Oh, wouldn't that be lovely? I would love to see the look on her face if I brought a couple of pigs home to her. Maybe for Christmas!" Anna said with a wicked smile on her face. "No, we would like you to consider doing an adoption event during the carnival portion of the party. There will be tons of people, tons of families, and impressionable children for us to put the idea into their little heads that they need a new pet! I would help you the whole time. I would have some flyers printed up beforehand and we could include it with the invites. I think it would really be a good thing."

Barbara thought for a moment. "I think it would be great! Sounds great. I am in. We have had so many puppies and kittens

IT'S IN THE BAG

being brought in, we are about at capacity. I am having an event at the local pet shop and I hope to find some good homes there for some of our longest residents." Barbara came around the counter once again, headed toward the door to the outside path that led to the Dog House. She motioned for Anna and Tony to follow.

"Now we will have to remind people we have an application process, and while our prices are quite low, we do provide all first shots, spay or neuter, and first vet checkup. We have just the cutest litter that just came in from just a little south of here." Barbara opened the door to the Dog House, and immediately all the dogs got excited and barked; some even were jumping around. Such a cool place; it was all done to make it look like a big yard. Each kennel was made into its own doghouse and it was very clean. Off to one side was the area for the youngest puppies. That was exactly where Barbara was headed. She stopped just beside a little area made to look like a little doggie nursery. Just inside was what she wanted Anna to see.

"Do you remember telling me years ago that the dog you wanted was on the smaller side, shaggy and cute...? Didn't have to be a pure breed and just needed someone to love it? Well, look right in here."

Anna gave Barbara a look and then she looked into the pen. Inside there were four tinny pure-black puppies. They were shaggy little things, three almost the same size and one just a little smaller. The smaller one looked up and met eyes with Anna. Anna looked at Barbara. "Can I...can I pick this one up?" She motioned to the smallest one.

"Of course. Just be very careful when picking her up. The smallest one is named Daisy. The other three are Tulip, Jasmine, and Yellow Belle. They won't be ready to be adopted for about six weeks or more, but for now, this is their home. They are a terrier mix."

As soon as Anna picked up Daisy, the little puppy just put its head on her shoulder and nuzzled its nose into her neck. Anna was instantly in love. For years she had been looking for just this kind of dog. A shaggy little dog who needed a home. This was it. This had to be her dog. "Oh my goodness, I know now what they mean when they say love at first sight. I just fell in love." Anna held Daisy so that she could look at the little pup's face. It was so sweet, so tiny, but so perfect.

Tony watched as Anna was cuddling the puppy. His heart swelled as he watched how happy and how cute she was with Daisy. He couldn't help making a comment, though; he couldn't let this moment pass. "I thought you were talking about me when you said you finally knew what love at first sight meant." He winked at both ladies. "But I guess Daisy is a little cuter than I am. I get it, my ego is a little bruised, but I think I will live."

"Ha ha ha." Anna said out loud in a slow manner. "You are cute, but look at this little girl's face. It is the cutest face." She looked at Barbara. "I want to put in an application, today, right now. I know that there is a process. You can come to my house. I will buy all the things we need, I will, just please let me adopt her. Please…" Anna was at the point of groveling; so unlike her.

Barbara put up her hands and nodded. "Okay, okay, we will put your name on Daisy. Like I said, she isn't going to be going anywhere for at least six weeks, then she will have to be fixed and get her puppy shots. You have some time to prepare. Also I will do your home visit myself. You make the best snacks. It will be just a formality for the file. I already know Murphy. I think you are good to go."

"Are you adopting a dog or a getting ready to foster a child? A home visit, an application, what else do you need? Blood type, social security number?" Tony was laughing, but he really wanted to know. "Last time I adopted a dog, it was from the pound, years ago. I just signed a piece of paper, paid the fee and out the door we went."

"Well, I am supposed to talk to the family vet to check to see how well Anna keeps up Murphy's visits and if Murphy is up to date on his shots and all. Other than being a little obese, I think that will be okay too. Adoptions have gotten a little more intense, if you will. A process, but totally worth it when you find the one in a million, like I do believe Anna has." Barbara nodded over to where Anna was playing with Daisy in the pen, unaware of anyone else was in the world.

"I hope she has. I think I have." Tony didn't mean to say that out loud, but too late now. He was happy when all Barbara did was smile and send him a wink. She put her hand over her heart and patted.

Anna filled out all the paperwork and even went ahead and paid the adoption fee. She wouldn't leave until Barbara put the official "Adopted, I Am Going Home" sign on Daisy's door. Anna made Barbara promise with her life that no one would get Daisy and that she would protect her night and day. Only then did Tony open the door to the outside, and he and Anna left to head back to her house. Today had been a good day; not just a good day, but a very, very good day, and she hoped it wasn't over yet.

CHAPTER 16

Anna pulled into her driveway. They both had pretty much been silent most of the short drive home. She pushed the button for the garage door to open. While she waited, her phone buzzed with a text. It was from Jack; they were just finishing up with their round of golf and would be home in about half an hour. All the boys would be there. She told him to pick up five pizzas and she would handle the rest. Anna parked in her spot in the garage and turned off the van. She didn't want Tony to leave, but she also felt kind of like she had taken up most of his Saturday. Well, some of it he volunteered himself for.

"Well, looks like I am going to have a house full of teenage boys tonight. The guys and five pizzas will be here in about half an hour." She looked at her watch; it was quarter until four. Maybe he was hungry. "You are welcome to stay for some pizza. I am sure there will be a basketball game or two, some baseball on the television, and perhaps some video games. You are welcome to hang out with the guys, or Murphy, or me. I have got to make some snacks for tomorrow. Shellie and Peggy are coming over. We are getting our hair did." Anna threw up her hands thanking the Lord for her upcoming new highlights.

Tony rubbed the back of his neck as Anna opened her door and got out her key to the house. He opened the door and after he shut it he looked at her and really didn't want to leave yet. "Aren't you good and tired of me yet? I would love to stay, but if you need time to yourself, I understand." He waited for her response, pretty sure he already knew what she was going to say.

"Look, one thing I am shocked you haven't figured out yet, if I want rid of someone, I get rid of someone, in the office or at my house. So the offer stands. If you are leaving, thank you so much for helping me today, with Momma and everything. I had a really good time, a nice day. If you are staying, follow me and buckle up for an evening of teenage eating and loudness. You, my friend, may be the one who needs time to himself." She laughed and put the key in the door and opened it. She punched in her code on the security system, looked back, and smiled. Looked like there was going to be one more for dinner.

Tony wasn't really sure what he was walking into, and he had no real intentions of making a day of this, but so be it. He was having a good time, she seemed to be having a good time, and he wanted to see where this evening would go. He smiled as he walked into the house and into the kitchen. He watched Anna breeze through doing her usual things, her being her. He liked what he saw.

"So what can I do to help?" Tony tried to stay out of her way, but still wanted to help out. He could tell she was used to being in control of the situation and handling about fifty things at once. "I will be happy to help… I know from personal experience that teenage boys require a lot of food."

Laughing, she smiled and nodded. She thought for a moment. "Okay, can you grab the salad stuff out of the fridge? Anything and everything that you would put in a salad. I have some diced ham and some shredded turkey too. I like to put that on top. I also have a couple of hard-boiled eggs in there. Can you peel those?" Anna was happy to have help; she could get used to this.

Tony went to the fridge and opened it. He was amazed at how organized and clean it was. Not that he was a gross human or anything, but his had at least a couple of takeout boxes, a science experiment or two, and some food mingled in. Anna's was so bright, everything in its place. He grabbed the lettuce, tomatoes, cheese, eggs, diced peppers, ham, and turkey. He made quick work of shelling the eggs and placed them on a paper towel. Anna had laid out a bowl, and he washed and chopped, diced, and prepared a nice salad. She was impressed.

"Looking good over there. Here, let me get you the egg slicer. Hang on one second…" Anna reached around him and pulled out a utensil drawer. She grabbed the egg slicer and set it down in front of him. "Okay, rinse off the eggs and lay it in here and push this slider through it. It makes the cuts perfect every time. Then just lay the slices around the top of the salad and it can go back in the fridge." Anna smiled and returned to making some brownies.

Just as Anna was pouring the batter into the pan, the sound of the garage door alerted them to the boys' return home. "That sound, the garage door, is the sweetest sound to a mother whose kids are old enough to drive. Glorious. It means they made it home one more time." She scraped the bowl and then licked the spatula. She scraped up the last little remaining bit and held out the spatula for Tony to taste. "Wanna try it? You don't have to worry. I don't have cooties. I have been vaccinated against them." Anna smiled and kept holding out the ooey-gooey goodness.

Tony bent down and licked the spatula that Anna was holding. She was right; it was great. He wanted more. He must have had that look in his eye; she could read that look. She grabbed his hand and put it on the spatula for him to hold it. She turned and grabbed the bowl and handed it to him to hold. She put her finger in the bowl and scraped up a little from the very bottom. She put the finger in her mouth and shut her eyes as she licked it and decided that her work on the brownie batter was sufficient. He could look at that vision all day and he would probably think about it all night. That would keep him warm when he was lying in bed alone tonight.

The door from the garage opened, and an onslaught of teen boys entered the room. Johnathan and Jack and three large boys surrounded Tony and Anna. Anna laughed as Johnathan ruffled her hair and gave her a hug. "Hey, guys, welcome home. How was your game?" Anna spun around to meet Jack with his offering of a hug, and he dipped his finger in the bowl that Tony was holding.

"Yummy! I love brownies! Are they done yet? I'm starving," Jack said as he reached in for one more swipe. "John wouldn't let me have one slice of pizza on the way home. He made Fletch bring it in his car so I wouldn't steal a piece."

"That's right, Mrs. D. I am the only reason the pizzas made it home at all." Fletch was a handsome young man; her boys had been

IT'S IN THE BAG

friends with him since they were in kindergarten, so she had watched him grow, just as she had the other two boys. "You are really cool for letting us hang out tonight. Thanks!"

"Hello, guys! Well, I am glad that you all can hang out here and don't think I am as cringey as my boys do. Y'all are welcome anytime, you know that." Anna looked at Tony; the boys were kind of staring at him, so she had better introduce him soon. "I would like you guys to meet Detective Tony Philips. He and I are working on a case together, and he is a good guy. Be nice to him and don't fart around him. At least till you are around him for a while. Ease into it with him. Don't scare him off!"

Truck, Fletch, and Jacob all came and gave Tony fist bumps and greeted him in some boyish way. John and Jack were impressed that he managed to live through the meeting with their gram. Johnathan opened that can of worms right off. "Good to see you made it through the morning with Grams. You don't seem to be too worse for wear. She must have taken a liking to you. Some people aren't quite that lucky."

"She is always nice to us, when we have ever been around when she is here." Jacob spoke out in support of Grams. "She even made us some cookies the last time we were over there helping y'all clean out their garage."

Jack was quick with a comeback. "Yeah, man, she is always nice to 'special' people, Jacob. She has a weird love of cute little boys." Jack punched him in the shoulder showing he was just kidding.

"Hey, guys, I am glad you are all here. I have an announcement to make. Are y'all ready for this?" Anna looked excitedly over the group of young men with Tony standing beside her. "Our family is going to increase by one."

Johnathan looked at his mom with a questioning look on his face. "This is kind of sudden, Mom, since we just met Tony this morning. But hey, they say when you know, you know. Congrats!"

The rest of the boys just looked stunned, even Tony. Anna was laughing. "No, no, guys. Tony and I are not getting married. I just met him, like, not even two weeks ago. Geez." Anna looked at the group of guys, then at Tony. "No offense to you, Tony, but I have a strict policy of not getting married when I have known someone less than three weeks. Strict, I know." Everyone laughed.

"Good, no offense taken, and that is a sound policy. Good practice. You only really know someone after three weeks, not two." He winked at Anna.

"Guess again, guys. Our family is growing by one, very soon." She really emphasized *one*. Anna was so excited about the new puppy. She could not wait to be able to bring her home. "So cute, I cannot wait!"

Jack looked at his mom and smirked. "I got it. You're pregnant." Jack smiled and laughed loudly. "Grams is gonna love this. Her unmarried daughter, pregnant, with two almost-grown boys." He kept right on laughing.

"Mom, that is so gross. You had sex? Oh my goodness. You preach to us all the time about being careful, not having sex, not making you a grandmother while we are teenagers, or until we are at least thirty, and here you are, pregnant." Johnathan sounded more like a parent than a child.

Anna turned all shades of red; the heat was probably as visible as it was burning through her face. "Um, wrong again, on so many levels. I am not pregnant. *Do* I look pregnant? *No*. And another thing, I have not had sex in quite some time, so there. All that preaching that I have done to you, it still stands. I adopted a puppy today. A puppy. Two dogs had sex, and I adopted a puppy that resulted from them having sex. Not me." Anna started laughing in spite of herself. Good grief, that escalated quickly.

"Mrs. D, I wouldn't have had a problem if you were pregnant," the ever kind and sweet Truck said out of nowhere.

"Well, thank you, Truck. That is very kind of you to say. Although I am not, I appreciate you saying that." Anna smiled.

"I am glad you aren't. I am not about to share my bedroom with this slob." Johnathan put Jack in a headlock. "So tell us about the puppy. What made you do that?" Anna showed the group the photos she had taken at the shelter. She told them about how sweet and cuddly Daisy was and how little she was. All the boys instantly loved her, and Anna promised to take the boys to meet her soon.

IT'S IN THE BAG

Anna put out the paper plates, plastic silverware, and red solo cups, and they all said the blessing. When grace had sufficiently been said, she released the hungry mob onto the food. The pizzas, the salad, the breadsticks were attacked with gusto. When the crowd had thinned out and made their way to the den to eat and watch whatever sport was on TV, Tony and Anna were left to scrounge with what was left and the fresh pan of brownies that Anna had just retrieved from the oven.

Anna handed Tony a paper plate. "Only the best for my guests. Sorry about the paper plates, but with those guys, my real dishes would never make it. I would be loading and unloading the dishwasher all night. No thanks!" Anna grabbed herself a plate and started with some salad. "Feel free to help yourself to anything in the fridge. I will wipe off the table on the back porch. It is a nice night. I'd want to eat out there. It will be a little less loud too." Anna smiled.

"Sounds great. Be right out, thanks." Tony made his plate with a couple of slices of pizza and a small salad. He poured himself some sweet tea and grabbed his fork and napkin. He stepped outside and onto the back porch. The porch was off the first floor of the actual house, but it was up above the basement back on this side of the house. The view was nice; seemed like a nice neighborhood. No one right on top of each other, but close enough to know one's neighbors. Tony could easily tell why Anna loved this area and this house. Tony took the chair beside Anna's, where he could look out over the backyard as well. "You have a really nice deck here. I really like it."

"Thanks. This is almost my favorite part of the house. Especially in the evenings, it is a peaceful place to sit, eat, think, read, study. I like it. It is also a good, quiet escape when your home is full of loud teenage boys." Anna smiled as she took a sip of her tea. "I am glad you stayed for dinner. Otherwise, it would just be me out here, with the birds and the bugs."

"I have had a good day. I have to be honest—I was a little worried about meeting your mom, but she was great. I can tell where you get a lot of your sassy attitude from." He laughed. "I also loved meeting your boys, and their friends. They are really great. I think it is awesome that they are so close with you."

Anna almost snorted. "You mean how it seems they keep track of when I have sex and immediately thought I was pregnant? That is a little too much for sure." Anna laughed. "They are great. We give each other a hard time, and we keep each other on our toes. They are really good at that, but those two boys will never know how much they have made me a better person. Some days, they have been the only reason I got up and kept going." She then added, "And we don't talk about my sex life, or lack of one. I would never discuss that with them. As far as they are concerned, I have only had sex twice, to have them. That is fine. I talk to them about it, and about how they need to keep theirs in their pants till they have been married at least two years. Never can be too careful." She winked.

"You are really easy to talk to. When I first met you—well, after you got up off the floor in your dad's office, I didn't think that you would be so easy to talk to, but you are. I haven't really gotten out and made a lot of friends since I moved here. It's not that I don't like having friends, it's just that for so long I have only focused on work. Today showed me again that it is good to get out, see things, do things, and meet people. I bet I met more people today hanging out with you than I have met since moving here, outside of the department, of course."

"Of course, but it is important to know that friends are so important and can be a lifeline, especially when you don't have family close. Even when you do have family around, friends can help you not take yourself so seriously, help you see things for what they are and just have fun. I love the close friends I have. I wouldn't take a million bucks for any one of them. They have seen me through all the good and bad times in my life. I hope that they could say the same for me." Anna smiled. "The four of us, my closest group of friends, we are like a really small gang. My peeps."

"I couldn't agree more. I hope to form my own little gang soon too. Would be nice to hang out and eat pizza and shoot hoops with some guys. To have a few I could really count on. That would be nice."

"I am totally going to change the subject. I hope that is okay." Anna looked at Tony, and he nodded. "Do you think you could help

IT'S IN THE BAG

me get the financials on Maria before I meet with them on Tuesday? As soon as you can get the numbers, that would be great." She looked hopefully at him.

Tony could tell her mind was working, planning, scheming a way to get this woman to screw up. "I will call in some favors. I can even send out a few emails tonight. I will try my best to have all the information I can get on her by Monday morning, noon at the latest. Do you want me to call you or just come on by the office? I could go over them with you and see what you think. Would that be okay, just come on by?"

"That would be awesome. I don't have anything scheduled for Monday until the afternoon. I am free up until about two. I have a couple of appointments then, but I will have the evening too if needed... Well, wait, Daddy usually comes to eat with us on Monday nights. Momma goes to the ladies' thing at the club. Daddy could never understand why she likes to hang out with all those 'snobs,' but that is her gang. So Daddy doesn't think I know, but he always ends up eating here with us on Monday nights. It's like an 'unofficial' official thing." Anna shrugged her shoulders. "We have done this unofficial thing for about three years now. If there are still things to go over, we can just meet here, have dinner, and then we can talk things over with Daddy too. He would love to be in on what we are thinking."

"Okay, sounds good. I will plan on being at your office on Monday morning, then here, later, if needed." Tony looked around. "Let me help you clean up this mess and then I am going to head home."

"Oh, you don't have to help. The mess will only expand before it gets better tonight. I am pretty sure I have a full house for the night." Anna could see he actually did want to help. "Well, okay, let's clean up this out here and then put up things that will cause food poisoning if we don't. Deal? Then you will be free to go." Anna smiled as she stood. She was already dreading this day with Tony ending. "Remind me one day, I owe you a huge favor in return for today."

The two of them made quick work of cleaning up the kitchen, putting the few dishes in the dishwasher and sealing the salad in a bowl and putting it in the refrigerator. Anna wiped down the island

and stacked the pizzas on top of the oven and placed paper plates, cups, and napkins beside so that the guys could easily find them, knowing there would be a second meal needed before turning in for the night.

The cleaning done, Tony walked past Anna toward the table by the door. Anna could smell his scent, a mixture of clean soap and his aftershave. She could get very used to that smell. Anna only snapped out of her wandering thoughts about his wonderful aroma when she remembered she needed to run to the potty. Ah, the life of an ostomate. Eating equaled needing to go to the bathroom. All right, she needed to pull another smooth move.

"I think the guys are out in the garage and the driveway. Run talk to them a minute. I need to pee. I will be right out and will say bye then. Be right back." Anna scooted down the hall and into her bathroom before he could respond.

Anna made quick work of her bathroom excursion. She had this down to a science. NASCAR pit crews had nothing on her. Anna knew that she should just tell Tony about the bag. It was really nothing to be ashamed of, really. It was just a medical necessity, something she needed to live. That was it, and if he couldn't get over that and see her as the same person who he thought pooped just like him, then he wasn't worth her time. She was strong and said that to herself while locked in the bathroom, safe in her own home. One day she would tell him, one day, but not today. Why upset a day like she hadn't had in years? An easy, fun day, with a sexy man. Why upset that She finished up and went out to find the guys.

Anna walked outside to find the boys, including Tony, shooting basketball and having a great time. All the teens had either taken off their shirts or were just in a T-shirt, losing the golf shirts quickly. Tony had taken off his overshirt and was only left in a white T-shirt and jeans. He looked happy, comfortable, and able to almost hold his own with the younger guys. Anna sat down on the steps to the porch to watch.

"Oh no, Ms. D, get out here. You are usually our best weapon. Get out here and help us." Fletch yelled over to Anna.

IT'S IN THE BAG

Anna waved them off. "No, no, not tonight. You have just enough to play. I will stay over here and be a cheerleader. It is a dream I never realized in high school. The cute cheerleader. I was the nerd with glasses."

Johnathan came and pulled his mom's arm so hard it almost popped out of joint. "C'mon, Mom, don't be such a loser just because you have a new friend. Come show him what you've got. It ain't much, but it is something." He let go of Anna's arm when he was pretty certain that she wasn't going to retreat to the stairs. "Hey, guys, y'all step out for a minute. Mom won't last too long. It will be Mom and I against Tony and Jack. This will be quick."

"Hey, one of you guys come in for me. I have got to see this. I will miss the best parts if I am trying to play. One of you come on in."

"All right, all right, we will just play, us three to ten. Whoever gets to ten first wins…deal? This is how we usually play when it is just us. I am certain the neighbors love those shows of my lack of athletic abilities." Anna grabbed the ball and started to dribble it.

"Done. You are on. You might as well sit down now and watch with the rest. You will be better off over there." Jack tried to tap the ball away from his mom; no luck.

"All right, let's get going… It's getting late and I am old. I need my beauty sleep and take my vitamins. Move along, little doggie." Anna bounced the ball to Johnathan.

Tony laughed at the banter between Anna and her boys. He could tell they must do this quite often; they looked as if they knew each other's tricks and ways to try to get the best of each other. No rules, no calling fouls, no actual basketball rules were being followed, but it was a good show. Anna held her own, mostly, until she started laughing. She did make a couple of good shots, but mostly for her, it was just fun. The boys were rough with each other, bumping, shoving, and the occasional out-and-out foul, but when they went up against their mom, they treated her with a little less of the rough play. These would be great memories for them, all of them. Johnathan scored the winning point. He gave his brother a high five and his mom a comforting hug and consolation of her losing the challenge.

"It's always wonderful to get beat by those two." Anna laughed as she tried to catch her breath and sat down on the steps by Tony. "Get back in there, guys. I have shown you how it's done, so go do it! Don't be slackers."

"This has been a really good day. I know I keep saying it, but it was. You and your family have been great. You have some great kids. Their friends seem great too. I really appreciate the invite to hang out." Tony looked at Anna. She smiled. He started to get up, and Anna followed suit.

"I will walk you to your truck. Watch out for the game here. I wouldn't want you to get injured, you are so close to an escape." Anna laughed but was actually serious.

Tony looked at the group of guys. They paused when they could tell he was leaving. "Hey, great game, guys. It was nice meeting all of you. Hey, Johnathan and Jack, take care of your mom." Tony waved and opened the door to his truck. "I hope you have a great rest of your night. Hanging out with you has sort of whooped me. I am going to go home and take a shower and relax. I will send out those emails tonight and see where we get from there." He climbed in and shut the door. He started the engine and rolled down the window. "I will let you know when I hear something. Thanks again!"

"Welcome. Have a good one. I will talk to you soon. Thanks again. Be careful!" Anna said as she backed up a little to let him pull away from the curb.

Tony looked out the window and only said one word as he drove off: "Always."

Anna watched him as he drove to the end of the street and disappeared. She had had a great day. Unexpected how good, but good nonetheless. She felt a little sad in her heart that he wasn't there anymore, but her heart was also full as she headed back up the driveway into the chaos of a boys' basketball game. She was thankful for a good life. Everything wasn't perfect, nothing ever is, but today had been pretty darn close.

CHAPTER 17

Anna woke with the sun filling her room with its warm goodness. She had slept soundly and felt refreshed. It was still early, and the newness of the day welcomed her into a new day. Sundays were one of Anna's favorite days of the week. She loved the slowness of the morning, church, and the restful feeling of only doing what she wanted. She very rarely worked on Sundays, only in dire emergencies. She held on to the teachings of her youth; Sundays were the Lord's Day, and work was not to be done. Her momma always said, "If even the good Lord needed a day of rest, then how much more do we need it?" Anna never quite understood that while she was young, but she fully grasped its meaning now and tried to practice it every chance she got. Today would be a good day. Church, and then the girls coming over to have fun, laugh, eat, and, more importantly, do hair. She needed it something terrible; she needed some highlights and a good trim.

Anna made her bed and replaced all the pillows that served no other use than to decorate the room and use the bathroom. She kept on her comfy pink pajama pants and the matching T-shirt. She did brush her hair. There was her boys to think of; she would hate if she scared the guys who slept over last night with them. She would start breakfast soon, enough for a small army, or at least five teenage boys. Right now, she just wanted her caffeine and the morning news. First she checked her phone; no new texts or no missed calls. That was good news. No one had died during the night; all must be well. Next, a quick scroll through Instagram; nothing too earth-shattering there either. On to the most important news of the day, only fifteen minutes away: *Sunday Today*! A Sunday morning must, watching Willie Geist with her *Sunday Today* big yellow mug...didn't get much better than that.

Anna and the boys had to leave the house at 10:30 to make it to church on time. Plenty of time to watch the only show on television worth watching, and then breakfast and getting ready. Now that the boys were older and much more self-sufficient, Sunday mornings were not quite as hectic. Lionel Ritchie's song made sense once again: "Easy Like Sunday Morning." That just ain't possible when you are the single parent, or heck, probably married parents of toddlers or of a child of any age for that matter. Anna was thankful the boys had never given her a hard time about going to church. They had so many good friends there, their own group to meet with for Bible studies and outings. She was also very thankful to know that they had both asked the Lord into their hearts, to be saved by his grace. That was what truly mattered; she knew they were settled with eternity. Now she just had to keep praying that they make it through life with the least amount of problems and missteps as possible. No one ever prayed as hard as a mom. Pray like a mother. Anna thought that was pretty good. She needed to write that down.

Anna's phone buzzed with a text.

> Good Morning. Sunday Today is about to start. Didn't want you to miss it. Waiting on reply from emails. Tony

Anna held the phone and reread the text about fifty times. She thought it was sweet that he remembered that she loved *The Today Show* and all its entities. Well, she had just told him the day before, so if he didn't remember, there might be something wrong with him or he just didn't care. She needed a quick reply without too much thinking. She positioned her bright yellow *Today* mug on her knee, with her pj's pants showing, and clicked a quick photo. She set it up to send and typed,

> Already sitting here waiting on Willie Geist... Thanks for the reminder! Have a great day! Anna

IT'S IN THE BAG

Anna hit send. Hopefully, that was okay. She sat back and smiled. She felt like a teenager who just got a text from a crush. So goofy. She needed to stop it. She wasn't looking for a relationship. She wasn't even thinking about anyone that way until she met Tony. Well, really, until she felt his hand on her arm. Something stirred in her that day, and she had felt drawn to him ever since. Silly thinking; she had to put that thought away; she couldn't get into a relationship with him. She was working with him, she pooped in a bag, and it would just be way too complicated. Honestly, she just didn't think she could stand the thoughts of him being disgusted by her body. She couldn't take a chance. She was going to be proud to be his friend and that will have to do.

*****

Anna was ready to get her hair done. She had about cried when an older lady, Mrs. Russell, at church that morning asked her if she was just going to let the gray take over and go with it. She told Anna how she wished she had not spent so much time and money on dying her hair all those years. Anna smiled and said she was considering it. Anna really loved when people tried to pay a compliment but sometimes it felt like a stab in the eyeball, with a hot crochet needle. Anna had held her tongue since she was in the Lord's house, and old Mrs. Russell was crotchety, even on her best day, and obviously, this was not a good day. Anna wanted to tell Mrs. Russell that she liked her helmet of curls and that the shade of blue for her hair she had chosen went so well with her skirt, but she didn't. Older people were kind, sweet, and gave out candy. Mrs. Russell missed that memo, every week; didn't even get the message. Anna had a soft spot in her heart for the elderly. Heck, when she and Mark were married he used to joke that Anna would stop to help an old person or a dog on the side of the road but everyone else was just out of luck.

Anna was staring at the gray stripes that were making their way throughout her hair when the doorbell rang. Party time! Anna went and opened the door. Shellie and Gigi stood there with smiles on their faces and bowls of yummy food in their hands. "Hello, ladies, come on in!" Anna grabbed what she could to help and moved aside as the girls came on in.

"Hello, Anna. Can we just set all this down on the island? I love that we went with a Mexican food theme. I am going to eat until you have to roll me out of the house and down the street," Shellie announced as she walked into the kitchen.

"Sure thing. Anywhere you can find will be great." Anna took the chips and a bowl of guacamole from Gigi. "I am so glad you guys are here!"

Gigi sat down her famous nachos and her homemade Pico de Gallo. She could sell that stuff. "Thanks for letting us come hang out here today. I needed this. I have been looking forward to this for days." Gigi gave Anna a hug and then just melted onto one of the barstools at the island.

"You okay?" Anna asked as she just stood and looked at her.

"She has been like this since I picked her up this afternoon. I think we all just need an afternoon hanging out and not having to worry about anything. Just a good time with good friends. Right, Gigi?" Shellie looked at Gigi and smiled.

"Right. I just need some time where no one needs me, or anything from me, and who isn't constantly calling out Mom. Mommy. I love my kids more than life itself, but dang, they can be needy." Gigi finally let the cat out of the bag. Momma needed a break. Easily fixed. "Have either one of you ever wanted to just get in your car, drive for however long you wanted to, and just, like, go somewhere, by yourself…but then you get there and all you do is miss your kids?" Gigi looked close to crying. They had to intervene…no crying today.

"Every single day when I go to work, to the office. When I look forward to going to the grocery store, alone… But then you know what, a few minutes into my day at work, or even at the store, and my mind immediately wanders to what they are doing, how they are doing, and that I am a horrible mother for needed some time to myself. Then I come home, I get over it, and by the time we all go to bed, all is well. You will be fine. There is nothing wrong with needing some time. Enjoy it. Do not let the guilt win." Anna squeezed her shoulders and went to get her dishes out of the fridge.

IT'S IN THE BAG

The doorbell rang once, the front door opened almost immediately, and the girls heard Johnathan talking to Peggy. Her laugh was unmistakable. John walked down the hall with her and greeted all the girls. "Hello, ladies! Smells good in here. I see Gigi's famous nachos." Johnathan was a sucker for Mexican food. He could sniff it out like a hound dog.

"Hello, everyone. Sorry I am a little late. I had to get all my supplies, then I had to talk to my mom, then I forgot half my stuff, and now I am here, after a return trip home and a stop at Sally's Beauty Supply. Whew. I need a minute." Peggy gave Johnathan a hug. "Anna, I think I am gonna marry this one. He is just so handsome." Peggy gave him a kiss on the cheek.

"Sure thing. As long as your husband is okay with it, sounds good to me." Anna smiled and sat down her taco shells, lettuce, cheese, onions, and sour cream. Then she stirred the ground beef seasoned with taco seasoning. "Hey, I would be your mother-in-law. That would be so much fun." Anna smirked at Peggy.

"Sorry, Johnathan, I am married, and I already have one mother-in-law to contend with. I think you are sweet as sugar, but I can't put up with your momma too much more than I already do." Peggy shrugged her shoulders. She laughed and winked at Anna.

Johnathan picked up a chip out of the nachos and came over and kissed his mom's cheek. "Once dork face gets down here, we are going to go over to Chandler's house for the afternoon. Too many girlie things going on here today. We will be back by dinner. Save me some leftovers, please?"

"Sounds good. Tell his mom hello for me. And, John, please don't call your brother dork face in front of company. Act like somebody. I told you to only call him that when it was just us here." Anna smiled at John and gave him a big hug.

Jack walked into the kitchen and snuck up behind Shellie. He pinched her sides, and she jumped and squealed. "Gotcha, Shel!" Jack was definitely the jokester in the family. He was always trying to get the best of anybody and everybody he could. He lived on that thrill. "Hey, everybody! Bye, everybody!" He gave his mom a quick hug and smooch and also grabbed a chip and broke into the guacamole. "Love you, Mom."

"Bye, guys. Be careful." Anna hollered after them as they opened the door to the garage. "See you this evening. I love you!"

"Love you too. See ya!" both boys yelled as they shut the door. Anna could hear the garage door going up.

"Well, ladies, should we dig in?" Anna put the napkins by the paper plates and cups. She led the saying of grace, and they all made their plates. They made their way to the back porch and found their seats. Laughter and the occasional scream with laughter engulfed the air around them.

"So." Shellie cut her eyes to Anna. "You need to spill it about how yesterday went with Tony. Everything."

All three ladies were now totally focused on Anna and, more importantly, her reply. "It went good. Good day," Anna said with a sly smile. She might as well have fun with this if they were going to be expecting some lurid tale.

"First of all, someone needs to catch me up here. I am out in left field. Are we talking about Mr. Hot Pants? The detective guy? Why would he be with you on a Saturday? I am so confused." Peggy had driven herself to Anna's and missed being filled in by Shellie like Gigi was. "Help a sister out, please."

"Yes, Detective Hot Pants. I couldn't go with Anna to be her scapegoat at her momma's yesterday while we were at lunch on Friday. Tony, the hot detective guy, offered to help out. There, all caught up. You're welcome." Shellie was so good at just giving the facts without a lot of words.

Again all eyes were waiting impatiently for Anna to spill it. "He came over yesterday morning, had breakfast with the boys, we went to Momma's, and we were out of there before noon. Done and done." Anna took a chip and scooped up some guacamole.

"Done and done? No and no! What did he think of your momma? What did he say, how did he act, and what did he wear? What did the boys think of him?" Peggy seemed to catch up with the conversation rather quickly. She apparently missed her calling as an interrogator. "Speak up, sister."

"The boys liked him. Before he left last night, the guys and Tony were playing basketball in the driveway. They talked yesterday morning, and then when they got back from Etowah yesterday evening, they talked some more. Even the boys' friends chatted with him. He helped me make dinner for all of us and then hung out for a little while, and he left. No big deal."

"No big deal? You spend an entire day with Detective Hot Pants and not one of us get a text, a call, a picture? Nothing? And what exactly did y'all do all day, from your momma's house until the boys got home for the dinner y'all made together?" All Shellie needed was the bright light to shine in Anna's eyes. She wanted facts; cold, hard facts. A minute-by-minute itinerary.

"Well, we left Momma's. She had given me my marching orders when it comes to Daddy's fiesta. I needed to go to order the cake. Tony didn't have anything pressing to get back to, so he came with me. We went and saw Pamela at the Heights Bakery. We picked out and ordered the cake. It was a little after noon, so we grabbed some lunch there and ate outside." Anna was telling God's honest truth, but the girls didn't look impressed. "I needed to go to the animal rescue and work out a plan to have an adoption event at the party also. Instead of a stinky petting zoo. All done with my chores, we came back here. I needed to make a salad and some things for the guys when they got home with the pizzas they were bringing, and I told him he was free to go or he could stay and have dinner with myself and five teenage boys. He stayed. We had a nice evening and played some basketball, and he went home."

"Is that the truth?" Gigi was smiling. "No fooling?"

"No fooling, cross my heart." Anna actually crossed her heart like she was in the seventh grade. "Oh, I also adopted a puppy. I fell in love with it while I was talking to Barbara at the Shelter. Her name is Daisy and she will make your heart melt. I get to bring her home in a few weeks. She is tiny."

"So no sex? No quickie before the boys got home? No sneaking to your old room at your momma's? Nothing?" Shellie would be the one to ask.

"Gross, not at my momma's house. Good Lord, Shellie." Anna shivered at the thought. "Although I did play the piano, and he seemed to like it, and I made my momma cry. Good times."

"He likes you. A lot," Peggy said, getting up from the island to put away her trash. "Look, a guy just doesn't spend an entire day, offer to help out at a lady's momma's house, then spend time picking out a cake—and a dog, it seems—if he doesn't like the woman. He likes you."

"No way. He just didn't have anything else to do yesterday and got caught up in helping me with all those things. Then last night, I guess he was just hungry and didn't want to have to pick up something or make anything for just him. So not a big deal." Anna tried to justify his actions as anything but him liking her.

"Okay, here is the test. Have you heard from him since last night?" Gigi was always, usually, the voice of reason in the group. Except today. Today, she was being no help.

Anna knew she was about to be in trouble. "Yes. He texted me this morning, before *The Today Show*. He didn't want me to miss it because he knows how much I love *The Today Show*. He does too. He has the mugs, just like me. That is not weird at all. We are both *Today Show* freaks…*and* he is calling in some favors to pull the financials on a suspect in a case he is helping Shellie and me with. So there."

The other three ladies all looked at Anna and said together, "He likes you."

"He likes me. So what? He likes me as a friend. Nothing more. I know it. If he liked me that way, I would know." Anna had thought, maybe, but never let herself even go too far with that thought. It would never happen, it couldn't. "He does smell so good, though. And he looks really good in just his T-shirt—well, a T-shirt and pants. He really fills out a pair of jeans really nicely."

"You like him, and I do think he likes you. Get used to it, girl. You might just have to buckle up and enjoy the ride of a relationship, and I for one think it is about dang darn time." Shellie had spoken her mind, again, as usual. And as if she felt immediately better after getting that off her chest, she suddenly seemed to remember why

IT'S IN THE BAG

they were all there today: highlights. "Can we get to the hair-doing part of this shindig? I for one look like a wooly mammoth."

"Peggy, you go ahead with Shellie. I will clean up the kitchen, then you can go in between us. Does that work?" Anna started to pick up napkins and things that could be thrown away. "*And* if no one minds, I will make the boys a plate apiece, that okay?"

"Sure thing, sweetie. I'll help. That way they can get started." Gigi hopped up with Anna and started making one of the plates. "We can have this done in no time and then we can sit and chat until it's your turn."

Peggy made quick time of setting up her makeshift hair station on the back porch, perfect place to give the haircut portion and then inside to do the color. Gigi and Anna made the plates, covered and put away all the food for now in the fridge, cleaned up the island, and poured themselves a fresh glass of sweet tea.

The two ladies took a seat in the den while Peggy worked on Shellie outside. "You okay? I mean I know you were a little stressed when you got here, but is everything okay?" Anna loved Gigi; she was her most adventurous friend, in life and in her career, and loved extra special for it. She had in the past had some moments of depression, and Anna liked to keep a close check on that. "I know some days can be overwhelming, but you know what? So far you have survived every single one of your bad days. This one is no different."

"Thanks, and I am okay. I just get too worked up sometimes about my business, the kids, worrying about money. You know how I am. This has been a really nice escape. It helps me slow down, listen to you guys talk about your things going on, and then it helps me put my life in perspective. I guess I just try to do too much, all at once… What's new, right?" Gigi wasn't known for her calm, calculated handling of anything really. She was the fly-by-the-seat-of-your-pants kind of girl. So far, every time, somehow, Gigi had fallen backward into some of the best business deals, things for her kids, everything. For her, it worked.

Anna admired that part of Gigi, not so much that she wanted to throw all caution to the wind, quit her job in law, and open a business in, well, there isn't a business for being a sassy ostomy awareness speaker…so she better keep her day job. "I am proud of you, Gigi. You bust your tail every day, you love your kids and your hubby, and you do so much. I am happy for all you have accomplished." Anna smiled and bumped her shoulder into Gigi's.

"Thanks, that really means a lot. I needed to hear that, thanks." Gigi was getting the look on her face that meant a pep talk was coming up. Anna could spot it a mile away. "Look, can I be honest with you?"

"Yep, like I could stop you…and besides, your left eye does that stupid twitch thing when you lie. Remember, that is why I can't take you on a client interview with me. And I will never take you to Vegas if I ever go. Your poker face sucks." Both girls laughed. Anna was ready for whatever it was. "Go ahead, sister, tell me that truth you were talking about."

"Okay, don't get mad at me, but look, Anna, you need to let yourself explore having a relationship if that is something you want. I know, I know, you poop in a bag. Big flipping deal. Did we stop loving you? Did your boys stop loving you? Your family? Did you stop getting clients because you don't have a butthole anymore? Is your lack of being able to fart causing you to not be able to support your family financially? Did the world stop spinning? *No!* You did not stop living. You just poop in a bag. Get over yourself." Gigi must have taken lessons from Shellie; she was more direct than usual.

"I get all that, I do, but I don't look like I used to. I wouldn't say my body before would have knocked anyone's socks off back then, but I was more confident about my body. Even when the disease was at its worst and I would spend hours a day in the bathroom, have to cancel plans, be so weak I couldn't get out of bed, I knew that my body at least looked normal." Anna shifted in her seat. "I am not comfortable with the way I look, and I can't imagine trying to one day have an intimate relationship with a man and have that just there. A bag of poop just there, between us. Simple as that. I couldn't imagine letting someone close enough to have that kind of relationship and then him being disgusted with me, which would crush me, permanently. Forever."

IT'S IN THE BAG

Gigi shook her head. "I know, but, Anna, just don't let something good pass you by just because of the what-ifs. If a man, Detective Hot Pants or whoever, is worth his weight in fluff, he will not bat an eye at that bag. He will just see you. Think about it. I want you to be happy. You are an incredible woman. You deserve to be happy, in all ways."

Anna was about to say something when the back door opened, and Shellie burst in with an awesome new bob. Peggy followed her inside. "Anna, your turn in the hot seat. I will do your cut and your foils out here, then you can process while I do Shellie's color. Come on, girl." Anna scooted past Shellie and disappeared outside with Peggy.

Anna's phone buzzed with a text.

> Hey, got some info. Shocked. You will like. T

Peggy knew that sound well. "Everything okay?" That was code for asking who that was without seeming nosey.

"It's from Tony. He has gotten some information about that case we are working on and he thinks I will like it. I need to write him back. Hmmm, let's see." Anna tried to keep her head in the position that Peggy needed it in, so it made her look like she was looking at her boobs typing back her reply.

> That's great, what is it? I am intrigued. A

Her phone buzzed his reply before she even put the phone back in her lap.

> Can I run by and bring it to you? This evening? T

"He wants to come by tonight and bring the information to me. It must be really good." Anna was chewing on a cross that she wore around her neck, a nervous habit; she had many. "I think it must be some pretty incredible stuff if he can't even wait to come to the office tomorrow."

"Please tell him to come now. Right now. Please, give this lady something to make her day? I so need to see someone who fills out his jeans well. C'mon. Do it." Peggy was so funny. She was married to her own hottie. They had been in love since the beginning of time and had no problem with the romance.

"Let me think." Anna's wheels were turning in her head. "Okay, watch this." Anna started typing away.

>	Sure, give me an hour or so, getting hair did. Come on by. A

"Now work your magic, sister. You are now on the clock." Anna put her phone on the table and helped hand Peggy the foils. She needed to be done and beautiful in *t* minus ninety minutes.

*****

Anna heard the doorbell ring. She looked at Peggy behind her in the reflection of her mirror. Peggy smiled and nodded. Anna felt almost giddy that Tony was coming over this evening. She was excited to get the information about the case, but she was more excited to see him again, even though it had been less than a day since she had seen him last. This was not good.

"I'll get it." Anna took one last quick turn and glance in the mirror. Peggy had helped her pick out some skinny jeans that still had the tags on them, a cute halter-cut top, some silver bangle bracelets, and some cute silver hoops for her ears. Her new highlights were amazing, no sign of the gray stripe that used to shine through. She was happy with the way she looked. Of course, she had clothes on. She started toward the door. "No one better touch that door. I will get it."

Anna's breath caught when she opened the door and saw Tony there, on her porch, holding a couple of files and his laptop. He was dressed in a worn NASA T-shirt and jeans. His arms were well-de-

IT'S IN THE BAG

fined, and his chest showed NASA a thing or two. The jeans—ah, to be that pair of jeans, wrapping up his wonderful lower half... How did denim become so lucky? Anna was snapped back into coherence when Tony spoke.

"Hi, I hope I'm not busting up your party? Your hair looks great, by the way." Tony smiled and stood there in his awesomeness.

"Come on in, Tony, good to see you." Anna tried to breathe him in as he walked by her into the foyer. Anna shut the door and turned to see her three friends gawking at him as if he were on display at the zoo. "You will have to excuse the peanut gallery staring at you. Well, you know Shellie, but it is a very odd thing for a handsome man to be at my house. I think the other two are actually in shock." Anna swatted at Gigi to shut her mouth. "Let me introduce you to my friends, who were just about to leave… This is Peggy. She is the amazing hairstylist who does wonders with my hair." Tony waved. "And this is Gigi. She is one of my best friends in the whole world who does amazing things with furniture."

"Nice to meet you ladies. Shellie, nice to see you again too." Tony smiled, and all four women just stared. "Shellie, it's good you are here too. I would like you to hear what I have found out about the Logan case."

"Oh, I don't think I can stay. I gave Gigi a ride here. I will need to get her home." Shellie remembered and started for her purse and keys.

Peggy waved her off and motioned for her to sit down. "I can give Gigi a ride home, no worries. Hey, since the boys will be home later, and since Shellie and Tony are here, why don't you keep the food with you? I will get my bowls later. That okay with you, Gigi?"

"Sounds good. Hey, wanna go grab a quick coffee on the way to my house?" Gigi grabbed her purse and picked up some of Peggy's supplies. "I can help you get this to the car. Let's get out of here so that they can get to work."

"Anna, just give me the money for my expertise when I get the bowls. I know you are good for it, and I also know where you live. I will see y'all later, and hopefully you too, Tony." Peggy waved with her one free hand. With that, she and Gigi were out the front door and gone.

Anna plopped down on the couch beside Shellie. Tony sat in one of the oversized leather chairs that sat opposite the coffee table. "So, must be some pretty interesting stuff you got on her. Let's have it. Wait, I have to get my notes and a pen." Anna ran into the kitchen and grabbed a pen and her workbag. Back on the couch, she was ready for him to lay it out.

"Okay, so, Melanie has cleaned up over the last few years. She is quite a wealthy woman. Look." Tony laid out some printed-out emails from the estates office. "This is just what I got when I asked a couple of questions, but this is more than enough to get you started with your conversation with them on Tuesday. I thought the sooner you had it, the more time you would have to plan your meeting."

Anna and Shellie took some papers and started reading. They spoke and pointed and shared, and Anna started making notes. Tony watched them work and talk, and checked his email to see if anything else had come in. Anna sat back and read; Shellie took a page from Anna's legal pad and jotted down a few things too.

"This is crazy. Absolutely crazy. She is sitting on roughly over two million dollars, and there is still some property in her name. You guys were there the other day. Mr. Logan didn't give any indication that she was loaded or that he knew that she had this kind of money. Right?" Anna was dumbfounded. That didn't happen too often. "Where is she keeping it?"

Tony had tried to piece as much together as he could before heading to Anna's. "It seems that the homes that she inherited are still actually in the name of the deceased. As you know, until they draw up another deed, the will of the deceased acts as the deed. She would only have to change it if she went to sell it. So the cabin in the mountains is still in the name of Mr. Hampton. The home of Mr. Chambers, her husband before Mr. Logan, is still in his name." Tony shuffled some papers. "And as best as I can tell, she probably has an account in one of her aliases, or previous names, maybe maiden, and it isn't in her actual name she uses now. Does that make sense?"

"She is a nut. A dangerous, greedy nut." Shellie struck again with her quick summation of the information before them.

"This will be great to help me when I talk to them on Tuesday. This will be really good. I will just need to craft how I bring this up and start to question her about her assets when she wants him to change his will to give everything to her." Anna sat staring at the notes as she talked. "I think Ms. Melanie might have just met her match with the Logan family, and we are going to make certain of it."

"Just be careful. All three of us know what she is capable of, and if you bring up information that she isn't wanting Mr. Logan to know, you may make a quick jump up on her list of people she wants to off. Just watch yourself. You too, Shellie. Just don't put yourselves in any undue danger. Let this system work and watch yourself," Tony cautioned Anna and Shellie. "Once this is opened up and the deceit is brought to light, you won't be able to stop her anger. Just like when you peel an onion, you can't put the layers back on the way they were. Once you expose her, then the game is on."

"Got it." Anna winked at Tony. She smiled at Shellie. "We can be professional and careful. No doubt about that. We will shock you at how professional we are."

"All right, sounds suspicious, but good. Just see that you are careful." Tony stood up and gathered his notes. "I am going to get out of your way and let you guys talk and hopefully enjoy the rest of your Sunday. By the way, your hair looks good too, Shellie. You guys think Peggy could do anything for my hair?"

"Ha, your hair is perfect just the way it is, very nice. I like it a lot." Anna just kept right on talking long after her brain had told her to shut up. "You look good. You don't need any fixing." *Shut up.* Anna's brain actually just told her to shut up.

"Well, thanks for that. You look good too." Tony cleared his throat and turned toward the door. "I will see you guys tomorrow if I get any new information. If not, I will check in after your meeting on Tuesday. I hope this really helps get her away from Logan. He does not need that kind of crazy, and I hope he makes it out of her grasp."

Anna and Shellie followed him to the door. "Thanks again for coming over. We really appreciate it." Anna watched him walk out onto the porch and turn around. "You have been a real help, a godsend. Thanks!"

"You know what," Shellie said, "I am going to head home too. I need to do a few things to get ready for tomorrow. Thanks for everything today, Anna. I will see you in the morning." Shellie picked her purse up off the hall table and grabbed her keys. "I will get my bowls later. Let the boys clean out the food. I know how much they love Mexican." Shellie was out on the porch with Tony.

"Well, fine, y'all just leave me all alone. Fine." Anna smiled, then she noticed the boys pulling into the driveway and heading toward the garage. "I guess it is later than I thought if my hoodlums are home. Thanks again, both of you. I will talk tomorrow." Anna stepped back to close the door. "Y'all be careful." Anna waved as she shut the door and then headed to meet her guys in the kitchen.

CHAPTER 18

Anna had prepared and thought, thought and prepared, until she had a headache. She needed to calm herself before the meeting with Mr. and Mrs. Logan. She had been a hot mess all day yesterday at work, and her Monday-night dinner with the boys and her daddy had been a good break from all the worry and fret over this meeting today. Her boys and her daddy had always been able to get her out of just about any funk and bring her back around to realizing the world will keep right on spinning, the sun will rise and set, no matter how much she worried. That she needed to stop herself and enjoy the moment. That was what mattered; truly that was what mattered in life.

What mattered most in life right now was this meeting. She had her mind prepared on how it was going to go. She had not prepped Mr. Logan at all; didn't want to risk losing the shock value of him finding out about his wife's years of windfalls from her previous ill-fated husbands. She needed that raw emotion of hurt, confusion, and anger to drive the meeting in the direction that she was hoping it would take. This was not the nicest tactic in the world, but it was proven in wars and in other legal cases. Shock and awe: shock them with information, and then awe them with whatever chaos ensues.

Anna made sure she looked amazing. You have to look your best when you are going to face down a lying, conniving man-killer. Or at least that was how she thought about it. She had a very special part of her closet for just that. Usually she didn't deal with killers, but some divorces almost came down to that…so the section of her closet was born. Today Anna had chosen a black pencil skirt, a red-and-black silk shirt with a bow that tied just below the V-neck, and a little black fitted jacket. She had on her black Jimmy Choos, and with the red accent, his trademark, on the bottom of the soles, she was a force to be reckoned with for sure. Her hair was spot-on; half up, half down, highlights shining.

The morning had gone by swiftly, and she was only about a half hour away from the meeting. She stepped into the bathroom and retouched her makeup, brushed her teeth, and did a final check on her hair. She stopped by and sat for a moment in her chair by Shellie's desk. "So, this is make-it-or-break-it time. Okay, if when we go into my office, somehow the door gets closed, find a reason to bring me something and leave it at least a little cracked. I want you to be able to hear well when you're eavesdropping. You take good notes and even better mental ones. Those could really come in handy." Anna smiled. Talking with Shellie always calmed her before a big meeting. Somehow she thought this one would be the biggest of her career so far.

"When they get here, just IM me, tell me what they are like together, and act like you are very busy. I will come out and get them. Do not act like you have met Mr. Logan before. Remember, we are supposed to be just meeting both of them." Anna got up and walked across the room to her office door.

"Aye, aye, captain. Roger that. Ten-four. Crystal clear. Okey-dokey." Shellie was nervous, trying to hide it with cute little sayings. Nice try.

Anna went into her office and shut the door. She poured herself a Mountain Dew, sat back, and waited for the couple to arrive. She pulled up Pinterest on her phone, scrolled through it, and looked at yummy food ideas and cute outfits. She particularly loved the Kermit memes that said some of the things she wished she could say in real life. You go, Kermit! She was happy to live vicariously through that little green frog. An IM popped up on her screen.

> ALERT: The Birds have landed. I repeat, the Birds have landed, in the waiting area and are not talking at all. She looks pissy and he looks defeated.

IT'S IN THE BAG

Anna quickly typed a reply.

> OK, Be out in a few. Drinking my Mt. Dew. Making her sweat a little. And the correct saying is 'The eagle has landed.' For future reference. Make a note. LOL!

Anna stood up, downed the rest of her drink, and prayed she didn't burp like a sailor while she was talking to the couple. She used to pride herself on making the boys laugh with her burps and farts. Mommas of little boys. But since the bag and the absence of a butthole now…the farting was out of the question and her burping had taken on less fun and appeal. Now they just tell her how gross she was. The word they used is "cringe." Gotta love teenage slang. Anna was determined to use that correctly in a sentence one day before she died. Here goes nothing.

Anna stood at her door, took a deep, cleansing breath like they did on the videos she saw on Pinterest about relaxing and yoga…and opened the door. Her eyes focused on Mr. Logan, sitting with a very grumpy look on his face. He was doing wonderfully with the act that they had never met. As Anna walked toward the couple, Mrs. Logan turned in her seat. She was an attractive lady; her dress, her hair, and her nails, all beautiful. She was slim, but not too skinny. If Anna had just met her on the street or at a restaurant, she would think she was one of her momma's snooty friends or a corporate worker. Too bad she was a man-killer… She would have fit in nicely at the club on Monday nights.

"Good afternoon, Mr. and Mrs. Logan, correct?" Anna smiled as she stood beside them. They stood and nodded. "My name is Anna Dawson. I have been looking forward to meeting both of you. Come on into my office and have a seat. You can choose the conference table or by my desk. Whichever you prefer."

The couple both rose from their chairs, and Mr. Logan held out his hand to Anna. "My name is Richard Logan. It is nice to meet you. This is my wife, Melanie. We are happy you could meet with us. Our will has been something we have been discussing for some time." They both walked into Anna's office, and Anna followed. She was thankful she was able to leave the door mostly open.

Richard and Melanie took the chairs in front of Anna's desk. Anna was happy about that; she had played out the scene many times, and this had been how it was. She silently said a thank-you prayer to the Lord. "Can I get either one of you a beverage, water, tea, coffee?" Anna asked before she took her seat.

"No, thank you, I am just fine. I just came from a lunch with some friends," Melanie said, and Richard waved off the offer.

"We met each other here. I came from the house, and she already had plans to be in town today. This worked out perfectly." Richard was so very kind; he now smiled and seemed calmer. Melanie, on the other hand, looked like she was about to be booked into the county jail. If Anna had anything to do with it, that would be the case, sooner rather than later.

"Okay, it is my understanding that you, Mr. Logan, have a will that was prepared some time ago. Is that correct?" He nodded to Anna's question. "And Mrs. Logan, it is my understanding that you do not currently have a will to speak of, and for those reasons, you both are here today." Anna looked at the couple and specifically at Melanie. Doing this for years, Anna had become quite the judge of character.

"Yes, my first wife and I had wills made years ago," Mr. Logan began. "She passed away, and Melanie and I got married a little bit ago. I hadn't given it much thought, but Melanie thinks it would be a good time to redo the will that I have."

"As you know, life events can occur, and we have no control over those," said Anna. "It is sometimes necessary that a will needs to be updated, redone, or codicil your current one. With your first wife's passing, and with your remarriage, it would seem that one of those things is certainly in order. There are some questions I need to ask you before we begin." Mr. Logan agreed, and Melanie looked even more squirrelly. "Did you bring a copy of the current will that you have, Mr. Logan? If not, I can get one at the estates office. I have sent a request for information to be sent so that I can work with the information from your wife's passing. I saw that you started an estate

IT'S IN THE BAG

and acted as her executor. Correct?" Again Mr. Logan nodded, and Melanie looked like she was going to pass out.

"I did, even though most everything went to myself and the kids. We have three adult children. There were some distributions that she wanted made upon her passing to some charities and organizations. All debts in her name were paid in full and the estate is now closed." Mr. Logan looked at Melanie and smiled and even reached over and patted her hand. Nice touch.

"Now, Mrs. Logan, I assume you would like to do a will as well. I would highly recommend it. I have requested your information as well, so I can do one for you too. It will all be part of the same fee, so it is good to get yours done too. No one knows when they will be in their last day on earth, except the Lord, of course, and it is much better to die with a will than not. You do not ever want children or extended family fighting over every cent and lampshade. That can tear a family apart."

The first words Melanie had actually spoken in a sentence form at this meeting were very telling. "How did you get my information? I did not authorize that, and no, I do not want my own will done. We are here for his, not mine. I am perfectly fine. I have no children, and if I die, my husband will get my belongings. Done and done." Melanie was a feisty one for sure. Snippy was more like it.

"That is fine, Mrs. Logan, not a problem at all. So as it stands right now, all of your assets would go to Mr. Logan. That is how you want it, correct? There aren't any charities, entities, spiritual organizations, anything you would like to bequeath a gift to? I have records that you have in excess of two million in cash and two properties, is that correct? From five previous husbands' estates? All of whom sadly passed away shortly after marrying you?" Anna could be snippy too.

This divulgence of information apparently did not sit too well with Mr. Logan. He turned to Melanie and gave her a look that really didn't need words, but he threw those in too. "Two million dollars? You have two million dollars? And where is this property?"

Anna couldn't help but correct him. "Just to be clear, over two million, and there are two properties. One a house, from her marriage most recently—before yours, that is—to a Mr. Chambers.

There was a terrible boating accident, it seems. And there is a cabin in the mountains, not too far from Pressley Heights, just near the Tennessee line. Didn't even bother pulling the comps on the prices of those properties."

Now Melanie was shooting her icy daggers directly at Anna. Knowing full well she had just been outed in numerous lies, she finally turned her attention to Mr. Logan. "Honey, I just didn't tell you about the money because I wanted you to love me, well, for me. The money is nice and all, but I didn't want it to cloud your feelings for me. We can work all that out later. We are here to fix your will, not worry about what I have or may have. This lady can just do yours really quick and we can talk about doing mine later."

"Mrs. Dawson, I really don't want to change my will now, with this new information coming to light. My children will inherit my business, and my oldest will inherit the house. At that time, he can decide whether to keep it or sell it. If he sells the home, he must split the profit from the house, equally, three ways. Seeing that my wife here is sitting pretty with her own nest egg, greater than what I could give her, what are my rights to it if she were to pass before me…and what can I do to protect myself, since I seem to think she has bad luck with husbands? Am I in some kind of danger?"

"Well, Mr. Logan, as far as being in any kind of danger, you have to be the judge of that. I cannot do that for you, but without your wife having a will, and not seemingly wanting one, it would stand to be that if no other heirs came forward with a right to the money or property, then by marriage, you would be entitled to it. That is barring any other legal claims on the property and funds." Anna was as truthful as she could be.

Melanie was getting hotter and hotter the longer she sat there. "Richard, I cannot believe that you would even think I had something to do with any of my husbands' passing. I am appalled that you would even spend a moment thinking I would ever do anything to hurt anyone, especially people I love. I cannot believe you."

"Quite frankly, Melanie, I am appalled that you have been married, what, over five times, and they are all dead now. That looks suspicious, and even more so since you didn't have the decency to be

IT'S IN THE BAG

honest with me and tell me how many men there have been that you have sent to an early grave, whether by your hand or just bad luck of being married to you." Richard sat there for a moment. "And you are the only reason that we are here. It was your idea for me to change my will. What, am I next on your list? Are you going to off me?"

"Oh my Lord, Richard, would you listen to yourself? Let's go home and talk this out, in private. I don't think this is the proper place to work out our differences. Let's go home and talk." Melanie wanted out of there fast.

"I don't think it is a good idea for you to come home tonight. I think I need some time. You need to get a room somewhere, and I will pay for it. I just need some space to think. I do not want you at the house tonight." Richard was doing well.

"Where in the hell do you think I am going to go? I am not staying in a hotel room. I am not. I am coming home. That is my home too. We are married. You cannot do that to me." Melanie was getting rather flustered. "You better just watch yourself, Richard Logan. When you said, 'I do' to me, that sealed it. I get whatever you have."

"I really don't care where the hell you stay, but you will not be at the house tonight, I assure you that. If you show up there, I will call the police. Don't try me, Melanie. I did marry you, and I cannot for the life of me figure out how you snowed me into that, but it must be the same way you did all those other poor saps who married you. You will not do to me what you did to them." Richard was a champ at being strong and forceful.

"I swear, Richard, you will be sorry. I really hope you come to your senses quick. If you don't, you will regret it. I assure you that. I could be the best thing that ever happened to you. You really don't want to mess with me." Melanie just realized she needed to rein it in a little; she was letting her inner psycho show. She flipped an internal switch; total calm and reassuring replaced anger and threats, instantly. "Okay, honey, it looks like we have some things to work out. I will agree to stay at the Hilton tonight. You go home, relax, think, and we can talk tomorrow and put all this silly misunderstanding over money and things behind us. We can totally put off the will change and look into this another time, with another attorney." Melanie looked at Anna. "No offense, Ms. Dawson."

Anna shook her head. "None taken." Anna needed to get them to leave now. She had seen enough to know that if she didn't do something quick, Mr. Logan wouldn't make it through the night. He had done pissed off her inner demon. He had started his own clock of demise. Anna needed to think fast. "I think it is wise that you both take some time to cool off, regroup, and look at this with fresh eyes in the morning. Maybe even with a professional. Get everything out in the open, and I am certain all will work out for the best. Does that sound like a plan?"

"Richard, since we drove separately anyway, I will just go reserve a room and do some shopping. I will call you in the morning. Do you want to meet somewhere to talk this out then?" Melanie was getting up and collecting her purse. "I really want us to get past this. We can, you know."

Anna mentally willed Richard to agree to Melanie's plan, just do it, and get her out of here. Agree, get home, and set the alarms. Anna felt in her gut that the trap had been set, and Richard just needed to set it in motion to catch her in the act.

"Sound good, honey. I want to make this work. I do." Richard looked at his wife. "Let's meet at the diner on the bypass at ten. How is that?"

"Sounds great, Richard. I look forward to seeing you in the morning. Sleep well!" The couple headed toward the door. Melanie looked back at Anna. "Thank you for the meeting, Ms. Dawson. I hope you have a lovely afternoon. It was a pleasure."

"All mine. Best to you both," Anna said with a smile and a chill down her spine.

CHAPTER 19

Anna waited to hear the door at the bottom of the staircase close before she came all the way out of her office.

"Get your purse, Shellie. Grab the office camera, some snacks, and some drinks. We are going to have a long evening. We are going to make sure Mrs. Logan does her shopping, gets settled into the Hilton, and doesn't budge. If she does, we do too."

Anna turned and was in her office in a flash. She kicked off her Jimmy Choo's, slid on her most reliable flip-flops, and grabbed her purse. She stuffed it with granola bars, a few cans of Mountain Dew, and a pack of gummy bears.

Shellie did as Anna had asked, but she had so many questions. "What are we doing, Anna? Are we going to die? I really don't want to die tonight, because if I die, I really wanted to be better dressed. Have you ever heard that the outfit you are wearing when you die is the outfit you wear for all eternity? This is not my best look." Shellie smoothed out her black-and-white polka-dot shirt and her black pants. "I really didn't want to do dots for eternity."

"Oh my Lord, Shellie, we are going to follow a woman around for the night. We aren't going to compete in a cage match to the death. We will probably go hang out at the mall and sit in the Hilton parking lot near her car for the evening. We will need to grab your phone charger too." Anna was peeking out of the window down to the sidewalk. "Hurry up, woman, we need to go. We need to be able to head out when she does. They are having a lively discussion on the side of the building, right down below my window."

"All right, let's go. I have everything. Let me just say, this is the craziest thing you have ever had me do. Isn't this called stalking?" Shellie started down the stairs.

"No, this is not stalking. This is called good police work." Anna shut off the lights and started down the stairs too.

"Then why isn't the police doing this? Why are we?" Shellie stopped to look at Anna. "We don't know what we are doing."

"Good grief, Shellie, how hard is it? Come on and act natural. Let's just get to my van and then we can catch up to her. Looks like she is in that silver BMW." Anna made a mental note of the make, model, and license plate number.

The two makeshift deputies made their way to Anna's van and circled back around the block just in time to see Melanie pull out of her parallel parking spot and turn down toward the Hilton. The ladies followed her to the turn in to the hotel. Melanie made her way to the underpass, got out of the car, and went inside. The valet took her car and parked it in a spot close to the entrance. Anna found a parking spot in the lot across from the hotel, facing the front doors. Luckily, this fancy-schmancy hotel didn't have back doors, only the front main doors and the side closest to where Anna parked. It was well-lit; they would be able to see if she left out either door.

"Do you think we need to call Tony to let him know what we are doing?" Shellie, the ever-present voice of reason.

"No, and you had better not. There is no reason to call him. We don't know anything right now, and no crime has been committed. We don't need him. We have so got this." Anna looked at Shellie with her best "don't you dare" look. "I need to call the boys and my momma. They will need to stay with their grandparents tonight. I will tell them we are working late and that they need to eat there and whatever." Anna made the call to the boys, squared away that they would stay with Grams and Gramps and that Shellie and she were working late on the Logan case.

A couple of hours went by with less than anything exciting happening. Anna thought she had watched a drug deal, right in front of her, but she wasn't sure. Pretty sure something wasn't 100 percent on the up and up, but that wasn't her main concern at the moment. She was dead set on keeping her eye on Melanie. She wasn't going to let her try to do anything to Mr. Logan, not tonight.

IT'S IN THE BAG

"I am getting hungry. These granola bars aren't quite cutting it for me. It is past my dinnertime, Anna. We didn't plan this stakeout very well. Gosh, a steak sounds good right now." Shellie wasn't helping Anna or herself keep the hunger at bay.

Anna rustled in her purse. "Here, here is my stash of gummy bears. Do not eat all the pineapple ones, those are my favorite. The clear ones—those are all mine." Anna handed her the bag and watched her open it. Anna reached for a couple and popped them in her mouth. "I love gummy bears. I thought when I got this bag I would have to give them up, but no, and I still take my gummy vitamins too. All good!"

Shellie and Anna sat talking, laughing, and eating whatever they could scrounge up in the van. Anna caught sight of Melanie walking out to the valet from the front door. "Look, there she is. She is getting her car. Where could she be thinking of going?" The two watched as she tipped the valet, got into her car, and pulled to the entrance to the street. Anna started the van and slowly pulled to where she could see the direction Melanie was turning.

"So, we follow her and then what? What if she sees us?" Shellie was getting nervous and eating all the bears.

"First off, go easy on the bears, Shel. That is the last of the provisions that we have currently. It isn't exactly a balanced diet, but it will work." Anna maneuvered the van through the night just far enough back from Melanie to keep her in sight. "Did I ever tell you about when I was closing on the house and I had both the boys with me? They were, gosh, four and two. It was taking forever, and they were getting hungry. We had gone through all the snacks I had brought. Except for a bag of York Peppermint Patties. The kids love them to this day." Anna smiled at the memory. "Mom of the year right there, feeding your kids a bag of chocolate candies."

"Look, she is pulling into the hardware store. Who goes to a hardware store at eight thirty at night? Why would she go there? She is staying at the Hilton. She making repairs?" Shellie was getting into this now. "There she goes, into the store."

Anna took out her phone and opened the camera. She took a couple of photos of Melanie's car outside the store, then she zoomed in on the door, just enough to see when she came out. "I will try to get some photos of her and hopefully what she is getting. This might be some good evidence."

"Look, the door is opening. Here she comes." Anna snapped some pictures and then put the phone down. "What's that she has? It looks like a big roll of paper, like the kind you put down to keep weeds out of your flower beds. You know she doesn't need that for tonight at the Hilton, and their yard looks like they have it professionally maintained. You saw it. Hmmm."

"Looks like she's leaving. I wonder where she is going now?" Shellie handed Anna the bag of bears. "She's backing out. Get ready to go."

Anna started the van and looked down into the bag of bears. Only the clear ones remained. Such a good friend, that Shellie. "Thanks for the pineapple ones. You are the best." Anna popped a couple in her mouth and pulled out onto the street. She gave just enough headway for Melanie to get a couple of cars in front of her. "Blinker is already on...what? Look. She's turning into the gas station. I'm going to pull into the bank parking lot." Anna made an illegal maneuver and jerked the van into the bank parking lot. "Sorry about that."

"No need to apologize to me, but those three cars that about hit us. You might need to offer them one. Great job not drawing any attention to us, Anna. I bet no one heard all those horns honking." Shellie rolled her eyes. Good thing Melanie had quickly gotten out and gone into the convenience store of the gas station. "Maybe she got hungry buying all those rolls of paper. I bet she is getting a snack."

Anna snapped a few more photos and waited. Melanie emerged carrying three red portable gas containers. She stopped by her car and put her card into the gas pump, pushed a few buttons, and proceeded to fill each one up. Anna took more photos. "Those are what, five-gallon containers? That is going to stink to high heaven if she puts those in her car. This lady is a freak show. I know she isn't going to mow the grass, and she apparently doesn't need gas for her car... This is starting to get weird."

IT'S IN THE BAG

"Starting to? Please, this was weird from the time we met the three grown kids of Mr. Logan. Remember the spit cup guy? I bet he is a hoot. He seems like a honey badger, you know, those that don't give a shit." Shellie laughed at her own joke. Shellie loved the viral video of the honey badger narrated by a guy with a thick accent. "He looks like he knows how to have a good time, though."

"After all this, I could probably get you his number if you'd like. You could be his good-time girl." Anna laughed but was dead serious. Shellie needed to get out there. Broaden her horizons. Anna's attention snapped back to the task at hand. "She's getting ready to leave again. Watch for me while I get to the exit."

"She's turning toward the hotel again. You don't think she's just going back to the hotel now with all that gas in her car? She would never get that smell out of there if they sit in there all night." Shellie was pointing left.

"I don't think she is going back to the hotel at all. I just don't know where she is going." Anna followed, just close enough not to lose her. She followed Melanie back toward the hotel, but her BMW made a turn before she made it to the Hilton. The car slowed and turned into the French Toast Hut, the all-night eatery, obviously known for their French toast. "Looks like she's hungry." The two ladies watched as Melanie made her way into the diner and took a seat by the window, her back to the van parked at the end of the large parking lot. Anna turned off the van and the lights. "Looks like we are going to be here for a bit. Might as well sit back for a little bit."

"I'm starving. I could really go for some French toast right now." Shellie looked as if she would cry. "I might not make it, Anna. Those gummy bears have moved along and are gone. I need to pee too." Shellie was just a whiney ball of herself tonight. "What am I supposed to do about that? I wasn't prepared to do an all-night watch-the-crazy-lady adventure."

"There are some bushes behind the van. It's dark. Go do your business." Anna kept her eye on Melanie. She was placing her order now. Anna looked over at Shellie, who was staring at her. "What? Go pop a squat and pee."

"I am not peeing in the parking lot of the French Toast Hut. Nope, not going to do it. I will pee in your van before I do that," Shellie protested.

Anna looked at Shellie, opened her door, walked around to the back of her van, and proceeded to "pop a squat" and pee. When her business was done, she came back to the driver's side, slid into her seat, and shut the door. She looked at Shellie out of the corner of her eye. "Man, I really had to go. I feel so much better. Ahhh." Anna looked back at Melanie in the diner, waiting on her food.

"Sometimes you are quite the smartass, Anna." Shellie opened her door. "Be right back."

*****

Tony didn't have a good feeling, deep down in the pit of his stomach. He thought for sure he would hear from Anna after the meeting with the Logans. He knew it was that afternoon and that it would probably take quite some time, but it was now getting dark and he didn't like it one bit. He didn't plan on her to get back with him that evening, but he thought she would have at least one story to share about the infamous Melanie Logan.

He picked up the phone to text and immediately put it back down. He didn't want to seem like he was stalking her, but he couldn't shake that feeling. He had driven by her office after work and the lights looked like they were all off and he didn't see her van in any of the spots around the office. He knew sometimes she parked in the deck, but he did today, and he didn't see her van there either. Maybe she and Shellie had gone out to dinner, or maybe she had something to do at the school tonight. He was probably worrying about nothing.

A quick text to Jake would calm his mind. If anything were going on with Anna, he would be the first to know. Tony typed a quick text to him and hit send. It wasn't but a couple of minutes when the reply came through asking Tony to call. This couldn't be good. He dialed Jake's number and waited for him to answer.

IT'S IN THE BAG

The conversation wasn't long, but it was long enough. Jake had found out when he got home that the boys were staying with him and Darcy that night. Anna had called the boys after work and told them to stay with their grandparents that night since she and Shellie would be working on the Logan case late. Tony hadn't gotten to the bottom of where Anna was, or if she and Shellie were all right, but he had accomplished one thing. He got Jake riled up enough to start looking into where his daughter might be.

Tony decided to go by Anna's house, her office, and any of the places she had mentioned to him about liking to go. Maybe they were working on notes over coffee or something like that and just lost all track of time. That had to be it. Jake had told Tony to call him with any information, saying that if he needed him, he was headed back to the office.

*****

Anna was going to have to figure out something to feed Shellie. Shellie was looking in the glove compartment for random crumbs and stale french fries from when the boys were little and would throw them around the van.

"She sure isn't talking much to anyone, Anna. The waitress just scoots by, fills up her coffee, and goes on her way. No small talk, no chitchat. Isn't that odd?" Shellie stopped her scrounging for a moment to observe their person of interest.

"I am no expert in the life of crime or anything, but I wouldn't think that if I were planning to do something horrid to a person that I would want to chitchat about it with the waitress at the diner in town. That would just prove intent." Anna laughed. Then something caught her eye. "Look, Shel, she got her bill. She's getting up to pay."

"Well, at least she has the common decency to pay for her meal. I mean, I would think that if you kill people like it's nothing, you wouldn't have any difficulty walking out of the diner without paying. That whole life-of-crime thing." Shellie shut the glove compartment and put her seat belt back on.

"Okay, let's see where she's going now." Anna waited to start the van until Melanie had pulled out and turned right down the street. "Looks like we still aren't going back to the hotel. She is turning out to be a night owl."

Anna and Shellie followed the little car for quite some time, winding through streets, and then things started looking familiar, even in the night's darkness. They were heading toward the house Melanie shared with Richard. "We're headed toward Richard's. She isn't supposed to go there tonight. What time is it anyway?" Anna looked over at the clock on the dash. "It's almost 11:30 p.m. She has no business there at this time of night…and with all that gas, and the weird rolls of paper? Oh my, Shellie, I think I know what she is going to do. We have got to warn Richard. She is going to try to kill him, right there in his house."

"What do we do? What?" Shellie looked at Anna. "What do you need me to do?"

"Grab my phone and look up Richard Logan. Dial his number and put him on speaker." Anna stayed farther back now that she knew where Melanie was headed. She was going to let her do her thing to a point and then she would have her. Caught in the act.

Anna talked to Richard. He was the only one in the house. The house was locked and the alarm set. Of course, Melanie still had a key and knew the code, but that should work in Anna's favor. She instructed Richard on what to do, to stay quiet, no matter what he heard downstairs. That she and Shellie were just down the street and they would be keeping an eye on Melanie and the house. They would call back when they knew more and when it was safe for him to come down. With that squared away, it was time to park the van and head off on foot.

Anna parked the van on the side of the road, two houses down from the Logans'. Anna made sure she got her gun out of the purse and grabbed her phone. She also made a mental note to not wear skirts, especially on the shorter side, to meetings that may turn into stakeouts. Shellie and Anna got out of the van and slowly made their way toward the Logans' driveway. With it being a longer driveway and the probability that Melanie had driven closer to the house with

IT'S IN THE BAG

all that she had bought, it was a safe bet that they could go up the road and down the drive just a bit.

"Flip-flops are not the proper foot attire for this kind of walking. Do you know that those are murder on your feet? You always complain about how your feet hurt. Look at your shoe choices." Shellie shook her head and stayed in step with Anna. "I just try to help you out. Keep you from some pain."

"Thanks, Shellie," Anna whispered. "Let's come back to that topic when we are not sneaking through a neighborhood trying to catch a crazy woman killing her husband. Priorities. Now, shhh!" Anna took a detour, through the woods, in the dark. There was just enough room for the two to walk between the mature trees and thankfully not a great deal of low-growing plants to step over or around. "Wait, I can see the house, and there is the car. See? The outside lights were on by the front door. Thank the Lord the Logans liked outdoor accent lighting. See her? She's unloading the gas cans now, onto the front porch." Anna took out her phone and snapped some pictures, and the two women eased up closer.

"Anna, look, she's opening the front door. Looks like she just turned off the alarm." Shellie tapped Anna's arm and motioned that they could go closer. They made their way to the rock wall just between the two properties. Melanie was coming back out to her car. She grabbed the roll of black paper and walked back toward the house.

Anna got a few more photos, and they watched as Melanie disappeared into the house with the paper. The two ladies were totally fixated on watching what was going to happen next and didn't even notice the slow approaching footsteps behind them. In an instant, both Anna and Shellie's mouths were covered with a large, strong hand. The person behind them had a strong hold and only spoke once. They quit shaking. Anna was trying to get a good hold on her gun. "*Shhh!* It's me, Tony. Please don't keep reaching for your gun." His voice triggered an immediate sense of relief. His hands came away from the women's mouths and he wiped his hand on his pants. He looked directly at Anna. "Did you really have to lick my hand so much? It's such a weird feeling. Gross if it hadn't been you."

"What in the hell are you doing here?" Anna was mad as a hornet. "How did you know we were here? I specifically didn't tell you or anyone where we would be. We didn't even know where we would be."

"I can ask you the same thing, Miss Thang. You are not trained to handle a situation like this. What is even going on? I found your van back up the street and just followed the scent of your perfume." Tony sniffed her neck. "Yep, that is you."

Anna sniffed herself and didn't smell anything. "Well, since you are here and obviously not going anywhere, be quiet. We have watched her all evening. She is supposed to be staying at the Hilton tonight. Richard needed some time after our meeting. She has bought black tar paper, three gas canisters, and gas, and now she is in the house with the paper. I called Richard, and he is aware she is in the house. He is upstairs, waiting on word from me to come out."

"She is going to try to burn the house down, with him in it. She is counting on him being in bed asleep." Tony pulled out his phone. "I need to call and get some deputies out here for backup and put the fire department on alert. Don't worry, no sirens. Nothing until we have something to charge her with." Tony made a few calls, then returned his attention to the house.

"I have taken photos all night, every step of the way," Anna said proudly. "Look, she's coming out now…she's unrolling the rest of the paper there on the porch." The trio watched in silence as she looked back toward the entryway of the house. Then she turned and walked slowly toward the first gas can. She carried it back into the house, and in a few minutes, came out and got the second one. Anna snapped pictures as Melanie moved methodically, like a machine. With the third gas can, she only was inside for a few seconds, and then she stood on the porch and poured the gasoline all over the last part of the paper, then all around on the porch. She slowly made a trail out toward the driveway. "She is getting ready to light it. We have got to stop her." Anna started moving, and neither Tony nor Shellie could stop her. She was walking straight toward the house. She was making a video now, holding the phone with her left hand and she had placed her gun in her right.

IT'S IN THE BAG

Anna stopped and watched as Melanie stood there, in the driveway, pulled a pack of matches out of her back pocket, took a match, and struck it on the back. The glow of the match cast a warm light onto Melanie's face, her expression hard as stone. She was evil. She had to be stopped. Anna cleared her throat, and Melanie's head snapped in Anna's direction. She just smiled at Anna and then dropped the match.

Immediately, the gasoline ignited and surged toward the front porch. Soon it reached the paper, and a larger flame began to build. Anna dropped her phone and grasped her gun with both hands. Pointing it directly at Melanie, she yelled for her to stop. Melanie turned her body to face Anna and started to slowly walk to her car like she was just going to get in and drive away.

Shellie and Tony were down at the house and pulling the paper away and shutting the front door. Sounds of sirens were now audible in the distance and getting closer by the moment. Richard appeared with two fire extinguishers. Tony and Richard made quick work of putting out the fire. Anna still held the gun on Melanie. Once the fire was out on the porch, Tony came up beside the car and asked Anna to lower the gun. He placed his hand on Melanie's shoulder and asked her to turn and face the car. He quickly put handcuffs on her and sat her down in the yard to wait for the other deputies to arrive. Tony waved the deputies over, and they escorted Melanie to a waiting sheriff's car.

Tony walked slowly toward Anna. "Anna, hand me the gun. You did great. It's over. Let me hold on to that for you." Tony gently eased the gun out of Anna's hands and put it in his waistband. Immediately, Anna fell into his arms, shaking. "It's okay, Anna, everything is okay. You did great, the house is okay, and, most important, Richard is okay, and will be. Because of you."

Tony eased Anna up so that he could see her face. Her big hazel eyes were glossy with something like tears, but she wasn't crying. She had never looked more beautiful to him. Tony wanted so bad to lean in and place his lips on hers, even with all the chaos around them; he felt in that moment it was just her and him, for miles around. But even with his all-consuming want of her, he knew in his heart that this was not the time or place for such a declaration of his feelings.

"Come on, let's get you somewhere to sit down. You are really shaky."

Shellie was beside them and noticed Anna; she knew the signs of dehydration. "She needs something to drink. Quick. Water, please." Shellie bent down in front of Anna while Tony went to get some water for her. "You did great, girl. Now you need to get some fluids in you, and some food. You will collapse if you don't." Shellie brushed the hair back off Anna's forehead. "Look, here comes your dad." Shellie stood. "Hello, Mr. D, you should have seen your daughter. She is a badass." Shellie caught herself. "Sorry, Mr. D. I didn't mean to cuss in front of you."

"Dammit, Shellie, what did you two think you were doing? And Anna out here pointing a gun at a murderer? Good Lord, your momma will never let you out of the house again. She will probably kill me because she'll think I knew about this circus." Jake bent down and picked up Anna and hugged her like he was trying to smoosh her to bits. "I am proud of you, Little One, but damn, what were you thinking?"

"Daddy, I just need to get home. Please. I need something to drink and get home." Anna felt like she was going to collapse. "I just want to get home. My van is right over there, just a couple of houses up. Shellie knows where it is."

"Oh no, Missy, you are not driving." Jake looked around and found Tony. "Tony, I want you to take Anna home and make sure Shellie gets home too. I will get someone to follow me in the van, and I will drop it off at your house. Will you be okay once you get home? Do you need to come to the house and stay?"

Anna shook her head as she downed some water. "I will be fine. I don't think I can drive, but if you promise to have my van home by the morning, I will let Tony drive both Shellie and me home. Daddy, the keys are still in it. So is my purse." Anna looked at Shellie. "Do you mind staying at the house with me tonight? You can sleep in Johnathan's room. I'm sure he has clean sheets." Shellie smiled and put her arm around her friend.

IT'S IN THE BAG

Tony loaded the women up in his car. Jake went down to talk to Richard and to gather all the information for the necessary reports. Anna and Shellie were just ready to go to bed.

CHAPTER 20

Anna told Tony the code for the lockbox hidden on her porch. He quickly made the correct entry and retrieved the spare key to her house. He unlocked the door and let the women enter. Anna told him the code to the security system, and he disarmed it as well. He went outside and replaced the house key and made sure the box was securely locked once again.

"And, Shellie, if I haven't told you yet, we are officially closed tomorrow. How about that? I am the boss. I can do that." Anna smiled and went to get a Gatorade out of the refrigerator. "I am not long out of the bed, but I will tell you what I am coming out of right now." Anna wiggled and wiggled and then she simply pulled her bra out of her shirt sleeve. She had long since lost her jacket somewhere in Tony's car. "Wow, that feels so much better."

Tony snickered and knew he needed to make a gracious exit; quick but gracious. That was the single hottest thing he had seen in a very long time, in person. "While I would love to stay and see what else you can wiggle out of, I had better go. Do you think you ladies can keep it in the road, or at least in the house, tonight without a babysitter?" Tony winked at Anna.

"Yes, Detective Phillips, I do believe I can keep her under lock and key for at least twelve hours. Can't promise much after that. You will have to forgive her. She is a little on the dehydrated side and she hasn't eaten—well, except for half a bag of gummy bears—since lunch. She just needs to finish that Gatorade and get some sleep. She should seem less drunk tomorrow."

"If you need anything, just call or text. I can be here in just a few. I will check on y'all tomorrow. No more stakeouts for a while, okay?" Tony gave Shellie a quick hug, telling her he was glad it all worked out. He went to Anna, who was sitting on the couch, and sat next to her. "I am proud of you, Anna. Y'all did great work tonight. Take care of yourself, and I will check on you tomorrow." Tony was going to just give her a hug, but before he knew it, he had kissed her softly on her forehead. Her reaction was immediate; she leaned in and put her head on his shoulder. Her body relaxed, and she almost instantly fell asleep.

Shellie opened the hall closet and pulled out a blanket and arranged the pillows on one end of the couch so that Tony could lay Anna down off his shoulder. He did and lifted her legs and placed them on the couch. Shellie handed him the blanket, and he covered her and made sure she looked comfortable. He placed the bottle of Gatorade on the floor beside her head and stood and looked at her for a moment. He could feel Shellie's stare on him, so he turned and walked with her to the door.

"You know, she really does like you," Shellie said, and Tony stopped and looked at her. "She does. You'll just need to give her time. Anna can be stubborn, pigheaded, a little anal, but she loves like no other. Her heart is pure, and she is good, to the core. She is good. There are some demons that she has to battle, and I think you are just the one she will do it for. I have known her a very long time, I have been down every road she has, right beside her, and trust me when I say she sees something in you worth fighting those demons for." Shellie smiled and nodded, like it was the most important thing she had ever said. "And one more thing, if you ever hurt her, in any way, I will kill you myself. I look fabulous in stripes, and my favorite color is orange. Goodnight." Shellie walked back inside and shut the door. Tony could hear the deadbolt slide into place.

He stood there, even after Shellie had turned out the porch light, and thought to himself, *What in the world just happened?*

*****

Anna woke up, looked around, and realized that she was on the couch. She felt around, grabbed her phone, and looked at the time. Two thirty-three a.m. Then the pain hit again. Immediately, Anna's brain went into overdrive. She reached down and felt her ostomy bag. Empty. Nothing. Anna's next thought: *Please God no!* She dropped her phone on the floor and wrapped her arms around her stomach.

Her mind was racing. She immediately thought of the boys. She knew that they were safe her parents. Another pain overtook her. She got down on her knees and rocked slowly back and forth like she had been told to do. She needed her heating pad; that was supposed to help too, or a hot shower. She decided to try the heating pad first. She crawled into the den and thanked herself for leaving it plugged up beside the love seat. She rolled over on her back and clicked the heating pad on high. She laid it over her stomach and bag. She willed her small bowel to work.

The heat felt so good, and it did help to take away some of the sharpness of the pains that were coming in waves now. The pains reminded her of contractions when she was in labor with the boys. There would be moments of just a dull ache, and then the more intense and jolting pain would hit and last until the spasm was over. Anna lay there and kept checking her bag. In her mind, she knew now, without a doubt, that she had an obstruction. She had felt these pains before, and with her bag being flat and empty, she knew just how bad this could get if she couldn't get the obstruction to move.

Anna rolled around on the floor until she couldn't stand the pain anymore. She remembered that this movement, walking, and bending were known to help. She climbed up to her feet against the couch and held herself steady during the next rush of pain. She walked slowly, holding on to chairs, stools, and the island. She made what she thought were a million rounds of the island, stopping to bend and catch her breath, in intense bad. She bent over the island and prayed that the Lord would help this pass. She raised her head and looked over at the clock on the stove.: 4:28 a.m. A hot shower was next on her list of things to try.

Anna made it into her bathroom, turned on the shower, and put the temperature to the hottest she thought she could stand. She slowly peeled off the clothes she had on from the day before and checked her bag once again. Nothing. This was not good; not good at all. The last obstruction that she had was after her surgery. Her small bowel was very slow to wake from the seven hours of anesthesia. Finally, after what seemed like an eternity and a nasogastric tube into her stomach, along with people storming heaven with prayers, the obstruction passed, and Anna was able to go home a few days later.

She stepped into the shower and slid the glass door shut. The water felt so good, the heat surrounding her body and helping take some of the edge off. She stood and let the water hit just above her bag and let it run down her body. She then turned and let the water hit her back, just above her hips, as she leaned up against the back wall of the shower. She grabbed a washcloth and managed to wash her body between bouts of pain. Shaving her legs and underarms proved to be a feat that she was determined to accomplish. Not knowing what this day would hold but knowing some sort of doctor visit was in her near future, she needed this much done.

Anna stood there and made plans in her head. If this didn't work, she would need to somehow get ready, grab a few things, and get herself to the hospital. She would need to let the boys know, call Dr. Hyrd, and figure out what to do about her appointments the next couple of days. Anna stood there until the water started to cool and she began to shiver.

She grabbed a towel and slowly dried herself off. She got her hair dried and somewhat presentable. She made her way to her chest of drawers and found a nice pair of lace panties and bra that matched. She may feel like hot death, but she was not going to go down looking like a crazy lady in her granny panties. She had shown her ass to almost everyone in the state of N.C., but she was going to make sure that if she had to today, she was going to represent well. That was a lesson straight from Darcy Dawson herself. She could hear her momma's voice now: "Anna, always make sure you have on clean underwear, always. You never know when you will have to show your ass." Thanks, Momma. Life lessons.

Anna finished off her outfit with a Train concert T-shirt from years ago and some black yoga pants. Not her best look, but it would have to do. Feeling like death was almost imminent, she really didn't care anymore.

Anna checked again, hoping that all that she had been doing was paying off. Nothing. She made a mental note that the last time she emptied her bag was the afternoon of the day before, right before her and Shellie had left to keep an eye on Melanie. She knew that twelve hours without any output was not good. The pains were still enough to make her knees buckle and she knew that she was not going to make it until she is able to call the office at nine. She was going to have to go straight to the hospital. She would wake up Shellie, but first she needed to get her phone, charger, makeup, hairbrush, deodorant…and Murphy, poor cat. Had he been fed yesterday evening? She needed to find Murphy.

Anna got her bag filled with her necessities and started to head toward the kitchen. She ended up crawling and dragging her bag. All of her stirring around and moaning must have roused Shellie and Murphy. Anna found both of them looking at her like she had lost her mind when she made it into the kitchen. Anna stopped when she realized that Murphy was happily eating, and she sat back and leaned up against the wall. Murphy stopped eating for a moment and raised his head, looked at her, and made a loud, "*Meow*."

"You look like you have been out all night drinking… You are not okay, are you?" Shellie came and knelt down in front of Anna.

Anna couldn't speak right off; she was trying not to cry out in pain. Once the pain eased somewhat, she looked up at Shellie. "You need to drive me to the hospital. I have a blockage. I am certain of it. Been up most of the night. I have tried all that I know to do at home to help. I need to get to the hospital and get drugs. Soon."

"Oh, crap. Okay, let me get ready. I look like crap." Shellie was running her fingers through her hair, grabbing her phone. She ran to the front door and then back to the kitchen. She didn't have the heart to tell Anna that her daddy hadn't brought the van like he had promised. Shellie knew Anna would kill her if she (a) called an ambulance, or (b) called her parents. Shellie had only one option. "Let me run upstairs and change. I borrowed some pj's last night from your room. I will get you taken care of." Shellie left Anna on the floor, picked up Anna's phone off the floor by the couch, and ran upstairs to Johnathan's room where her things were. She ran to the bathroom, used the boy's brush to comb her hair. Makeup could be done in the car. Shellie took Anna's phone and looked for Tony's number. That was her only option.

Shellie pulled up his contact info and hit the button to call his cell. It rang, and she waited. After the second ring, he answered.

"Hello, good morning," Tony said, sounding happy to be getting a call from Anna so early.

"Tony, this is Shellie. Look, I need you to listen to me and not ask any questions right now, okay?" Shellie sounded very authoritative. "I need you to get here as soon as you can. Do not call anyone, especially Jake or EMS. Anna is very sick. We need to get her to the hospital very fast. Come now." *Click.*

Shellie ran back downstairs and sat with her friend, telling her that they would be leaving for the hospital very soon.

*****

Tony had just gotten back to his house after an early-morning run. He loved to head out in the mornings to think, clear his head, and work out things that he had been worried or anxious about. Funny thing; his phone rang, and the caller ID had displayed Anna's name and number. She had been on his mind like crazy this morning.

Tony was about to ask a question when Shellie hung up on him. He made sure he had his wallet, keys, and phone, and out the door he ran. He was in his truck and backing out of his driveway in less than a minute. Why didn't Shellie just call 911? What was wrong with Anna? Tony didn't pray too much, but he knew in his heart that there was a God up there handling things, so he said a prayer asking the Lord to help Anna, whatever the issue was.

His mind raced. It could be so many things. She didn't look that good when he had left last night, but he thought she was just tired and needed rest. He pulled into Anna's driveway in less than five minutes.

Shellie met him in the driveway. "You are going to need to help me get her up. I can't get her out here by myself. And Tony." She caught his arm as they walked in the door. "She might be a little mad, a wee bit snippy, but please just remember it is the pain talking, not really her." Tony looked at her and they ran into the kitchen. Anna had slumped into a ball on the floor. She was moaning and grasping at her stomach.

"Oh my God, Anna, what's wrong?" Tony was down at her side in an instant. "What happened?"

"Please just get me to the hospital. Shellie can explain. Please." Anna lifted her head to speak and then put it back down as the pain came back, slowly getting worse.

"Shellie, get her things and be ready to go. I am going to pick her up and put her in the truck. You get in behind my seat and sit with her, okay? Open the passenger-side back door." Tony scooped Anna up in his arms and carried her toward the door. "Just hold on, sweetie, we will be at the hospital in no time. Just hang on, okay?"

Shellie did what Tony instructed. They were in the truck, Anna's alarm had been set, her door locked. Murphy could make it with his gravity feeder for the day. Tony started the truck and started to back out of the driveway.

Anna lifted her head and asked Shellie for her phone. "Tony, I need you to call Daddy, on his cell phone, not the home phone. Tell him you are taking me to the hospital, that I am certain I have a bowel obstruction. Tell him to not tell Momma yet. Tell him he can tell the boys and tell them I will be okay. This is just like what happened last Christmas. Okay? Got it?" Tony nodded. "Shellie, look up Dr. Hyrd's number, under Collin Hyrd in my contacts. Text him that I am on my way to the hospital—obstruction, very bad pain. Nothing for over twelve hours." Shellie started typing away and hit send.

Anna could hear Tony on the phone with her daddy. She knew that Tony probably had so many questions, but she hoped that she could at least get some pain medicine in her before he started asking them. Shellie held up the phone so that Anna could see the reply from Dr. Hyrd. Anna nodded and lay her head back against the window.

"Just pull up to the emergency room entrance. Her surgeon will make sure a nurse is waiting there with a wheelchair," Shellie instructed Tony as he pulled into the hospital entrance. They pulled

IT'S IN THE BAG

under the drive-thru at the entrance to the ER and a nurse was there with a wheelchair. "Right here is good." Tony stopped the truck and put it in park. He got out and opened the door for Anna and helped her into the wheelchair. Shellie came around and pushed Anna's hair out of her face. "We will be right in, just as soon as they will let us back, okay? We are going to park, and I will bring in your bag"

The nurse told Shellie and Tony that it would be a few minutes but that she would come out and get them when they had Anna settled and had her vitals done. "Thanks, we appreciate it," Tony said as he started back around the truck. He climbed in, and Shellie did too, this time in the front seat; she knew there would be questions. Tony looked at Shellie with wide eyes. "Well? Will you please tell me what is going on? She looked horrible, and she is in so much pain. She has a surgeon on speed dial, and he had someone waiting on her to arrive? Spill it."

"Okay, remember last night when I mentioned Anna had a demon? This is it." Shellie started to explain. "Look, Anna has been very sick, for a very long time. She has had Crohn's disease for over twenty years. She also suffers with ankylosing spondylitis. She has been to the best doctors, taken all the best medicines, new medicines, done everything, but her body just wouldn't cooperate. The Crohn's would go into remission for a little while only to come back with even more of a vengeance. In a sense, her immune system sees even her organs and healthy tissue as an invader and works against her. It is fighting her from inside." Shellie took a breath and watched Tony as he tried to digest all this. "You okay?" He nodded. Shellie continued.

"Long story short, Anna has almost died a couple of times, it has gotten so bad, but she has always fought and come back stronger. A few years ago now, she finally had the surgery she was putting off for so long. She had her colon, rectum, anus, appendix, and fallopian tubes removed. They had to do a bunch of repairs internally to fix some of the damage that had been done. It was a seven-hour surgery, done by Dr. Hyrd. There is so much more to the story, but Tony, she was so depressed after getting the ostomy bag." Shellie patted her side, where a bag would be if she had one. "She went into a very dark place and only let very few in. If it hadn't been for her boys and her faith, I don't know whether or not she would have come out of it. But she did. She is still so worried that no one could love her or find her attractive, because of the bag. That is her demon. She has never had a relationship since her divorce. You are the first person I have seen her even consider the thought. That is something. She likes you. Let's just hope that this doesn't set her back. Let's go." Shellie hopped out of the truck, and Tony had to run to catch up.

Shellie and Tony walked into the ER; they took a seat nearest to the door that led into the inner space where the separate rooms were. "I can believe that she has been through all that. She looked so tired and was in so much pain. Will she be okay?" Tony asked, staring straight ahead.

"She has had obstructions before. We will know more when we talk to Dr. Hyrd and Anna." Shellie patted his knee. "I know you have been bombarded with information in a really short amount of time, but please don't give up on her. She will not be happy you found out, or in this way. She hates being here and messing with her schedule, but just don't give up on her. Okay?"

"I don't give up, Shellie. Especially on someone I intend to get to know better." Tony still looked straight ahead. "I just wish she had more faith in me and more confidence in herself. She has been through so much. It would take a mighty small man to find that a reason not to have a relationship with someone. She should know that about me, at least."

The doors to the waiting room opened, and Dr. Hyrd came out. "You both can come on back. Anna was right, she does have an obstruction. We have gotten an IV started and given her some pain medicine. Her BP and pulse were rather high, due to the pain of course, and she was very dehydrated. We had a really hard time getting an IV started. I have ordered an NG tube to be placed, and hopefully, that will relieve some of the pressure and we won't have to do surgery." He stepped aside. "Come on back. She's in room 4. I will be back in. Go on and sit with her."

IT'S IN THE BAG

Tony and Shellie walked down the hall and stood outside room 4. "You go in first. I will be right out here." Shellie nudged his arm. "Quicker war, sooner peace?"

Tony knocked and opened the door. He stuck his head in and saw Anna lying there on the hospital bed; an IV in her arm, dressed in a hospital gown, a blood-pressure cuff strapped around her upper arm, a pulse/ox meter on her finger. He watched for a moment as her heartbeat was mapped out on one of the screens. He looked back down at Anna, who was looking much more peaceful that she did earlier. Her arms were folded across her midsection, not grabbing or holding on to herself for dear life like before. He quietly walked a little closer and looked back at the screens.

"You stayed?" Anna spoke softly, and her eyes fluttered open and focused on him. "I am so sorry for all this."

Tony pulled the chair up close to the bed. "Of course I stayed, where else would I be? Don't worry about anything right now. Just relax and feel better. The doctor said he would be back in to see you in just a little bit. Just rest." Tony watched as her eyes shut, and the look of peace overtook her face again.

Anna's eyes popped open as she heard the door open and saw Dr. Hyrd and his assistant Jessica walk into the room. Tony stood, pushed back the chair, and stood against the wall. "Hello again," Anna whispered. "I sure could use another round of that pain medicine. It's starting to creep up again."

Dr. Hyrd nodded and asked Jessica to go tell the nurse to get another dose ready. "Sure thing. Coming right up." He sat on the side of the hospital bed. "Look, you have a blockage, that is certain, and the films show it is up pretty high. I have ordered an NG tube be placed, and we will hope and pray that relieving that pressure in your stomach will loosen the blockage and things will get working again. If not, we will have to go in and fix it."

Anna, now fighting the pain, which almost as bad as before, reached out and grabbed the doctor's coat. "I do not want anyone else cutting on me other than you. You know me. You have done all the surgeries on me. No one else. Promise?" Anna didn't let go.

Dr. Hyrd let out a little laugh. "You are in luck. I am here all week and on call this weekend. I promise to take care of you." He patted her leg and stood and reached out a hand to Tony. "It is nice to see that she had someone by her side other than the other forty people usually crowded in here anytime she is in the hospital. It is good to see she has someone to love her. She has long shut that part out. Glad to see she has opened that door. You must be some kind of man." The doctor turned back to Anna. "I will check on you once you get to your room. Oh, and by the way, you are being admitted. No ifs, ands, or buts." With that, he was gone.

Tony didn't know what to say or how to react to what Dr. Hyrd said, and Anna, slowly folding into the fetal position once again, didn't look like she was in the mood to talk about relationships. Tony peeked out the door just as the nurse walked in with a tray.

"Good morning, Ms. Anna." A very caffeinated but nice male nurse was putting gloves on before sitting down beside Anna. "I remember you from a while back. You remember me?" Anna nodded. "I am going to be doing the NG tube, and then it is time for another dose of pain medicine. We are also going to give you something to relax you a little also. Sound like a plan?" Anna nodded again. "Do you want this gentleman to stay or step out? Doesn't matter to me."

"He can stay if he wants. Up to him," Anna whispered and took the small cup of water that the nurse handed her. Tony sat down in the chair beside the wall, out of the way.

Within just a few minutes, the tube had been placed through her nose and down into her stomach. The pain medicine had been given, and just before the nurse pushed the plunger on the medicine to relax Anna, he looked at both her and Tony. "This is going to make her really loopy. I will have to put up the bar on the bed, but feel free to scoot up closer and sit by her. She may sleep for a while. I know it has been a long night for her, so sleep may be good." He pushed slowly, and the medicine was in.

Anna's eyes opened and caught Tony's. "I hear her. My momma. She and Daddy are here." Her eyes shut just as fast as they opened. She was officially high on painkillers.

IT'S IN THE BAG

Just then the door to her room opened, and Darcy, Jake, and Shellie all flooded in. Tony stood, trying to get out of the way. Jake took refuge by Tony, Shellie stood at the foot of the bed, and Darcy seemed to climb on top of her daughter, who was doing better than the rest of them, being in narcotic la-la land.

Darcy looked her daughter over and then at all the tubes, the monitors, and then at Jake. "See what all this work stress does to her? Why in the world were the two of you out catching a killer last night? That is not what attorneys do." Darcy now turned her focus to Shellie. "She is fragile, she is sick, and she needs to stop all this craziness. It is going to kill her. All this stress caused her to get this blockage thing again." Darcy was hysterical and crying now, lying over Anna like she had just breathed her last breath.

"I really don't think it was work that caused this, Mrs. D. I think it has something to do with the bag of gummy bears she ate last night for dinner. While we were out catching a killer lady." Shellie just told it like it was. "Pretty sure it was the gummy bears. She isn't fragile, Mrs. D. With all due respect, Anna is probably one of the strongest people I know. All company included in that."

"Now, now, ladies. Let's just know that she is in the best place that she can be, with the best doctor. She will never eat gummy bears again for dinner, and we will get her through this. Shel, have you canceled the appointments for today and the rest of the week?" Jake took charge, thank the Lord, and Shellie nodded. "Okay, I am going to take Darcy home so she can worry and fret in peace. Tony, do you mind staying here while I take Shellie to pick up her car at the office?"

"Not at all. I sent some texts out, and some of the other guys are covering for me today and tomorrow. That okay?" Tony pulled the chair back up beside Anna's bed.

"Sounds good, thanks. We will head out. I will be back later, and Shellie will be too. Keep me posted and let me know what room she is moved to. Should be on the seventh floor, her usual spot." Jake went over to Anna. "I love you, Little. Rest, you got this." He bent down and kissed her on the forehead and squeezed her hand.

Darcy stood next to Jake. She leaned over and kissed her only child and rested her forehead on Anna's. "I love you, Anna. Rest." Darcy stood and looked at Tony. "Watch over her, promise. We will come back later. I need to calm down and rest some myself. I just needed to see her for a minute." Tony nodded. He appreciated her trust in him to look over her daughter.

"I will walk y'all out." Tony looked at Anna; she was sleeping soundly. He walked the three to the door of the hospital. They stopped just outside the door. "Will she be okay? I mean, I know y'all have been through this with her, apparently numerous times, so she will be okay, right?" Tony looked more rattled than he had all morning.

"She will. The best outcome is that she will not have to have surgery. So far, she hasn't had to for an obstruction." Jake put his strong arm on Tony's shoulder. "She will be okay. She is tough." He laughed a little. "She is a hell of a lot tougher than you and me, and I assure you that." Tony started to get in his car. "Oh, when she isn't quite so high, let her know the boys are okay. They are at school and doing fine. We got them taken care of. I will call Mark and let him know what is going on."

"I will be back in a little while. Let me text you my number." Shellie took her phone and sent Tony her number. "I will go back to her house and get some things that I know she will want. I will go home and grab some things and then I can stay there, get things ready for when she can come home and take care of the cat." Shellie got into the back seat of the car.

Tony watched them drive away. He went to his truck and got his phone charger. He made his way back into the ER and into Anna's room. She was still resting. He closed the door as softly as he could. Still, she roused. "You're back. It is so sweet that you are here. You know, I have been through this before. You can leave me here alone if you want. When I get to my room, I will have a nifty little button to push for pain medicine. I like it here." Anna had the sweetest smile on her face. Tony could imagine her tipsy. She was probably a hoot.

"I won't go anywhere until you tell me to, deal?" Tony smiled and touched her hand. "Can I get anything for you? You doing okay?"

Anna nodded. She was quiet for a few moments; just the sounds of the machines and people walking in the hallway outside. "Do you know the first time I knew there was something about you? Something I really liked?" Anna looked at him with her big hazel eyes, kind of glassed over with IV drugs.

"Nope. Why don't you tell me, and I will tell you when I knew I liked you." He smiled.

"Remember when I walked into Daddy's office, you were wearing that really nice blue suit? Your butt looked really nice in that suit. Anyway, I fell down. Do you remember?" Anna looked up and saw Tony nodding as he smiled. "Well, when I was going to the bathroom and went the wrong way, you reached and grabbed my arm." Anna pointed at her arm, showing him where he had grabbed it. "I felt something, like electricity. It was you, your touch." Anna's eyes slowly shut.

"I remember. I felt it too," Tony whispered to her. He could have sworn he saw her smile.

*****

Anna was moved into a private room on the seventh floor, just as Jake had suspected. Anna also had full control of the pain medication pump, able to hit the button every ten minutes for medication, but she had had to do it only twice in the past three hours. Tony had kept track. Another dose of the relaxation medicine was given, and she was kept on IV fluids for hydration. Tony had not left her side, except for a moment long enough to get a cup of coffee while they moved her from the ER to the floor. She would wake up for moments, look around, and fall soundly asleep again. Nurses were in and out, taking blood, checking vitals, checking her bag. No change, but prayers were going up.

Shellie had called to say she would be back up in about an hour. Jake had called to check on Anna; he knew the drill. He said he would call again later and if all stayed like it was; he would be back up in the morning. Jake told Tony he didn't have to stay every minute, that he could go home, there were nurses to keep an eye on her, but Tony didn't feel as if he could leave her.

Tony had spent much of the day reading anything and everything he could google on Crohn's Disease, ostomy surgery, care, obstructions, surgeries. He talked to the nurses, talking about medicines and therapies. He was reading when Anna opened her eyes. She didn't say a word for a long time; she just watched him sitting there, entranced by his iPad. He was intrigued with whatever it was, keeping him drawn to the screen. She shifted her weight to her right hip and scooted back to see him better. He instantly put the iPad aside and was up and looking down at her so intently. "You okay? Do you need anything?"

"No, but have you been here the whole time? What time is it anyway?" Anna looked around but not actually trying to see a clock. She could tell that the sun was on the way down. "It has to be late afternoon at least. You don't have to stay here with me. I appreciate it, I really do, but I have done this before. I will be fine." Anna looked at Tony and smiled as she smoothed out her sheet and blanket. Her right foot was out of the covers, her coral toenails shining, just like how she slept at home.

Tony sat back down and scooted the chair up to the side of her bed. "If it is all the same to you, and I am not bothering you, I would not want to be anywhere else. Seems to me you might just need someone to look after you. You should know that gummy bears for dinner is not good for you. For anyone, really." Tony smiled so big it made Anna laugh. "I think I am just the person to keep an eye on you. At least until you get sprung from this joint. And maybe after too, if you will let me."

Anna was about to say something when there was a quick knock on the door and Jack's head popped in around. "You aren't naked, are you, Mom? I have all the guys out here and they are just dying to come in." Jack and Johnathan walked in as Johnathan smacked Jack in the back of the head. "Just kidding, Mom. Hey, Tony... So, you found out about Mom's second home?" Jack smiled and went over and gave his mom a gentle hug and kiss on the cheek.

IT'S IN THE BAG

"It seems I did. Heck of a place to hang out, but your mom must make quite an impression here. There have been a few nurses who have come by today because they saw her name on the admit sheet." Tony smiled and walked to the head of the bed to let Johnathan come around and be on the other side of his mom.

"How are you, Mom? You are going to be okay, right?" Johnathan rarely looked worried, but when it came to his mom, he was rather protective. "Dad called while we were on our way up here. I'm supposed to call him once we see you. He sends his best." Anna held the hands of her boys. She brought each hand to her mouth and kissed them.

"I will be fine, promise. I just ate a whole bag of gummy bears last night for dinner. Not a good plan."

Jack smiled and looked at his mom. "Gramps told us you helped to catch a killer last night. That you had her at gunpoint. Is that true?" Jack looked at both Tony and Anna for an answer.

"It is." Tony didn't give Anna a chance to respond, knowing she would try to downplay what she did, and he didn't want her to struggle to talk too much. "She was great. I saw the whole thing. What she did saved a man's life. You should be really proud of your mom."

"Mom, you rock…well, not for being in here, but, you know, for being you." Jack smiled. "When do you think you will get to come home?"

No one had noticed that Dr. Hyrd was standing in the doorway, watching them all visit. He cleared his throat. "I will answer that one… It seems that we need to put a time limit on the NG tube and pull the trigger on surgery if you have not cleared the obstruction on your own by, uh, noon tomorrow. So high noon." The three guys moved to the perimeter of the room and let the doctor get close to Anna. "How is the pain, manageable? The nurses said that you have used this pump pretty sparingly." Dr. Hyrd pressed along Anna's midsection, checked her bag, and looked at her chart. "Hopefully the tube and some more time will knock it out without surgery."

"Do you think it will be okay by tomorrow?" Anna looked up at the doctor. "I am sorry about the gummy bears."

"Don't apologize to me. You keep me in business. I get to go home to my wife tonight. You, you get to stay in this two-star hotel and get poked and prodded." Dr. Hyrd shook Tony's hand and smiled. He turned to the boys and gave each of them a fist bump. "I swear, what does your momma feed you? You have grown a foot since I saw you last. Lay off the Miracle Grow." He turned to look at Anna. "You know how to get ahold of me if you need me. You text me if you need anything or if it gets worse, okay?"

"I will. Thanks for everything." Anna smiled. She hated being in here, but she was so happy that the pain was manageable. She hated being away from the boys, but she knew that they would be okay.

Dr. Hyrd smiled and said his goodbyes and promised to come by before his office hours in the morning. The boys headed out soon after. They were having dinner at Truck's house tonight and then staying at the house with Shellie. Anna didn't know what she did to have such wonderful friends and family, but she was thankful beyond words.

Soon it was just Anna and Tony again. Another visit from a nurse and a CNA at shift change and another set of vitals were taken. The nurse said that Dr. Hyrd had ordered another dose of medicine to help her relax and sleep through the night, hopefully to ease the obstruction. Shellie called and told Anna that she was going to hang out at her house and wait on the boys to get home. She had called and rescheduled all the appointments for the rest of the week and, depending on how Anna did, she could do the same for the next week as well. A volunteer from the hospital came in with an enormous flower arrangement—roses, carnations, daisies, greenery, and lilies, Anna's favorites. Tony read the card. It was from Mr. Logan and his grateful kids. Tony did great fielding phone calls and texts that came in on Anna's phone. Anna then told him to let most go to voice mail; only for her boys, her parents, and Shellie did he need to answer.

Another knock at the door. It was Mark. Anna hadn't seen him in weeks, not since Johnathan had gotten his driver's license. Anna and Mark didn't have any real reason to see each other that often.

Sweet that he would come by. "Hey, Anna. I talked to the boys. They told me what room you were in. I just wanted to come by and check on you and see how you were." Mark seemed reluctant to come in now. He extended his hand to Tony. "Hello, I'm Mark, the ex-husband."

Tony stood and returned the handshake. "Hello, I'm Tony Phillips. I'm a detective at the sheriff's department. I've been working with Anna and Shellie on a case recently." Tony sounded strong and confident. "I have met your boys a couple of times. You have two great young men, and I know you are proud of them. They are great guys."

"Thanks. They are pretty great kids. Anna and I joke that they got all the good parts of us. The Lord put those parts together and there was enough for two awesome guys. By the way, the boys mentioned that you were on a stakeout and caught a woman trying to kill her husband? And you had the woman at gunpoint last night?" Mark looked puzzled. "Is that true?"

"Yep, short version. And I ate a bag of gummy bears for dinner…thus the current situation." Anna smiled. "Thanks for checking on me. I appreciate it."

"I was here doing some rounds and wanted to make sure you were okay, or as good as you could be. Rest up and pray for no surgery, but if you do need it, I can help any way you need me to. Take care." Mark turned to leave. He looked back and motioned Tony to follow.

Tony followed him to the door. "It was good to meet you. I am glad she has someone to be with her and take care of her. If she were to need anything, just let me know. The boys have my number. I will check in tomorrow to see how she is doing." Mark offered a handshake again, and Tony accepted. "She is a great lady. Believe me, I know. She deserves only the best. Take care of her." Then Mark was gone down the hall.

CHAPTER 21

The nurse came in and gave Anna the medicine, and she felt at ease almost immediately. She had hit the button for more pain medicine just before, so she was good for the night, or until more vitals and blood work had to be taken. Anna lay there and just looked at Tony.

"I can't ever thank you enough for being here today. For helping me this morning and staying here all day. I know you had much more important things to do. I owe you big." Anna was really starting to get loopy now.

"You don't owe me a thing, but if we are keeping tabs, then you owe me pretty big." He laughed.

Anna reached out her hand toward him. "You can go. I will be asleep soon, and I won't be any entertainment at all. You need to go and get some rest. Please?"

"I will go when I know that you are resting well and are not in too much pain. I will go home, later. I need a shower in the worst way. Shellie called this morning right when I had gotten done with my run. I didn't even change my clothes. All I could think of was getting to you." Tony gave her hand a little squeeze.

"I want you to know something." Anna's words were slowing down, but still crystal clear. "I would love to see if you would like to take me on a date. I have thought about it a lot, but I was scared that you would think I was really gross, with my poop bag. That's what I call it. I think you are hot."

Anna stopped talking. Tony opened his mouth to say something, but Anna shook her head. "I have got to tell you the truth. I have not been with a man since my marriage ended. I was so hurt, so centered on the boys, school for me, and my career, I shut off that life. Then I got really sick and about died. I had to have the surgery,

IT'S IN THE BAG

and then I buried that part of my life. I was fine with that until I saw you. You touched me, and all of those feelings came flooding back. I have had some really nice thoughts about you. I love your butt. It's hot. I like spending time with you. You are a good, good man." Anna seemed happy with her proclamation. "Now your turn. Wow me." She beamed a smile in his direction.

Tony's heart was about to beat out of his chest. "I will make you a deal. You get better, and I will take you anywhere you want to go. Just you and me, on a date. Okay? But you have to get better."

"To bed, will you take me to bed? You take me to bed. Just you and me, and yep. How about that." Anna seemed loopy but determined to get her message across.

"Nothing would make me happier than to take you to bed, and all in due time, my dear. All in due time." Tony knew the drugs were inducing her talk, but he smiled, leaned in, and kissed her gently on the forehead. "I want nothing more than to make you happy. Sleep well, Anna."

Tony stayed for another hour, and when he was certain she was asleep and resting well, he walked softly out of the room and pulled her door shut. He would go home, shower, grab some food, and sleep for a couple of hours. He wanted to be back up at her bedside before dawn.

*****

Anna woke early, before the sun had even started to grace the sky with its presence. Her room was pitch-black; the only light she saw was just under the door, from the hallway. Instinctively, Anna reached down for her bag as she did each morning. This morning, it was filled almost halfway. Tears formed in her eyes. The blockage had passed. She knew that the Lord had heard her prayer. She was so happy. She reached for her phone. She immediately typed a text to Tony.

> It passed, all will be ok. No surgery needed.
> Thank you for praying! A

Her phone almost buzzed instantly in reply.

> Can I turn on your light? I am sitting right beside you in the chair. T

"Yes, please, yes," Anna shouted. "Please! I didn't know you were still here."

"I'm here. I went home for about an hour. Took a shower and tried to rest there. I couldn't. I wanted to be here, with you." Tony sat on the edge of her bed. He wiped away the few tears that had left streaks down the side of her cheek. "I needed to be here with you." Tony took her hands in his.

"You make me smile. I am so happy. I was so very scared." Anna looked at him intently. "You…you made it better, just knowing you were here. You made the bad not so bad. Thank you."

"I never imagined our first night we spent together would be in a hospital. I had far better other plans in my mind. Less clothes, visitors, and tubes." Tony smiled, bent down, and gently kissed her on the lips, still smiling. "I promise, our next one will be much better."

*****

Anna was released from the hospital two days after the obstruction. Dr. Hyrd wanted her to be able to eat and not have any issues. She was to stay on a soft, modified diet for a week or so before she could cautiously add more and more foods—except gummy bears.

Anna took care of herself. She worked a modified schedule for a couple of weeks, to let her strength build back up, and then she seemed to feel back to normal. Better than normal, actually; she let herself explore the possibility of a relationship. Anna continued to open up her heart and herself to Tony. It wasn't an overnight change; she was just letting him in after being so resolutely closed off to a romantic relationship, but he was up for the challenge. He went to appointments with her, talked to her doctors with her, really tried to understand what he could do to help, and learned all he could about the disease and how to help.

IT'S IN THE BAG

With the weather now warm, outdoor activities were great to help Anna gain back what she had lost in her most recent hospital stay. She and Tony walked almost every evening, at the park, around town, or just in her neighborhood. He spent evenings with Anna and the boys—dinner, activities—but never stayed overnight. That was something that Anna and Tony were adamant about. They both wanted to do this right and set a good example for the boys. Anna cautioned Tony, early on, that if he wanted a relationship with her, it was with her boys as well.

Also, there was another aspect: her disease. There was no cure for either Crohn's or AS. There would be times she didn't feel well and needed to be in the hospital. He needed to know that, first and foremost. He wasn't getting a whole, completely healthy package. She literally had baggage. Forever baggage, at least one bag. Tony assured Anna that he was strong enough to handle and carry any baggage she had and that he wanted nothing else but to be the one by her side.

Each day that they spent together seemed better than the one before. Slowly but surely, they were growing closer and closer. Anna started to tear down the walls that had kept her heart safe for years, the walls that had kept her new body and the way that it functioned a secret to everyone except the ones who had to know or whom Anna chose. She was learning to accept the change in her body as the gift that it was. She still wasn't overjoyed with how she looked or the fact that she had gone through so much, but she was becoming more and more proud of her scars. The scars proved that she was stronger than what came up against her.

Tony helped Anna to realize that she was still the intelligent, caring, beautiful, loving woman she was before she got the bag. The bag helped her to continue to be all those things and allowed her to grow to be able to be and do more. The only thing that made Anna feel bad was that she had wasted so much time being worried and ashamed of being different, feeling less than the beautiful woman that the Lord had made her to be. Anna found comfort in knowing that everything happened in the Lord's perfect timing and that he had sent Tony to her, when she was ready to receive the gift of him.

"Tonight, I have a special surprise for you. You will love it." Anna was so happy. "Be at my house at five. I will drive."

It was Saturday. Tony had some work to catch up on this morning, but they had planned to be together that afternoon. Barbara had called from the animal rescue and told Anna that Daisy was available to be picked up, a week earlier than the big party next weekend. Anna was so excited. She needed to go to the pet store before meeting Barbara that afternoon. She wanted Tony with her when she picked Daisy up. The boys were out with some friends but would be home in the evening. Anna had planned a special dinner at home so that they could spend the evening welcoming Daisy to the family. This was a surprise for the boys too. Anna was so excited!

"I'm sure I will love it, as long as you are there with me." Tony was as sappy as he was strong. "What are we doing?"

"Currently we are on the phone while we watch *Weekend Today*..." Anna was as sassy as she was smart. "And as far as this evening, you will find out soon! We won't be naked, and we will be with other people."

"Dang... I wanted naked." Tony loved her sense of humor. They had long ago agreed to take it slow and wait as long as humanly possible before being totally intimate. It wasn't easy, but it was important to both of them. "I will wear clothes just for you. You, totally optional."

"Gotcha. Now, go do your work and get that good-looking butt over here by three." Anna laughed.

"You drive a mighty hard bargain, Ms. Dawson. I will do my best not to disappoint. See you later."

*****

Daisy was so sweet. She was sassy and loved riding in the van. She looked great in her pink harness and leash. The bright color popped against her all-black fur. She was still tiny, only about seven pounds. She looked like a little black bear cub. Anna giggled like a little girl, which made Tony laugh, when she held Daisy. She called her a little wiggle butt.

IT'S IN THE BAG

The evening was so much fun. They walked around the backyard; since it was fenced in, they were able to let Daisy run and play until she couldn't run anymore. The boys loved the puppy. It was so sweet to see these two teenaged over-six-foot-tall young men laugh and roll around with a little puppy. Tony and Anna sat on the porch and watched the three play. Finally, Daisy had played herself out. She just flopped over and rolled onto her back as if she was asking for a belly rub. Jack scooped her up and carried her to his mom.

"She looks so sleepy! She is just precious." Anna took Daisy in her arms, and Daisy laid her tired little head on her shoulder. "So sweet. This reminds me of when you guys were babies. My favorite thing was to hold each of you while you slept. It was the most wonderful time."

"Nice. Hey, Jack, Mom just called you a dog." Johnathan laughed.

"You too, smarty-pants. You are a dog too!" Jack retaliated.

"Okay, okay, you both missed the sentimental moment I was having and tried to relay. Take your love fest inside. You are going to wake up your sister. Shhhh!" Anna laughed. "Did you have a good evening? Get enough to eat?" Anna turned her attention to Tony.

"This has been great. I have had the best time, watching you, the boys, Daisy. She seems like she is going to fit right into the family. She is definitely your dog, that's for sure. She seems to know you rescued her from that shelter." Tony smiled and took a sip of his tea.

"You seem to fit right in with us too. I like that. A lot." Anna laid Daisy down in her doggie bed, and she rolled over and snuggled down in the fluffy softness. Anna stood up and went over to Tony's chair. She sat down on his lap, facing him. "You know what, Mr. Phillips?"

"No, what, Ms. Dawson, what?" Tony took the ties that tied at the top of her shirt in his hands. He slowly untied them and let them fall, allowing the top part of her shirt to fall loosely open down to where the buttons started.

"I am in love with you, Tony. So in love with you." She could feel the warmth growing all over her body. Anna cupped his face in her hands. She could feel the stubble of his unshaven face, rough and sexy. "Can I kiss the stuffing out of you?"

Tony's hands fell to hold tight onto her behind, pulling her as close as he could to his chest. "I want nothing more than you to kiss me, because I was just thinking about kissing you." He then slid his hands up her back and into her hair, wrapping his fingers in her silky locks.

She let out a sigh and bent down to meet his mouth with hers. Gently at first, but then Tony quickly took over and kissed her with all the need and want that could be translated into a kiss. They kissed until they were both breathless. Anna rested her head Tony's forehead. "I really want you to make love to me. I want to feel you inside me. I can feel that you want me too."

"Soon, baby, soon." Tony kissed her gently and smacked her behind. "Not tonight. I wish, but not tonight. Time isn't just right yet, but I promise you, soon."

Anna slid off his lap and placed one more kiss on his lips, and she lingered there until she heard the back door open and Johnathan stepped out.

"Get a room, guys. Geez. Impressionable young children are present. What is Daisy supposed to think of her parents acting like teenagers?" He laughed.

"No teenagers I know better be acting like this." Anna bent down and kissed Tony again.

Johnathan quickly changed the subject. "So, next weekend is Gramps's party, right?"

"Yes, yes, it is. We need to go pick up your and your brother's suits for the dance." Anna went over and tousled Johnathan's hair. "Maybe you will find you a woman at this dance, well, not a woman, but a cute, nice, nun of a young lady who has sworn not to kiss or have sexual relations…"

"Okay, gotta go back inside. Can I take Daisy?" he asked, turning red.

"Sure, we will be in soon." Anna smiled.

IT'S IN THE BAG

Next weekend was going to be hectic and a night like no other. She could just feel it. And she was in the arms of the one she knew would be responsible.

CHAPTER 22

The week before the Carnival of Shenanigans went by with all the mayhem, cuss words, and violent outbursts that one would imagine before a Carnival of Shenanigans. Not one thing was up to Darcy's standards, not even the cups that the caterer brought for the shaved ice treats for the kids. Anna had gotten her calmed down from that catastrophe when Darcy was told that the DJ had come down with the flu but was sending his nephew in his place.

"Well, I just hope he speaks English and can use those turntable things, you know like they do." Darcy was beside herself. Kind of entertaining really. "I really hope he does well, not a lot of that rap-gangster stuff. A little is fine, but we need variety. Do you think you could talk to the nephew when he gets here, tell him not to be a rap gangster? And who gets the flu in the dead middle of summer?"

"First of all, Momma, please quit saying 'rap gangster.' Never say that again. That is inappropriate. Secondly, they don't use turntables much anymore since, like, the eighties. Third, plenty of people get the flu in the summer. Medical fact. And yes, I will speak to him and make sure that the music is of the variety nature. Got it." Anna hoped that at least her momma heard the part about not saying "rap gangster." All they needed was that to get around. Bless.

Everything else seemed to be going as planned. The daytime part, the carnival part of the day, was to begin at 11:00 a.m. with lunch and festivities. They had been at the Country Club since the good Lord woke up the sun that morning, and as far as Anna was concerned, things were in a good spot. Momma was on the verge of a nervous breakdown, but that was par for the course actually. Cause for concern would be the lack of Darcy running around like crazy.

IT'S IN THE BAG

Anna had on a short jean skirt, her trademark flip-flops, and a white T-shirt. Her hair was up in pigtails with red ribbons tied around. She was nothing if not patriotic. She had her evening gown and heels in the van. She had chosen a skintight royal-blue dress, strapless and one of Anna's favorites. She hoped that Tony would wear his blue dress suit; they would look amazing together.

Tony and both the boys had volunteered to help Barbara and Denise with the animals for the pet adoption event. They were helping transport the puppies and kittens and setting up the separate spaces for each. They were happy to do that and be away from the craziness for at least a little bit. Anna thought that if Tony made it through today with her family, he was certainly a keeper and fit for the job. It wasn't a job for the weak.

The club and grounds looked amazing. Tastefully decorated with red, white, and blue balloons and tents for the day part, and the ballroom was set and beautiful for that night; it would be gorgeous with all the twinkle lights. It will look like a dream, perfect for dancing. The ballroom opened onto the pool deck, and the big green space below would serve well for everyone who stayed for the fireworks over the lake, and if last year was any indication, just about every square inch would be covered with revelers. The more people, the better, which was how Darcy judged success: if everyone showed up and looked like they were having the time of their life.

Anna saw that her boys were back, all three of them, and she headed over to see the progress on the animal corrals. "Looks good, guys. Where are all the puppies and kittens? Let me get my hands on those little fuzz balls."

Tony whistled, stopped what he was doing, and watched her walk up. "Hello, darling, you dressed like that sure makes me rethink my career choice. I think we should buy a farm, and you can dress like that all the time." He winked and gave her a big kiss on the cheek.

Anna laughed and smacked Tony on the behind. "You sure don't want to see eighty-year-old me dressed in this getup. My boobs will be dragging the floor." She winked.

"Try me," Tony challenged her with a smile.

*****

The carnival festivities went splendidly. There were families and kids from the whole county. All the families who had very small children and who wouldn't want to stay out till midnight really seemed to appreciate the fact that the daytime part of the party was geared toward the children. Laughter and squeals could be heard from every direction.

Anna checked, and the most popular station, other than the ice cream truck and the dunking booth, was the animal shelter. Anna checked several times throughout the afternoon, and Barbara and Denise were both shocked at how many applications they had gotten. All of the animals they had brought with them were spoken for. This had been a huge success. Anna would have to remember this and talk to the girls about doing this event every year.

It was getting close to the time for Anna to change and get ready for the night. The evening crowd would be there in about an hour for dinner and dancing...and that gigantic birthday cake. Jake had been on cloud nine all day. He loved seeing all the families and children having such a good time. This was the perfect way to celebrate his birthday.

Anna was walking up to the clubhouse toward her daddy and Tony when there was the most horrible sound of crashing metal and screeching. Screams filled the air, and smoke was seen coming from around the side of the enormous building.

Anna ran toward the sounds and the smoke. "What in the world was that?"

Tony caught up with her, and they got to the scene. Just then, Darcy arrived to witness her worst nightmare. It sent her momma over the edge and into the rocky bottom of the pit of despair. Jake looked at Tony and Anna and went to his wife's side. He turned her away from the wreckage and walked her back into the club.

Tony took out his cell phone and dialed 911. Anna ran over to the driver's side of the car that was now half in and half out of

IT'S IN THE BAG

the Country Club ballroom. Nice. Anna looked in at the dazed but seemingly okay driver. "Hey, buddy, you okay? What's your name?"

"Ahhh, Wilkes." He rubbed his head and jaw. "My name is Wilkes. What happened?" The young guy looked at Anna and then back at the building. "He is going to kill me, kill me dead."

"It's okay, Wilkes, no one is going to kill you, I promise. Not today and not here." Anna tried to calm the guy and keep him from making any sudden movements. Tony was by her side before she knew it.

"This is Wilkes. I'm getting him to stay put until the paramedics get here." Anna looked at Tony, then she looked back at Wilkes. "Is that pot I smell? Are you high?"

Wilkes looked up at Anna and Tony. "Yeah, I drive high all the time, but I guess I was a little more stoked this time. I'm supposed to fill in tonight at some party for my uncle. He is going to kill me."

Anna laughed. "Help me, somebody. You're the DJ? That sounds about right. You don't have the flu, do you? That would just be perfect." Anna looked at Tony. "Can you handle this debacle? I have to find Momma, find a new DJ, and make sure she doesn't have a stroke in between A and B."

Tony smiled his steadfast and sure smile. "Go do your thing. I got this. No problem." The sirens were getting closer by the second. "I will find you when this guy is taken care of."

Anna left Tony to deal with Wilkes, who may or may not have been a good DJ, but he would have to try his skills in the cell tonight. At that point, Anna would be happy with some straight-up rap music, bluegrass picking, or the choir from the Baptist church. Some people got down to gospel music. She had nothing. Johnathan came up beside his mom with Jack hot on his heels.

"Great party, Mom. This is so cool," Jake said as he surveyed the damage. "Who is that 'bot' who ran into the building?"

"To be exact, he is the DJ for tonight, but he will be spending the Fourth of July downtown, in jail. He is high as a kite and in a heap of shit." Anna cringed. "I mean a heap of crap."

"It's okay, Mom, we have heard that word before. We aren't scarred for life or anything. I think we will be just fine." Johnathan put his arm around his mom. "You know, Jack and I know how to do the DJ thing. We can play some great music on our phones and pipe it through the sound system in the building...if it stays standing."

Anna looked at her children, her pride and joy. "Wait, what, you can? That would be wonderful. I'm sure Grams would give you the fee she was paying Mr. Flu Guy and his pothead nephew."

"Yeah, Mom, we can handle it. Not like it's hard. We have great playlists. You've heard them. We can pull up other stuff too, some slow stuff, old stuff, groovy stuff..." Jack would have kept going, but his mom cut him off.

"Look, I don't care if you play four hours of game-show themes or 'The Star-Spangled Banner' a million times...just do it. Go, go get set up or whatever you do." She hugged them both, and off they went. Anna needed to make sure her momma was coherent and get both of them ready for whatever else this evening was to hold.

Anna found her momma crying in the rather large and plush women's bathroom. Anna had retrieved both of the dresses they were wearing for the evening. She had her bag with makeup and tools for turning her pigtails into a sweeping updo. Anna hung up the dresses and went to sit beside her momma.

"Momma, look… I know that this evening hasn't started off like you would have wanted it. Granted, there is a car in the side of the building that happened to be driven by the nephew of the flu-ridden DJ, but your grandsons have taken it upon themselves to perform the responsibilities of the DJ. Whatever they do will be better than no music, and I told them they could have the fee that you were going to pay the other guy." Anna noticed that her momma had stopped crying. "The cake is being set up as we speak, and if I do say so myself, Tony and I did an amazing job picking it out. Pamela worked her magic and baked another masterpiece. She and Robert have it almost up and ready for you and Daddy to see. So let's get our sexy Dawson butts up and go show this place how to party! We already almost brought the house down, let's go finish the job."

Darcy looked at her daughter with such pride. "Thank you, Anna. I know I give you a hard time, all the time, but it is because I love you. I never want anyone to be able to take advantage of you, and I think you have shown me over and over what a strong woman you are. I am proud of you. I hope you know that."

"I do, Momma. I do." Anna hugged her momma, the sweetest moment they have had in about, oh, a lot of years. Anna would take it as a win. "Now, let's make ourselves look drop-dead gorgeous. I want you to knock Daddy's socks off, and I want to knock all of Tony's clothes off." Anna smiled, jumped up, and took her hair out of the pigtails.

"Anna, I taught you better than that…but hell, tonight, I am rooting for you to be happier than you have ever been. Let's do it."

In less than thirty minutes, both Darcy and Anna looked amazing. Darcy wore a champagne-colored, floor-length sequined dress. Anna gave her momma a lot of grief for being a member of the Country Club and hanging out with all her snooty friends, but her momma was in her element—not her snooty element but with her friends. Anna was happy that her momma was happy and had good friends she enjoyed doing things with. Now it was time to go greet the town, family, and friends.

The ladies walked out together, Darcy meeting up with Jake, who looked stunning in his tux. This was his night, and she was so happy to share it with him. Anna scanned the room, and then her eyes met his. Tony's mouth turned up in a sly smile, and they walked toward each other. They finally met in an embrace.

Tony whispered in her ear, "I will make it so worth your while if you duck back into that bathroom with me. You won't regret it." Anna looked into his eyes and could literally feel his want and need of her; his gaze looked on her as something he wanted to ravage.

"My first time with you, and my first time in years, is not going to the in the women's bathroom at the Pressley Heights Country Club. I am a lady, not a teenager. Been there, done that. When I have you tonight, it will be on a blanket in my backyard…or on the porch, or on the…" Anna winked and took his hand. They started toward the ballroom.

Her words hit Tony's mind like a lightning bolt. "Wait, what?" Anna looked at him and blew him a kiss.

Anna looked at the DJ stand. Her handsome sons were doing a great job, laughing, dancing, and keeping the crowd happy. Impressive. Tony and Anna waved at Robert and Pamela, and Barbara and Denise. Shellie and Gigi came over; they had their drinks in hand and were on their way to a very happy night. Peggy and her hubby were cozied up on a blanket out on the veranda, a bottle of wine chilling between them.

Mr. Logan came over and gave Anna a big hug and shook Tony's hand. Anna thanked him for the beautiful flowers he had sent while she was in the hospital, and he thanked her for saving his life. Anna saw the older couple, the Mullins, who she had helped with the stick problem in their yard. They were talking to the neighbors they had almost sued.

Anna's waved at Mark and Lindie, who were dancing, looking very happy. That, in turn, made Anna happy. Mark pointed to the boys and smiled at Anna as if to say, *Look at our boys!* Anna nodded, showing she shared the admiration of their guys.

Tony took Anna by the hand and led her out to the dance floor. He spun her around, and they came together in a kiss. The music slowed, as if someone knew it was time for a slower song, and they began to sway, seeming to move as one. Anna looked up at Tony, smiled, and couldn't think of anywhere on the earth she had rather be. She knew in this moment, in her arms and in this place, she had all she needed to live a completely happy full life, bag and all.

ABOUT THE AUTHOR

J. C. Adley lives in the beautiful mountains of western North Carolina with her wonderful husband, her amazing children, one rather moody cat, and one super-sweet rescue dog. She works as a paralegal for county government, and when not working, she loves to spend time with her family and friends, cook recipes she finds on Pinterest, and do just about anything that can be done outside. J. C. is an avid fan of *The Today Show*, *Chrisley Knows Best*, and black-and-white *Gunsmoke* reruns.

It's in the Bag was the culmination of J. C.'s love of writing and her actual path in life. Diagnosed in 2000 with Crohn's disease, J. C. began the long and at times dark and scary journey to her own "baggage" and a new and happy lease on life—from the moment she sat in her surgeon's office when he told her that colon removal and a permanent ostomy was her last hope; to today, being able to tell her story and share that life does go on, many times for the better, even with the baggage that one collects in life.

Much like the main character, Anna, J. C. uses humor, faith, family, friends, and a wonderful online community of other ostomates to love, live, and share her life with others. Her main goal is to encourage and help others to know that there is so much life to be lived and love to be given and received. No matter what you have going on (not just an ostomy bag), it will all be okay; keep going, keep trusting, hold on to your hope, and never let anyone steal your joy. You are worthy of all the love and good this life has to offer, no matter what baggage you may have.

CPSIA information can be obtained
at www.ICGtesting.com
Printed in the USA
BVHW040600130722
641927BV00007B/182

9 781638 810247